HINDUSTAAN

What if the British never conquered India?

Mainak Dhar

Vitasta

Let Knowledge Spread

Published by Renu Kaul Verma for
Vitasta Publishing Pvt. Ltd.
2/15, Ansari Road, Daryaganj,
New Delhi - 110 002
info@vitastapublishing.com

ISBN 978-93-80828-47-3

Reprint 2013

While many of the characters are real and borrowed from the real history, actions and words attributed to them are purely a figment of the author's imagination.

Layout by Vitasta Publishing Pvt. Ltd.
Cover Design by Geetali Baruah
Printed by Vits Press, New Delhi

As always,

For Puja & Aadi

Author's Note

Every writer has two major sources of inspiration- the people and the books he surrounds himself with. For me, the people who helped make this book happen were many.

My wife, Puja, always for being my greatest inspiration, a rock-solid pillar of support and the best muse a writer could ever want. My son, Aadi, whose requests for repeated readings of his Pooh and Mickey storybooks will one day be repaid when he has to listen to iterations of my plots and jottings. My father, Maloy, his second innings as a bestselling writer after retirement is an inspiration of how to keep one's passion for writing alive; My friend Rahul, whose shared love for history and historical novels sparked the whole idea of *Hindustaan* and finally my mother, Sunanda. Ma, I know you're up there smiling as you see this book join the others on my shelf–I'm keeping the promise I made–a book per year.

My book, *Hindustan*, would not have been written, but for four authors–Abraham Eraly and William Darlymple, whose books breathe life into Mughal India as never before; Harry Turtledove, who introduced me to the fascinating world of asking a simple 'what if' and then creating a whole retelling of history around it; and finally Conn Iggulden, whose books got me really passionate about the possibilities of historical fiction.

A note to readers–you will encounter several terms, ranks and units of measurement that were current during the Mughal era. I desisted from just putting in their modern English translation or equivalent in the spirit of keeping the authenticity of the story alive. Most of these will be self-explanatory in the context of the story, especially to Indian readers, but in case of any doubt, just turn to the Glossary at the end of this novel. While many of the characters are real and borrowed from the real history we know, actions and words attributed to them are purely a figment of my imagination.

— **Mainak Dhar**

Historical Note

It seems fashionable nowadays to talk about the 'rise' or 'emergence' of China and India as if this were a new or surprising development. Any serious student of history will tell you that far from rising, what we are witnessing today is perhaps the resurgence of these two nations to the kind of status they enjoyed not too long ago. In 1600, China under the Ming Dynasty was the world's largest economy, accounting for close to 30 per cent of total global income, and the second largest economy was that of the Mughal empire in what we today call India, accounting for almost 23 per cent.

That mighty economic colossus was built on the seemingly incongruous foundation of the descendants of none other than the Mongols (a corruption of which in fact led to them being known as the Mughals). Arriving initially as raiders, but fast becoming conquerors and emperors, the Mughals ruled over an empire that covered most of the modern Indian subcontinent for almost three hundred years.

To give a sense of perspective of just how big the Mughal Empire was in economic terms, the total revenue of the Mughals in 1600 is estimated to have been greater in absolute terms than the total revenue of the British Empire two hundred years later.

As most empires go, the Mughals too became a victim of their own hubris. Infighting and overstretch deeper into India (especially the guerrilla warfare waged by the Marathas) had severely weakened the Mughals by the beginning of the 18th century. The low point came when the capital, Dilli, was sacked, first by the Marathas and then by Afghan raiders, showing just how impotent the Emperor had become.

Also, being smug about their position and superiority led them to be totally inward focused, to the extent that they remained clueless about a new threat that arrived in the form of English traders. The intentions of the British became clear at Plassey in 1857 when a British-led and supported force defeated the Nawab of Bengal, who had not been doing their bidding when it came to trading terms. What began as jockeying for trading privileges soon took on imperial overtones as the British understood just how brittle the Mughal Empire was at its core.

By the 18th century, as a result, the Mughal Emperor was for all intents and purposes, an Emperor only in name, with large parts of the empire effectively out of control, and the British East India Company essentially running an Empire- down to raising and maintaining armies and meddling in the affairs of Indian kingdoms.

The Mughal Empire's last hurrah came in 1857, when a revolt by the East India Company's sepoys (in part sparked by rumours of greased cartridges) led them to rally to the Mughal Emperor. Many Indian princes and rulers (including those mentioned in *Hindustaan* such as the Rani of Jhansi) took the opportunity to seek revenge for their own grievances against the British and joined the fray. Much bloodshed later, the British prevailed, the Mughal Emperor Bahadur Shah Zafar was exiled, and his male descendants executed, effectively marking the end of the Mughal era, as the British Crown formally took over the newest addition to its empire.

But what if the later Mughal Emperors had not been so near-sighted? What if they had not squandered their immense resources in their own never ending `wars on terror'? What if they had not let the British gain a foothold and sent a force to aid the Nawab of Bengal? The victory at Plassey was the spark that led the British to first believe that their ambitions in India could extend beyond trading profits- and a defeat at Plassey would have perhaps changed the course of history as we know it.

Hindustaan is a fictional episode from that history that never was.

— **Mainak Dhar**

One

Compassion towards an adversary's compulsions should never come in the way of killing him as efficiently as possible.

That had been one of the earliest lessons that his father had drilled into Ranveer Pratap during his training, and he found himself thinking back to those words as he contemplated his current mission. The men he was going to face were not standard bearers of an invading army, nor were they even professional soldiers. Most likely, they had been peasants who had been driven to banditry by yet another poor Monsoon. Be that as it may, they had written their own death sentence the day they had ambushed a baggage train carrying supplies straight to the Royal household. Two Royal guards had been killed and much of the contents of the baggage train looted. This had proven to be the last straw, coming as it did after weeks of attacks on caravans coming into the capital. The normally soft-spoken Emperor had pronounced that such an outrage could not go unpunished, and as was usual in the Royal Court, the mere whiff of a suggestion by the Emperor had been magnified into increasingly blood-curdling pronouncements by multiple layers of underlings till a contingent of the Royal Cavalry had been sent out on a punitive mission.

'Sir, is it true that what these men looted were dried fruits and nuts from Kabul meant for the Harem?'

The question was asked by Ranveer's deputy, a crusty old man called Iftiqar. While technically he reported to Ranveer, he had seen at least twenty summers more than the young officer, and had been one of the men Ranveer's father had entrusted with his training when he was younger. Ranveer suspected that Iftiqar's being in his unit was no accident. It was yet another unspoken way in which his father was trying to make sure his son had trustworthy eyes watching over him when he went into harm's way.

While a few of the men around them chuckled at Iftiqar's words, Ranveer knew better than to belittle their mission or the Emperor in front of his men.

'Iftiqar, I don't care if all they stole were your undergarments. We've been ordered to hunt them down and that we will.'

The men chuckled even louder and Ranveer thought he caught an appreciative smile forming on the edges of his old teacher's lips. Iftiqar looked at the young man standing next to him. He had been Ranveer's teacher, mentor and bodyguard all rolled into one since the boy had been no taller than his knee. Iftiqar was known for his imposing height and build, but his pupil had surpassed him even in height. Unlike many sons of nobles who went soft due to the many indulgences available in Dilli, Ranveer's body was trim and toned from constant exercise and riding. Many of the younger nobles in Dilli liked to sport extravagant beards and kept their hair long. Ranveer's hair was cropped short and he allowed himself no more than a short moustache. Iftiqar remembered that a noble had once told Ranveer that he looked more like a common soldier than a noble's son, to which Ranveer had replied that the only purpose long beards and hair served were to provide easy handholds for an enemy to drag you down during battle. Iftiqar smiled as he realized that the small boy he had once taught had now become a full grown warrior. That was till you looked at his eyes. Iftiqar had seen Ranveer in action, and knew that those eyes could become cold and focused, but most of the time, they were dreamy, as if he were elsewhere, thinking of something else. Beneath all the bravado and strength, he was still quite naive about the ways of the Mughal empire, with its many layers of bureaucracy and constant intrigues, where a whisper could kill a man surer than an arrow fired at point-blank range.

Ranveer caught Iftiqar looking at him, and asked him what was on his mind. Iftiqar leaned in close so the men would not hear.

'Ranveer, I hear that the baggage train that was looted contained gifts being sent by one of the Princes for the upcoming celebration in Dilli, where the Emperor is expected to appoint his successor. Every noble has dispatched men to recover the stolen goods so they can impress the Court.'

Iftiqar noticed that as usual when talk veered towards the intrigues and politics of the Court, Ranveer's eyes glazed over. Ranveer's father had often chastised Iftiqar for not drilling into his son that there was more to becoming a successful officer than swordplay, and Iftiqar had tried, but the boy had no interest in, or understanding of, how the Court worked. Endearing if you had known and loved him since he was a boy, as Iftiqar did. A fatal weakness, if he found himself unprotected before the sharks of the Court.

His thoughts were interrupted by a shout from one of their men.

'Sir, I can see a group of armed men about two *kos* to the West!'

The cry came from one of the scouts Ranveer had sent ahead of his main force to look for the enemy. The man was galloping towards Ranveer's position, his horse sending a cloud of dust flying around him.

'Iftiqar, after we're done today, remind that idiot that the dust he's raising will be seen for many *kos* in the open desert.'

Iftiqar merely nodded, though Ranveer knew well that the burly man's 'reminder' would likely take the form of a robust beating that the young scout was not likely to forget soon.

'Men, mount your horses!'

Ranveer's command galvanized his men into action, and

without a word, twenty-five men fastened their weapons and climbed onto their war horses. All that could be heard was the snapping of weapons into place, the scraping of barrels as bullets were stuffed down them and the occasional clang of a sword jostling against chainmail armour as they prepared for the battle that lay ahead.

'Men, remember one thing. We are the Ahadis, the Mughal Emperor's own cavalry. We kill better and faster than any other fighting unit, but we fight with honour. No men who are willing to surrender will be killed, and no women and children will be harmed. Now, let's go and show these sons of whores who owns the desert.'

Ranveer led his men in single file, in order to maximize the chances that they could approach their quarry unseen. Their horses trotted along at a leisurely pace so as not to raise dust clouds that could be seen in the barren expanse of the desert. After a few minutes of riding, Ranveer saw some figures appear over the horizon. He picked up the pace till he was close enough to see that the group consisted of about fifty men. His job would be made simpler- there were no women or children to worry about. What he did however have to worry about was the fact that every single one of them seemed to be armed. A dozen or so seemed to be carrying rifles, and the others had bows, swords or lances. Several of them were carrying big sacks over their shoulders and even from this distance Ranveer could make out the fact that a few of them were carrying elaborately embroidered boxes, of the sort that may have adorned a noble's home in Dilli, but looked totally out of place here.

'Steady men. Attack only on my command and take out the *bandookchis* first.'

The Mughal riders were now less than two dozen paces away from their quarry, and as they fanned out behind Ranveer, the bandits stopped and turned to face them. Ranveer wondered if this was because they realized they had no place to run in the open desert, or if they intended to make a stand. Ranveer rode a few paces ahead of his men. He took in the men they had been following. They could have easily passed for ordinary peasants, dressed as they were in little more than loin cloths. But the fact that they were travelling in such a large group, and carrying such a complement of weapons, made that a remote possibility. Even then, Ranveer had to give them an opportunity to surrender.

'We are soldiers of the Imperial Army. Allow my men to inspect the goods you are carrying.'

Some of the men seemed to hesitate at his words, but a tall and well-built man, presumably their leader, stepped forward towards Ranveer. He had an ancient matchlock pistol slung in a belt at his waist, and a long spear in one hand.

'Officer, we are just members of our village patrol out looking for robbers who have been stealing our animals.'

'Then you should have no problem with us checking your bags.'

The man smiled at Ranveer, his eyes scanning the Mughal ranks, perhaps assessing his chances.

'Officer, perhaps we could come to an arrangement here.

You and your men could share in what we have.'

Ranveer rode even closer to the man. Now they were no more than a dozen paces away.

'Fool, you do not know who you are dealing with. I am not a provincial guard who will give in to your bribery. Don't waste my time. I will ask you one last time- surrender to my men.'

The man's eyes changed, the pleading look replaced by one of cold fury. He cocked his right arm back and loosed his spear at Ranveer. It was a good throw, and the spear came in straight and fast, but Ranveer was ready. He had already loosened the straps holding his leather shield against the left flank of his mount and brought the shield up with his left hand, deflecting the spear. His arm rocked back at the impact, but ignoring the pain, he took out the pistol hanging from the right flank of his horse and fired, hitting his attacker on the chest. As the other bandits scrambled to bring their weapons to bear, Ranveer's men opened fire with their rifles. A dozen bandits fell dead or wounded. At such close quarters, there was no time to reload, and Ranveer and his men took out their swords and waded into the bandits.

Ranveer's face was an emotionless mask as he went about his work with deadly precision.

Block, thrust, parry, cut.

He could have been at his barracks practising with his men, except that his sword was covered in blood. The bandits they faced outnumbered them, but it was more of a slaughter than a battle. Unarmoured and largely untrained, they were no match for the heavily armoured Ahadis. Within minutes, the killing ended, and Ranveer took stock of his losses. More than a dozen of his men had been wounded, but not a single bandit remained standing.

'Iftiqar, have the worst of the wounds tended to. Let's collect the looted goods and make our way to the nearest *caravanserai*, so the men can rest and recover.'

Ranveer could see scarcely disguised pride in Iftiqar's eyes. Too many nobles were content to let their men do the fighting, but Ranveer, like his father before him, led from the front. One of the lessons Iftiqar had taught him was that rank could buy you a soldier's obedience but fighting shoulder to shoulder with him was the only way to earn loyalty.

Within a couple of hours of riding, they could see the red brick walls of a *caravanserai* over the horizon. The ride had been a difficult one, with the scorching Sun beating down on them, and the sands of the Rajputana desert blowing into their faces. Ranveer had it a bit easier than his men- if only because his earliest memories were of riding in exactly such a desert. He put those memories aside as they approached the *caravanserai*. Ranveer could sense a lightening of the mood among his men. They looked forward to a hot meal, some well-deserved rest, and they also knew that they would then be on their way back home.

'Sir, a messenger approaches!'

Ranveer looked ahead to see a thin young man running towards them, his approach announced by the ringing of bells attached to his waist. This, and the plume tucked into his headband marked him out to be an Imperial messenger. When he approached Ranveer, he handed over a thin bamboo tube. Ranveer opened the tube to find a *firman* addressed to him, inviting him to join a superior officer for dinner at the *caravanserai*. The document was signed by *Amir-e-Azam* Shameem Qureshi. His father.

***

In theory all *caravenserais* were meant to be identical, offering weary travellers rest and security throughout the Empire. In practice, any rule went as far as the men charged with implementing it. So while *caravenserais* closer to the Capital were indeed exactly in keeping with the rules, since senior officials would likely visit them often, an outpost such as this one, almost two hundred *kos* from Dilli, tended to reflect the kind of men who frequented it. As Ranveer entered the walled compound he knew this was not one frequented by merchants or nobles, as it had no plush interiors or carpeted floors. But there were men who immediately came up to help him and his men take off their armour and took away their horses with practised precision. Ranveer thought that while they may not get the best of comforts, at least their hosts would know what soldiers needed most- some real food, and rest.

A portly man, presumably the caretaker, came up to Ranveer and saluted him, bowing low in respect.

'The Amir-e-Azam is in the quarters upstairs. He asks that you join him when you are rested and ready.'

Ranveer nodded and in an hour or so, bathed and with some

minor cuts and abrasions tended to, climbed the stairs to the room where his father was staying. When he entered, he saw his father hunched over a table, studying some documents. When he looked up at Ranveer, a broad smile spread over his face.

'My boy! How are you?'

'I am fine, Abba-*jaan*. What brings you this far out into the desert?'

As his father got up, Ranveer noticed that he was limping a bit. Qureshi walked up to his son and clasped Ranveer on the shoulder. Even at this age, his grip was strong, and while Ranveer had grown to be a full head taller than his father, Qureshi was the one man he was still afraid of.

'It's nothing. I'm just getting on in years. And oh yes, I came here to tell you that you should plan to spend some time in Dilli this time. Don't run away like you always do. I think you need to get some exposure to the senior officials there. It will be good for your career. Also now that you have recovered the Emperor's stolen treasure, you should make quite an impression at the Court.'

Ranveer smiled in return.

'Father, you know that's no place for a soldier. All the perfumed nobles make me sick. I'd rather ride in the open than get soft sitting in my barracks and get dragged into the politics of the Court.'

Qureshi sat down, motioning Ranveer to sit down across the table from him.

'You know my son, there will come a time when you can

no longer ride down any enemy and then you will need a life beyond being a soldier. As a father, it is my duty to help you prepare for that.'

Their conversation moved to banal pleasantries for a while as attendants brought in dinner and placed it on the table before them. Steaming hot *biryani*, lamb cooked in saffron, fresh fruits. After days of surviving on frugal army rations, Ranveer could barely wait to tuck into the feast before him. As the attendants left, he responded to his father.

'Don't you think we have too many politicians, and not enough soldiers? Isn't that what almost led to our ruin?'

Qureshi motioned to his son to start eating as he scooped a handful of *biryani* into his mouth.

'Ranveer, what our history teaches us is that we need strength, true enough; but strength combined with foresight. That is what led the Emperor to disregard his bickering Amirs and send an army to aid Siraj-ud-daulah against the British at Palashi a hundred years ago, and crush them. And then again, repeat that in the Battle of Kolkata later that year. That same foresight allowed the Emperor to join forces with other Kingdoms to repel the invasion of Ahmed Shah Abdali three years later. If not for that foresight, I have no doubt that the British would have been our masters today.'

Ranveer continued eating soundlessly. He didn't want to let this old debate sour his meeting with his father, but he was beginning to realize that the two of them were very different men. Growing up in awe of the man before him, Ranveer had not given much thought to doing anything other than following his father's advice and direction. For the longest time, it had actually felt good to have opportunities come his way seemingly of their own accord, to have people bow down before him, just because he was his father's son. But of late, as he had begun to understand for himself how things worked, he wondered if that was all he wanted to be for the rest of his life.

Qureshi sensed what was on Ranveer's mind and instead of continuing the debate, tried to steer the conversation to more neutral ground.

'Dilli is abuzz nowadays with the preparations for the grand celebrations to mark the hundredth anniversary of our victory over the British. I hear the Emperor is likely to announce his heir-apparent during his speech.'

'Father, what do you think will happen once our Emperor decides to pass the mantle on?'

Qureshi paused, taking a deep breath, and answered.

'That my son, is what keeps many of us in the government awake at night. The Emperor is an exceptional man, wise, compassionate and yet shrewd enough to see through his adversaries. His sons may not have all their father's virtues.'

Ranveer had ridden through enough of the empire to know that the only danger to stability came not only from infighting in the Court. He told his father that unrest was growing in the provinces, and that the old enemies of the Mughal Empire, the Marathas, were stirring again.

'Ranveer, we have enjoyed a hundred years of peace, but

peace earned through the power of our sword. When the other powers saw a resurgent Mughal Empire, they decided that the best course of action was to make their peace. Now they too can smell the whiff of instability in Dilli, and no wonder they are trying to test our resolve. Even the British are just biding their time; they are a people hungry for lands to conquer. See how they reduced the mighty Chinese Empire to a nation of opium eaters and lorded over them when they were frustrated in Hindustaan. So now, they trade with us, supposedly as equals, but any sign of weakness, and I bet they will be back as conquerors.'

Ranveer finished his *biryani* and answered with the confidence of youth.

'Our army can crush them. Let them just try.'

Qureshi looked at his son, perhaps seeing that despite all his bluster, he was but a young man just growing into manhood. He smiled and touched Ranveer affectionately on his arm.

'Ranveer, when you speak like that, I am so reminded of your father.'

They both fell silent for a while. This was not something they talked about often, but Ranveer's biological father had been a Rajput chieftan, and a great friend of Qureshi's. When Ranveer's parents had been killed in an attack by Afghan raiders, Qureshi had adopted the seven year old boy, bringing him up as the son he never had. Especially in the last few years, when Qureshi's wife had died after a prolonged illness, the two men had little by way of family but each other. Ranveer knew just how much he owed the man before him, and just how much he respected Qureshi's decision to never ask him to change his religion or name.

Which is why, Ranveer thought to himself, despite all their differences, he sought his father out when he needed someone to unburden his soul to.

Ranveer got up to retire for the night, realizing that he had an early start to the next day as he and his men would need to start their journey back to Dilli. Qureshi turned to him as he reached the door.

'Just remember that every man and every army has its strengths. But those very strengths hide the root of its fatal weakness. Our army is massive, with the ability to hammer and shock any enemy into submission in open warfare, but it is like a giant elephant, its mass is its weakness. All it takes is a few smart hounds to snap at its heels and get out of the way before it can bring it's lumbering strength to beardown on them.'

'And the Ahadis are the wolves who guard against those hounds, right?'

Father and son smiled as they parted for the night.

***

Ranveer and his men rode at a fast trot, refreshed after the night's rest and also feeling much lighter now that they were not wearing their armour, which was rolled into a cloth bundle behind each man. The day was just beginning and Ranveer planned to travel at least fifty *kos* by noon, when they would take a short break at the *caravanserai* near Bikaner. This far from any unfriendly border, a column of armed Mughal cavalry had little reason to expect trouble, but refusing to let his guard down, Ranveer had instructed two scouts to ride ahead of the rest of the unit.

Ranveer and Iftiqar rode side by side, a few paces ahead of the other men. Sure that nobody would hear them, Ranveer whispered to his crusty deputy, using the term of endearment that he had always used for Iftiqar, though one he had been asked by the old man himself to never use in front of the men.

'So Iftiqar *chacha*, what was actually in those Imperial boxes and bags we rescued from those bandits?'

Iftiqar scratched the back of his bald pate, and replied with a wry smile.

'Figs, dates and nuts from Kabul. And oh, yes, some silk undergarments for the Harem.'

Ranveer laughed out loud.

'Such is the lot of us mere soldiers. I hope those nuts taste good after the blood we shed for them.'

Iftiqar brought his horse a little closer to Ranveer's and said,

'The news is that you will not be a mere soldier much longer. They say you will be appointed a *hazaari* when we reach Dilli. One of your father's scribes told me that it is a foregone conclusion now that you are the rescuer of the Harem's undergarments.'

Ranveer looked at Iftiqar to see if he was joking.

'A *hazaari*? Even if they did see me fit to command a thousand men, I don't know if I could find enough men willing to risk their lives to rescue silk undergarments.'

Iftiqar burst out laughing, slapping Ranveer on the shoulder. Suddenly his mood changed to one of concern when he saw one of the scouts riding back.

'Sir, there's been some trouble ahead!'

Ranveer and Iftiqar rode with the scout to a small cluster of trees a *kos* ahead where they could see two dead horses. The stench was overpowering and the three men covered their noses as they surveyed the scene of mayhem before them. Both horses bore multiple injuries, but a few paces away, there were clues that the horses had not been the only ones to bleed that day. Two Sikh turbans lay on the ground, near pools of blood, next to a *palki* that lay half buried in the sand. Iftiqar dismounted and looked closer.

'Sir, the blood is still fresh. Looks like two *Khalsas* were killed or kidnapped and their horses killed.'

One of them pointed to the left, and just a few dozen paces away, Ranveer could see blood trails leading to the East. Ranveer thought about the decision that lay before him, and his mind made up, turned to Iftiqar.

'This is not part of our mission, but these are Mughal lands, and if someone is in distress we need to help. Men, put on your armour and follow me.'

As the men prepared themselves, Ranveer loaded and primed his flintlock pistols that he kept hanging from holsters on either side of his horse. His horse, like many of the other mounts, had become quite agitated at the sight and smell of death, and Ranveer nuzzled close to his mount's ear, whispering.

'Shh, my friend. There's nothing to worry about.'

Then the twenty six Mughal warriors mounted their horses and set off, following the blood trail. They did not have to travel far- just a couple of *kos* later, they came across the bodies of the two Sikh men whose turbans they had seen before. Both were splayed across the desert, bleeding from cuts, their long hair partly covering their faces like ghoulish masks. Ranveer guessed that both men had been wounded too badly to continue, and their captors had disposed of them. However, that still left whoever had been the occupant of the *palki*. Their pursuit was far from over.

Knowing that they were up against men who would not hesitate to slaughter unarmed captives, Ranveer spurred his horse at a full gallop, followed by Iftiqar and the rest of his men.

They caught up with their quarry in about half an hour. Ranveer could see six strongly built men just over the horizon, naked from the waist up, dragging along a figure draped in a sari. All six men had matchlock rifles slung across their backs and swords hanging at their belts.

'Those bastards were abducting a woman!' Iftiqar roared near Ranveer's ear. Ranveer had seen his share of battle and violence, but in the Mughal Army, if there was one thing to be taken for granted and was drilled into every recruit's head on the direct order of Emperor Bahadur Shah Zafar himself, it was that women were to be shown the highest honour. To see a woman being dragged along like this by six rogues, most likely to be raped and killed, or sold as a slave, made his blood boil.

One of the bandits turned, and seeing the horsemen in the distance, alerted his friends. Realizing that they were hopelessly outnumbered and outgunned, the bandits dumped their captive on the desert floor and ran.

'Should we chase them down?' Iftiqar asked.

Ranveer considered briefly before shaking his head in response.

'They will have a head start and the men are already tired and wounded. No point in spilling more blood needlessly since it looks like the woman they were kidnapping is safe.'

Ranveer and his men rode at a fast gallop till they reached the woman. She was sitting on the desert, her face obscured by a veil. Ranveer now looked at the woman the bandits had been carrying away and approached her to ask if she was okay.

As he came within a couple of paces of her, she took off her veil, and to his shock, Ranveer saw himself facing a gaunt, tall and unmistakably European man wearing thick spectacles.

To add to Ranveer's shock, the man addressed him in flawless Hindustani.

'Praise the Lord! I thought I was going to join those poor *Khalsas* soon enough. Thank you for saving me.'

Ranveer was still struck too speechless to say anything so the man stuck out his hand and as Ranveer extended his tentatively, the man introduced himself. 'Hello. I am Theophilius Metcalfe. But you can just call me Theo.'

After Ranveer had introduced himself and his men, he asked the man what he was doing out here in the middle of the desert.

'Oh, I am a teacher. I was employed to teach English to the children of one of the *Omrahs* in the Imperial Court. They were visiting relatives in Multan and I had accompanied them. The food there didn't agree with me so I was headed back and I employed two *Khalsas* as bodyguards. Somewhere along the way, these bandits happened to chance upon us.'

Something in the story didn't ring true, and this time it was Iftiqar who spoke. Ranveer and many of the younger generation had got used to seeing European traders, teachers and ambassadors, and regarded the British as little more than another empire to trade and do business with. Iftiqar and his generation had however heard tales from their parents and grandparents about the British designs on India and the bitter battles that had put them in their place. So it was natural that he regarded their new companion with suspicion.

'If you were employed by an *Omrah*, why didn't he send his attendants or guards with you? And what are you doing dressed in that ridiculous sari?'

When the man seemed to hesitate, Ranveer stepped towards him. The man flinched as he saw the tall Mughal knight walking towards him, wearing armour and with a sword in one hand.

'Look, I'll tell you everything. You see, it's a bit of a delicate matter. One of the *Omrah's* nieces was, how shall I put it? Err, quite of a friendly disposition, and as it happened, I ended up being more intimate with her than the *Omrah* would have liked. I heard that he had got to know, so I was getting away before he flayed the skin off my back. Just help me get to Dilli and you will not hear from me again.'

Iftiqar roared in laughter, and Ranveer found himself smiling.

'Theo, you would not be the first man to have got yourself into trouble over a woman. But I must say, your chosen escape plan is the most scatterbrained I have ever seen. Now wear a man's clothes and join us. If you keep wearing that ridiculous sari, one of my men may get amorous in the loneliness of the night and do to you what you did that to that *Omrah's* niece.'

That broke the ice, and soon, Theo had changed into some spare clothes Ranveer was carrying, and sat down behind Ranveer on his horse. Together with their new English companion, the Ahadis continued their journey to Dilli.

***

Two

As they approached Dilli, Ranveer reminded himself of how someone had once written that coming into the Mughal capital was like approaching the scene of a shipwreck. You would see the flotsam and jetsam well before you got to your destination. In Dilli's case, that took the form of urchins, beggars, mendicants, self-professed fakirs and astrologers, and small stalls selling everything from food to clothes, all working together to fleece anyone entering or exiting the capital. They gave the Mughal force a wide berth, though a couple of enterprising urchins ran up to the horsemen, offering lucky charms for sale, only to be shooed away.

However, what made the group of horsemen the object of much attention was the presence of an Englishman in their midst. People gathered around the roadside, cautious not to get too close to the dour faced soldiers, yet not able to contain their curiosity. The only Englishman most of them had seen were rich merchants or diplomats who travelled in palanquins or carriages, cocooned from ordinary Hindustaanis. But this Englishman wore old Hindustaani garments and was riding with a group of heavily armed soldiers. Most assumed that he had been arrested for some crime. An old lady walked up to Theo and considered him with a sad expression on her face, saying,

'Whatever it is you have done, repent and you may yet escape with your life in there.'

Theo answered in chaste Hindustaani, '*Chaachi*, if I start recounting all my sins, the Emperor's youngest son will sprout gray hair before I finish.'

Ranveer and the soldiers laughed out loud as the astonished crowd dispersed. As the riders approached the city, they began to see more Mughal troops and some of the men exchanged pleasantries with familiar faces. Word of their desert skirmishes had spread, and while a group of heavily armed Ahadis was hardly expected to do anything other than decimate the sort of riff-raff they had encountered, Ranveer's exploits in recovering the stolen Imperial treasure had in particular caught the imagination of the troops.

They entered the city through the southern gate, passing two immense stone elephants carved into the wall, and entering a street that was divided by a narrow canal. On either side sat merchants going about their business, sitting in front of mounds of grains or cloth. Ranveer led his men through alleys passing the Jama Masjid, before they reached their destination–the Qila Mubarak, which to common folks was simply known as *Lal Qila* or the 'red fort'.

'Well, Theo, we are at our destination. You are free to go your way now.'

Theo thanked Ranveer and his men profusely before dismounting and disappearing into an alley as the Mughal riders entered the citadel. After ordering his men to rest for the remainder of the day and to report for duty at sunrise the next morning, Ranveer rode straight home.

Home was a palatial *haveli* near the banks of the Jumna, not very far from where the Royal Quarters were. As befitted a man of Qureshi's stature, the house was in itself a small fortress, surrounded by a small moat, and guarded by more than a dozen heavily armed troops. There was also a veritable army of servants, and as Ranveer rode in, he found himself being literally mobbed by them–one brought him a cool *sharbat* flavoured with rose water, another handed him a cold cloth to wipe his face with, a third relieved him of his weapons, while yet another hovered in the background just in case he wanted anything. As Ranveer entered his room, he realized just how much he hated being here alone. Sure, he had every comfort he could have wanted, but the sheer size of the house seemed to mock his loneliness. His father was forever travelling on work, and with his mother no longer there, he had nobody to talk to or share what was on his mind. That was why he preferred to be at the barracks, sharing in the rough camaraderie of Iftiqar and the men, or even better, riding in the open with the wind in his face. His father may have dreamt many dreams for him, but Ranveer knew his heart lay somewhere very distant from climbing up the ranks of the Mughal bureaucracy.

Ranveer ate his dinner just after sunset, and then retired to his room. Many men his age would at this time have been stepping out to enjoy the forbidden pleasures that the Dilli night had on offer, but Ranveer had never acquired a taste for concubines or wine. Once an associate of his father had told him that it was perhaps good to have one or two conspicuous weaknesses, since men without obvious vices were either too good at concealing secrets or just too honest, both of which were not exactly virtues to have in the Court. That, Ranveer felt, was exactly the sort of politicking that made him detest the ways of the Dilli political system.

When he retired to his bedroom, he dismissed the three attendants who normally sat outside the room operating the *punkhah* over his bed. It was warm but he didn't want the creaking of the fan to interrupt his sleep. Every bone in his body seemed to ache after the exertions of the last few days, and his left leg hurt terribly from a glancing blow he had taken in the last skirmish. As he lay down on the bed, he prayed that he be granted a dreamless sleep. As with many young men from Mughal aristocratic families, Ranveer had been baptized in war from an early age, and in the field of battle, killing came without a second thought. It was only when he was far from the battlefield that it came back to haunt him- when he was asleep. That night, as with many others before, sleep did come to him, but not the peaceful, dreamless slumber he had prayed for. Rather, he dreamt of his sword dripping blood, and of corpses rising from the grave to ask him why he had killed them. If his father's associate who had lectured him about the importance of weaknesses had known, he may have corrected himself and said that there was one vice that was certainly not an asset–that weakness was having a conscience.

As was his habit, Ranveer woke before sunrise to exercise. Dressed in only a loin-cloth, he whirled around the small gymnasium behind the house, sweat covering his entire body. His sword flashed around him, almost too fast to see anything more than a glint of silver. The layman would have thought him to have lost his mind. The professional would know that he was assiduously practicing the moves that had been drilled into him by his masters through his years of training. When he finished, he winced at the pain in his left leg, and as he stood before the mirror, he saw dozens of scars and bruises across his body, each marking some occasion when an enemy blow or shot had penetrated his defenses.

His black hair was flat against his scalp, caked with sweat, and while he may not have the muscled bulk that many other officers favoured, his toned body and wiry muscles meant that he had both speed and surprising strength, as many adversaries had found out. While sons of other nobles still trained for largely ceremonial shows of individual bravado through sword fights between champions, and led their armies into battle sitting in tents at the rear, Ranveer knew that the old way of warfare was obsolete. Now it was down to mobility and surprise, and he wanted to be able to lead from the front.

Ranveer's father had often cautioned him about putting his life in harm's way. Couldn't he learn from the other young officers who didn't wade into the enemy like a maniac before any of their men? Leading from the rear was a job for cowards, had been Ranveer's retort, triggering yet another debate between father and son.

When Ranveer reached his barracks, he found that Iftiqar had already been putting the fifty men of his squad through their paces. Iftiqar's loud voice boomed across the ground and his bald head was glistening with sweat, 'Stay sharp, you move like a pregnant buffalo.'

After overseeing his men's exercises, Ranveer and Iftiqar strolled down Chandni Chowk to get some food. At Ranveer's insistence, lunch was going to be at Ghantawala's, reputed to be the best sweet shop in all of Hindustaan. The two of them feasted on steaming hot *samosas* and *kachoris* before Iftiqar declared that his stomach would burst if he ate another morsel. The two of them entered a neighbouring *kahwa-khana*, ordering cups of coffee as they sat down to plan the exercises for their men while they were in Dilli. They both knew that the men would expect some time off with their families, but Ranveer wanted to make sure they didn't lose their edge. Iftiqar had long come to accept that his former pupil was a very hard taskmaster. They were sitting in a secluded area of the coffee shop, cut off from the rest of the patrons by a thin canvas screen, and had barely begun their discussion when Ranveer heard a familiar voice.

'Even the biggest imbecile in Hindustaan knows that the Emperor wants to name Jawan Bakht as his heir apparent.'

Another voice chimed in, 'But he is only sixteen years old. He would be a puppet.'

'Whom would you want him to pick? Mirza Abu Bakr? Everyone knows he covets the throne, and carries a big grudge since his father, the eldest son of the Emperor, died last year. I hear he siphons off revenues and massacres innocents in the Afghan lands, but the Emperor turns a blind eye since nobody else can keep those tribes at bay.'

'Or is it just a guilty conscience that makes the Emperor tolerate Abu Bakr's excesses since his father was supposedly poisoned at the orders of the Queen?'

'Is it true Mirza Fakhru was poisoned?'

'Who knows? But the fact is that it is a good thing that Abu Bakr is away with the Army of Kabul. With his reputation for drunkenness, I dread the day he sits on the Peacock Throne.'

'So what if he enjoys a drink? Every Prince has his own vice.'

Ranveer had been listening in silence, but finally could not contain himself. He emerged from behind the screen.

'Englishman, you gossip like a woman!'

The two Mughal soldiers, the two men who had been sitting with Theo, ran away leaving the Englishman facing Ranveer.

'Please join me for some coffee and you may learn a thing

or two about your Empire.'

When Ranveer sat down next to Theo, he leaned forward towards him to smell his breath and then sat back.

'You must be suicidal, Theo. You are drunk in the middle of the day, blabbering about the Emperor and his sons. If another officer had overheard you, he would have had you thrown into the dungeon by now.'

'I say it's still not too late to do that', said Iftiqar.

Theo glowered at Iftiqar before addressing Ranveer.

'You see my friend, the occasional drink serves a most therapeutic purpose by cleansing my body of the various afflictions that accompany your climate. But forget me, shouldn't the two of you be preparing to guard the Emperor's procession next week or are they not involving the Ahadis in that?'

Ranveer leaned forward towards Theo, and spoke in a whisper.

'You know way too much for a disgraced English teacher. Now try and stay out of trouble, we have work to attend to'

As Ranveer and Iftiqar left the coffee shop, Iftiqar shook his head as he spoke.

'That Englishman is impertinent and irritating. You should just lock him up.'

'Iftiqar *chacha*, relax. He just talks too much and thinks too little. If we started locking people up for that, half of Dilli would be in the dungeons.' Iftiqar would have grumbled more if one of their men had not ridden up to them, dismounting before Ranveer and greeting him with a bow.

'Sir, you are to report home immediately. Your father is back and wants you to get ready.'

'Ready for what?'

'For your audience with the Emperor this evening.'

***

'Father, stop fussing. I am not a child anymore!'

Ranveer's patience had finally snapped after putting up with more than half an hour of non-stop advice from his father while they rode to the Qila Mubarak from their home. Qureshi looked at Ranveer and smiled.

'My boy, this is the proudest day of my life. You are to be promoted in the presence of the Emperor himself. So of course I am going to fuss! Especially when I have to present this hot-headed son of mine in the Court.'

Ranveer said little after that, realizing that his protests were going to have little effect anyways, and Qureshi kept haranguing him about making sure he showed the right level of respect and did not talk out of turn.

Attendants took their horses and immaculately dressed doormen, wearing gold and saffron headbands ushered them into the *Diwaan-e-khaas*. For all his bluster, even Ranveer was well and truly intimidated now. He had never been in the inner chambers before and seeing the sheer opulence of the Emperor's Court, he began to appreciate that the Mughal Emperor was not called the richest man in the world for nothing. The walls were covered in brightly coloured precious stones and the fabled Kohinoor diamond shining like the Sun itself adorned the Peacock Throne where the Emperor would sit. The hall was still half empty but looking around Ranveer saw a veritable who's-who of the Mughal aristocracy.

'Father, is that Ghalib himself?,' Ranveer pointed to an old man sitting in a corner, a fur cap on his head, scribbling away on some parchment, oblivious to the hustle and bustle around him.

'Shh...that is the crude street name- only the Emperor is so familiar as to use that name with him. In here, we refer to him only as Mirza Abadullah Khan or as Mirza Ghalib. If you're lucky today, you may hear him read one of his new poems.'

Ranveer took his position beside his father, sitting on richly embroidered mattresses on the carpeted floor, leaning back against some cushions that had been placed against the wall. Attendants were scurrying back and forth, serving *sharbat* and sweets to the nobles, and Ranveer was about to help himself to a glass when his father stopped him.

'Keep it at your feet. Nobody should drink or eat anything before the Emperor does so.'

'All rise. The Emperor is on his way!'

At that announcement, every man in the hall rose. As Ranveer rose, he tripped on the edge of the carpet and bumped into the man next to him.

'Watch your step, you clumsy oaf!'

Ranveer's eyes burned with fury as he looked up at the man

who had spoken those words. The man was tall and well built, with a thick beard, and wearing a black uniform and turban. Ranveer knew from the uniform that he would be from the Army of Kabul.

'I am sorry, I tripped. So you have my sincere apologies, but it seems you need some lessons in manners, my Afghan friend.'

The man stepped closer to Ranveer, murder in his eyes, when a smaller man stepped between them.

'General Abdali, the young man meant no disrespect, I am sure. Plus, I see he is accompanied by Amir-e-Azam Shameem Qureshi, an old confidante of the Emperor, so please let the matter rest.'

The man who spoke could not have been much older than Ranveer, was slight of build and had a nasal, almost feminine voice. Yet at those words, the burly Afghan bowed and stepped back. Qureshi had now stepped beside Ranveer.

'Prince Abu Bakr, it is a surprise to see you here! I thought you and your men were still in the land of the Afghans.'

'Qureshi-sahib, the Emperor wanted me to be back, and as always, I am at his service.'

As the two men walked towards the throne, Qureshi poked Ranveer in the ribs.

'Very smart, we're here less than a heartbeat, and you pick a fight with the General of one of the Prince's armies. General Abdali may be out of place in the niceties of the Court, but word has it that he saved the Prince's life in the Afghan hills. Since then, he has become the Prince's right hand.'

Ranveer was about to say something when his father continued.

'These are not men you should make enemies of, as odious as their behaviour may sometimes seem. The Afghan lands are still wild, but for all their brutality, men like Abdali ensure that the hordes do not encroach on the Emperor's lands, so he has a lot of favour here.'

Before Ranveer could say anything in his defense, a loud voice boomed across the hall.

'His Divine Highness, Caliph of the Age, Badsaah as Glorious as Jamshed, He who is surrounded by hosts of Angels, Shadow of God, Refuge of Islam, Protector of the Mohammedan Religion, Offspring of the House of Timur, Greatest Emperor, Mightiest King of Kings, Emperor son of Emperor, Sultan son of Sultan, his Royal Highness Bahadur Shah Zafar, is here.'

Every man bowed as deeply as they could, Ranveer needing another sharp poke from his father, so engrossed was he in watching the ceremony unfold. When he raised his head, he saw the man he had seen innumerable times on portraits and occasionally from a distance during parades. But now for the first time in his life, he saw the Mughal Emperor up close. Zafar was wearing an intricately embroidered coat, inlaid with rubies and diamonds, and a crown that was no less ornate. He had a soft face, looking more like a poet than the descendant of fierce Mongol warriors, and gently stroked his salt and pepper beard as he sat down on his throne. As all the men sat down, Ranveer realized he had been holding his breath.

'So Darogah-sahab, what is the order of business today?' asked Zafar to a young, clean-shaven man sitting to his left.

'That is Zahir Dehlavi, the Emperor's closest aide', whispered Qureshi into Ranveer's ears.

'*Jahapanah*, first we would like to welcome back Prince Mirza Abu Bakr and his Army of Kabul.'

As Abu Bakr stepped forward and bowed before the Emperor, Zafar spoke to his grandson.

'My Prince, you have done us proud. Ten years ago, the Afghan borders were unsafe for any Mughal trader or army, infested as they were with bandits and war-mongering tribes. Under your leadership, there is unprecedented peace there. I welcome you back- I wanted all the Princes to be here when I announce my successor.'

The Prince bowed even lower and said, 'I am always at your service, *Jahapanah*.'

Ranveer whispered to Qureshi.

'Is it true that the Emperor puts up with Abu Bakr's siphoning off revenues only because he is the only Prince brutal enough to keep the tribes at bay?'

Qureshi glared at his son, willing him to shut up.

After Abu Bakr sat down, several more nobles were called up and honoured with awards of lands or money for services they had rendered in the previous year. Ranveer was beginning to get bored when Dehlavi called out his name.

'Mansabdar Ranveer Pratap, son of Amir-e-Azam Shameem

Qureshi, please step forward.'

Ranveer stood before the Emperor, his head bowed just as his father had asked him to.

'For your services, you are granted the title of Amir, and promoted to the rank of *hazaari*. You will receive a monthly allowance of Rupees eleven thousand for yourself and your men.'

Ranveer's mind was still boggling at the amount, when the Emperor addressed him directly.

'Come to me, young man', he said in a soft voice.

Ranveer's heart was beating like a drum as he walked towards the Emperor.

Young man, did your father ever tell you that he saved my life on the Afghan border by fighting off four Pathan tribals single-handedly?'

Ranveer shook his head, as Zafar continued.

'I owe him my life, and trust that you will do him proud.'

Ranveer was expected to just mumble some niceties and sit down, but without thinking he blurted out.

'I never knew you saw battle against the Pathans, My Lord.'

Murmurs of disapproval at the young man's impertinence spread through the chamber, but Zafar just smiled indulgently.

'Ask him the story. We were both younger and stupider then.'

'My son, I am so proud of you but you do need to learn to control your tongue if I am to make a noble of you yet' said Qureshi as Ranveer sat down next to him

'Father, you fought off four Pathans and saved the Emperor? Why didn't you ever tell me before?'

'Well, you know now. And that was a long time ago, when I was young and hot-headed like you!'

As the day's proceedings ended, father and son rode back home in silence. Qureshi's heart was bursting with pride at his son's promotion, while Ranveer was even more in awe of his father than he had been before.

***

The next week passed by in a blur, as Ranveer tried to work through with Iftiqar the logistics of raising a force of a thousand men. Being promoted was well and good, but the logistics of raising, training and maintaining such a large force were complex. Sitting at their barracks one evening, Ranveer told Iftiqar that he just wished he could ride with his small force again without having to worry about such administrative matters.

'That is the cost of moving up in life, my friend. Maybe they will make a noble out of you after all.'

Ranveer scowled at the thought and got back to his planning, when his work was interrupted by a messenger from his father.

'Amir-e-azam requests that you join him tomorrow morning at the Emperor's speech.'

The next morning, it seemed like the whole of Dilli had but one destination- the vast open grounds outside Qila Mubarak on the banks of the River Jumna. When Ranveer reached the area, he was escorted to a special raised enclosure for officers and nobles, where his father was already waiting for him. Before him, he could see thousands upon thousands of people stretched out as far as the eye could see.

'My God, there must be tens of thousands of people here!'

'Son, this may be the only time in most of our lifetimes that we get to see the Emperor pass on his mantle.'

Ranveer remembered something that Theo had mentioned at the *kahwa-khana*.

'Father, why are the Ahadis not charged with security this time?'

'Son, it seems the Emperor wanted to honour Abu Bakr by letting his men take charge of security. He has a delicate balancing act to play–there are many contenders for the throne, and whoever the Emperor appoints will earn the instant hatred of the others unless the Emperor can keep everyone's ego satiated.'

'Father, who do you think should be appointed the new Emperor?'

Qureshi looked around to make sure nobody was within earshot, and then whispered to Ranveer.

'Be careful when you ask or answer such a question. Many a good man has been ruined due to imprudent speculation on such matters.'

Normally Qureshi would have ended the discussion there, but perhaps because he was still so elated at Ranveer's promotion, he continued, still barely whispering.

'If I were a betting man, which I am not, my wager would

be on Jawan Bakht being appointed the chosen one.'

Ranveer started to protest, but Qureshi raised his hand to continue.

'I know, I know, he is but a child yet, but the Empress Zinat Mahal favours him and you will learn one day, my son, that what a woman wants is often what her man ends up doing. Also, while he is still a boy, don't forget Akbar inherited the mantle at an even earlier age.'

Any further discussion ceased when a group of nobles came and sat near them, exchanging greetings with Qureshi, some of them congratulating Ranveer on his recent promotion.

The blowing of a dozen trumpets announced that the Royal Entourage was about to arrive, and then Ranveer was treated to the unforgettable spectacle of the Mughal Emperor arriving in all his splendour.

First came dozens of emissaries from foreign lands. The usual suspects were there- the British, the French, the Portugese and the Dutch, all of whom spent considerable money and time lobbying with the Mughal Court for trading rights. After the conflict of a century ago, the Mughals had been understandably cagey about extending too many rights or privileges to anyone lest a trading company again harbour notions of turning conqueror. Since the ceremony this day was also meant to commemorate the victory over the British, the presence of a large number of the Queen's envoys was also a signal that the British were keen to put the past behind them.

Then came a full regiment of soldiers of the Army of Kabul,

dressed in black, all heavily armoured and fully armed. Each man seemed to have been selected for his height and build, and atop their huge warhorses, they presented a fearsome spectacle. Largest of them all, his flowing beard marking him out even at this distance, was the General whom Ranveer had argued with in the Court. Ranveer felt a jolt of envy, since he knew that if in keeping with tradition, the Emperor had chosen the Ahadis to be the Honour Guard, he may have been one of the horsemen leading the procession.

Finally, in marched the main body of the Royal Entourage. In front were dozens of *choubdars*, carrying ceremonial maces, flanked by servants in bright red tunics carrying *punkhas*. Behind them came six elephants carrying the dynastic insignia of the Mughal Emperor. The first carried a flag showing the rays of the Sun embroidered in real gold, the second two golden fish suspended on a golden bow, the third a lion, the fourth the golden head of a Falcon, the fifth a horse's head, and finally the sixth, the golden Imperial umbrella. It was a display meant to inspire awe, and in that it did not fail. The roar of the crowd made any speech impossible, and Ranveer looked on with mounting excitement as the full regalia of the Mughal Emperor came on display for the first time since he was a young boy and had witnessed a victory procession in the capital.

The Emperor himself came mounted on a giant elephant that seemed to dwarf the six that had preceded it. Zafar had always enjoyed a reputation as being more of a poet and statesman than a warrior but seeing him with all the symbols of his power made it easy to imagine him at the head of his vast army. As his elephant approached the specially constructed platform near the ramparts of the fort, Zafar dismounted and then climbed up a short flight of stairs to the vantage point from which he would address his people. All the Princes were already there, and bowed low as Zafar approached. Ranveer did not envy them their position at this moment, as he knew that each of them must have their hearts in their mouths, waiting for the words from Zafar that would decide their fate.

Zafar acknowledged each Prince and then stood, motioning with his hand for silence. As if by magic, every voice stilled in the sea of people before him, as Zafar began speaking.

'By the grace of the Almighty, I have the good fortune of addressing the people of Hindustaan on the occasion of the hundredth anniversary of our victory at Palashi. Many people believe that this is an occasion to celebrate our victory over one power or the other, but I do not think that is so.'

At this, he seemed to tilt his head at the British emissaries seated a hundred feet below him to his left.

'We belong to the house of Timur, and when challenged, we fight to protect what is ours, but we are also the land of poetry, of culture, of the *din-e-ilahi* that the great Akbar created to bind our various religions and races. So we hold no lasting grudge, and when someone holds forth a hand of friendship, we are steadfast in our loyalty.'

Then he straightened again and addressed the crowd.

'No, people of Hindustaan, this is a day to celebrate the day when we finally regained the core of what made us great, what made us strong- and that is our unity. Never again must we allow ourselves to be weakened by internal divisions and squabbles, never again must our Empire be seen as an easy prey. Those are the principles we have tried to live by in the last hundred years, and those are the principles I have tried to embody in my time as Emperor.'

Ranveer could see grown men around him tear up, as they all knew what was coming. It was a measure of the incredible charisma of the frail old man before him that in the midst of all the politicking and cynicism of the Mughal Court, he still inspired such genuine loyalty among men like Qureshi.

'But my time has come. I have laboured hard to lay brick by brick the foundation for a nation that I hope I leave stronger than it was before me, but now it is time stronger and younger hands take on the task of laying the next layer of this foundation.'

'They ask me, Zafar, who have you chosen to succeed you? I tell them that I hold no such power. All I did was hold onto the throne and ensure it did not fall into the wrong hands. The worthy successor will choose himself by his deeds, in God's eyes and in the eyes of the people of Hindustaan.'

That seemed to go down well with the masses, and many of them cheered till Zafar resumed.

'I am blessed to have many strong and talented sons and grandsons, all different, yet together making me confident that the future of Hindustaan is in capable hands. So I would like for them to work together to ensure that we step into this future with renewed confidence. As for me, they ask, what will the Emperor do? I will become Zafar again, a man who lives by his pen, and looks back with satisfaction on a life well lived and in anticipation of an end near his loved ones.'

Out of the corner of his eye, Ranveer thought he saw some movement in the crowd and for a few seconds he scanned the crowd to see what had caught his eye. Not seeing anything out of the ordinary, he turned his attention back to the Emperor and he saw that he was now flanked by the Princes as he entered what was undoubtedly the most eagerly anticipated part of his speech.

'Mirza Mughal, diligent administrator, skilled diplomat and dutiful son, I appoint Qiladar. He will be in charge of ensuring that our citadel is forever safe.'

A tall young man next to Zafar bowed at the honour. If there was any disappointment at not being appointed Emperor, Ranveer couldn't see any obvious signs. Then again, he reminded himself, Mirza Mughal was the fifth son, and hardly one of the leading candidates for the position.

'Mirza Abu Bakr, the one who brought peace to the troubled Afghan borders, the unsurpassed strategist, I appoint...'

At that point, all pandemonium broke loose.

Ranveer saw a flash of movement in the crowd just below Zafar, and his trained eyes saw a group of men sling out crossbows and let loose a volley of shafts. He had not been the only one to notice, and in a split second, a group of black-clad Afghan warriors led by General Abdali had charged into the crowd, hacking at all in their path. But it was all too late.

Ranveer looked on in horror as he saw two bolts hit the Emperor on his chest. One missed and another grazed one of the attendants standing near the Emperor.

'Please Lord, let him live!'

Qureshi's anguished cry was probably echoed by thousands of others as Princes and attendants rushed to steady the stricken Emperor. Ranveer hoped that if he could get attention soon, he would probably live, since the Emperor would likely have been wearing armour under his cloak.

But then Zafar swayed unsteadily forward and to the horror of Ranveer and everyone gathered there, the Emperor of Hindustaan fell to his death.

***

Three

The evening of Bahadur Shah Zafar's murder, the whole of Hindustaan seemed paralyzed with shock. The streets were deserted, the shops closed. It was as if everyone dreaded what the killing of the Emperor would unleash. That night, Qureshi walked home, carrying the court newspaper, *Siraj-ul-Akhbar*. There was only one item in this hastily published issue–a single poem by Ghalib that perfectly summed up the mood in the nation.

We smashed the wine cup and the flask,
What is it now to us,
If all the rain that falls from heaven,
Should turn to rose-red wine?

Among the hardest hit were the sections of the aristocracy who owed their loyalty, and their continued success to the patronage of the old Emperor. Ranveer had never seen his father so broken and seeing the strong old man look visibly older and frail within a few hours of the assassination made him very afraid for what was to follow. Ranveer finally broached the subject as he and his father sat down for dinner at their home.

'Father, what will happen now?'

Qureshi looked at his young son and sighed deeply. Then, he turned to the attendants around them and dismissed them all for the night.

'Son, what I fear most, what all of us fear most, is anarchy. Sometimes it does not matter if you have a good government or a bad one, as long as you have one that at least lays down some rules to govern society. With the vacuum the Emperor's death has created, we all fear that the order we have all worked to establish will collapse.'

'But surely father, one of the Princes will take the reins of power. I hear rumours that before breathing his last, the Emperor did utter the name of his successor.'

Qureshi looked at Ranveer, with a sad smile on his face.

'My son, I have worked all my life to shelter you from the ugly side of our system. I fear that now nobody will be able to shelter their children from it. Whatever happens now, without a clear cut transfer of power, we may well return to the age when brother slaughtered brother in the lust for power. And when that happens, we will be but mere pawns to be traded and sacrificed as they see fit.'

With his father's fears still fresh in his mind, Ranveer reported for duty the next morning. After several months, every single

Ahadi had been mobilized and called to the Qila Mubarak, where they were to be addressed by their Supreme Commander, Zorawar Khan. The imposing old soldier was pacing up and down, his hands clasped behind his back, as five thousand fully armoured Ahadis stood before him. Ranveer stood at the head of his squad of fifty, with Iftiqar standing just behind him. Every single man snapped to attention when the old General began speaking.

'Men, we are passing through times the likes of which we have never seen before. The Ahadis were created as the force that reported directly to the Emperor, and was above all the politicking that afflicted the armies whose primary loyalty lay with their commanding nobles.'

To hear a career officer like Zorawar speak so candidly in front of all his men made Ranveer realize just how dire the circumstances were.

'And we have failed. The Emperor has been killed, and we could do nothing to protect him. It is no consolation to say that we were not appointed the Honour Guard that fateful day. While we may have failed in that task, we cannot fail the nation. Men, over the next few days, you may hear and see all kinds of things. Things that may shake your faith in the system we have given our lives to protect, but one thing that I ask you to do- whatever happens, do not lose faith, because the moment we lose faith, then all is truly lost. There are now only five thousand of us, but we will be the last line of defence against anarchy and chaos. As long as one Ahadi breathes, our nation shall not fall prey to vultures and jackals scavenging for remains. Keep yourselves in the highest state of readiness. In a few days, I will assign orders for each unit. Dismissed.'

As the men filed out, Ranveer turned to Iftiqar, hoping that his old mentor would be able to reassure him.

'I'm sure you would have seen situations like this. How long before you think, things will finally get back to normal?'

Iftiqar waited till all the men had left, and then gently guided Ranveer by his arm to a corner. When he spoke, it was not as a subordinate speaking to an officer but as an older mentor speaking to a young man, who was as yet uninitiated in the ways of the world.

'Ranveer, I have no idea how things are going to turn out but if I were you, I would just stay close to your father and do as he says.'

Iftiqar's words stung Ranveer, and as he turned to leave Ranveer stopped him.

'I am not a child anymore. I am an officer in the Ahadis, and I need to perform my duties.'

Iftiqar had almost a sad expression as he responded before finally turning and leaving.

'There are times when the strongest of us count for nothing, and the most heroic duty one can perform is to stay alive for one's loved ones. Now, I must go and ensure my family gets out of Dilli before things turn really nasty.'

Ranveer was puzzled as to why everyone was behaving so strangely. All his life he had been brought up to believe that for all its ills, the system worked. There were always enough checks and balances to ensure that things kept moving, that order was maintained. He had grown up with the unquestioning belief that the Mughal Empire could be temporarily shaken, but never really moved off the equilibrium it had achieved for a hundred years. Now, seeing men like his father and Iftiqar so worried, he began to wonder if he had missed something.

The next morning was the funeral of Bahadur Shah Zafar and the whole of Hindustaan forgot about fears and misgivings about the future to unite in grieving the loss of its beloved Emperor. The long funeral procession snaked its way around the Qila Mubarak, pausing in front of the Jama Masjid and then making its way beyond the Nizamuddin Dargah to reach the gardens where many members of the ruling dynasty were buried- starting with Humayun. The black coffin carrying the body of the Emperor was accompanied by the Princes, all with their heads hung in grief. Zahir Dahlavi, the Emperor's closest confidante was not far behind, and the young man was sobbing inconsolably. The Empire's Poet Laureate, Ghalib, was with him, a comforting hand on his shoulder.

Ranveer witnessed the sombre ceremony from a few hundred paces away, standing next to his father. Seeing tears stream down his normally stoic father's face made him choke up with emotion as well. When the ceremony was over, the Princes retired to the Qila Mubarak, and just before noon, Qureshi received summons that all the senior nobles were to assemble in the *Diwan-e-Khaas* for a special announcement.

Time passed excruciatingly slowly as Ranveer waited for

his father to return or at least to hear some news of what was happening in the Imperial Court. When there was no sign of his father by four in the evening, he started getting concerned. When a servant came to ask if he would like to have something to eat, Ranveer said that he would wait for his father to return. An hour or so passed, during which time Ranveer paced up and down the length of the courtyard in front of his home. Finally, at about five in the evening, he spotted a lone horseman galloping towards his house. When he saw it was Iftiqar, he rushed forward to meet him.

'Iftiqar *chacha*, is there any news from the Palace?'

Iftiqar's face and bald head glistened with sweat and he seemed to be slightly out of breath as he dismounted.

'Ranveer, your father sends word that he will be needed there for several hours more.'

'That's all he said? Tell me, Iftiqar *chacha*, what is happening there?'

Iftiqar shuffled uncomfortably from one foot to another, but when he realized that Ranveer was not going to relent, he faced the young man.

'Look, Ranveer, I am not privy to what is going on inside there, but I have learnt that a sure way to survive is to keep one's eyes and ears open. And I hear that things are moving fast.'

Ranveer was losing his patience, 'Iftiqar, spare me the philosophy. What is going on there?'

'The Emperor's personal physician has testified that the Emperor was alive for a few moments after the fall, and that his last words were 'Abu Bakr'. Based on that Mirza Abu Bakr has proclaimed himself Emperor. He says that he will lead in collaboration with the other Princes, but there's something else afoot. He announced that the four assassins were all Marathas or Rajputs, and were part of a conspiracy to overthrow the Mughal Empire.'

'Were they?'

Iftiqar looked at Ranveer, once again both touched and surprised at his naivety.

'Ranveer, let's just say that they are all conveniently dead and are in no position to refute any allegations Abu Bakr brings against them.'

***

When his father was not back by six o'clock, Ranveer decided that instead of having dinner alone, he was better off going for a ride to think through all that had happened over the last few days. He changed from his uniform into a simple white tunic and trousers and rode his horse through the main road leading out of his home and towards Chandni Chowk.

The first hint that things were not normal was when he passed the imposing structure of the Jama Masjid. What struck him first was the eerie silence. For as far back as he could remember, the steps of the Jama Masjid had always been abuzz every evening with activity. There were the faithful streaming into the mosque to pray, and then there were the bards gathered on the steps of the grand mosque, reciting the *Dastaan-e-Amir Hamza*. Those fantastic tales about the adventures of one of the ancestors of the Prophet could sometimes stretch for seven or eight hours, and there was always a ready audience to listen to stories about travels to exotic lands, battles with fire-breathing dragons and rescues of damsels in distress.

Today, however, the steps of the Jama Masjid were deserted, except for a few young men huddled together in small groups. Ranveer rode his horse on towards Ghantawala's sweet shop, where he wanted to get something to eat. As he dismounted and approached the shop, he saw the fat owner gathering up his utensils, as if preparing to close for the day. The old man must have been at least eighty years of age, though nobody knew his real age. All anyone knew was that, as far back as anyone could remember, his sweet shop had been doling out the best laddoos and *jalebis* to Dilliwalas.

'*Ram Ram*, Ghantawala *ji*, are you in such a hurry that you cannot serve up some *jalebis* for one of your most loyal customers?'

Ranveer was surprised when he saw the usually jovial features of Ghantawala cloud over with fear.

'My friend, I think you should be going home. This is not a place for a Hindu to be out on a day such as this.'

It never crossed Ranveer's mind why his religion would suddenly matter.

'What are you saying? I have grown up on these streets, and what does anyone's religion have to do with anything? For a hundred years now, the Emperor had decreed that all religions have equality before law. And...'

The man cut Ranveer off.

'Look, I need to close my shop and get home, all I can tell you is what I have heard.'

'And what might that be?'

Ranveer was still angry at being brushed off the way he had been, and certainly was not going to leave unless he got a satisfactory answer.

'Have you heard of Maulvi Sarfaraz Ali?'

Ranveer shook his head.

'He is supposedly the Imam at one of the smaller mosques in town. An Afghan by origin, I believe, and Mirza Abu Bakr after appointing himself Emperor has just appointed him as his spiritual guide.'

Ranveer was temporarily stumped as to how a sweet shop owner could know details of what was probably being discussed in the Palace at that very moment, but then remembered how Iftiqar had often told him that the bazaar gossip was usually the most reliable source of intelligence in the Empire. Ghantawala continued speaking as he started pulling the shutters down in front of his shop. 'An hour ago, I believe Safaraz Ali said that the assassination of the Emperor was an act of war against Islam, an attempt by *kafirs* to overthrow the rule of Islam.'

'What nonsense!' blurted out Ranveer, but despite his own bluster, he was beginning to see just how fast things were deteriorating.

'My friend, I am on my way home. What you should also know is that every Hindu merchant and shop-keeper is going home to try and ride out the storm that will be upon us. Rumours are already floating in the market about how dead pigs have been thrown into the courtyards of mosques. They're just stirring the mobs- soon the killing will begin. You look like you're too young to remember how things were when Hindus had to live in fear- I think those times are upon us again.'

Ranveer rode away from the shop, his mind a swirl of emotions. All his life, he had never ever had to think of himself in terms of being Hindu or Mussalman. Qureshi had drilled into him that hard work and ability were all that counted, and once he had joined the Ahadis, he had taken on a broader identity that seemed to be much bigger than any one religion- that of being an officer in the Mughal Army's elite unit of cavalry. A full half of the Ahadis were Hindus, in large measure due to Bahadur Shah Zafar's exceptionally tolerant and open-minded policy towards other religions. So while many of the other units in the Mughal Army still predominantly reflected the religion or origin of the nobles commanding them, the Emperor had chosen a much more democratic and open approach to choosing the men of his own elite unit.

Ranveer had been so lost in his thoughts that he never noticed the group of six men following him on foot. When he entered a narrow alley just to the left of the Jama Masjid, the group encircled his horse. Suddenly Ranveer looked up to see himself surrounded by men carrying cleavers and clubs. As he scanned the group, he realized that all six of the men were wearing dirty vests and *lungis*, and were probably just robbers out in search of easy prey. He was stunned when the man directly in front of him, a short, broad-shouldered man with a huge gut asked him just one question.

'Are you Hindu or Mussalman?'

'What is it to you?'

The man seemed amused at Ranveer's defiance and repeated his question adding, 'It means more to you than to us. If you are a believer, then be on your way. If you are a *kafir* who has murdered our beloved Emperor and insulted Islam, then you will be butchered here and now.'

Ranveer unconsciously felt for the sword at his waist, and then remembered that he had left home unarmed and wearing civilian clothes.

'I am an *Amir* in the Mughal Army. Get out of my way.'

The man took hold of the reins of Ranveer's horse and looked up straight into Ranveer's eyes.

'I don't care if you are the highest noble in the land. If you are a *kafir*, you die!'

Infuriated, Ranveer lashed out with his right foot. The man was taken by surprise as the kick connected with his jaw and sent him reeling back. However, before Ranveer could get away, he felt strong hands pull him off his horse. One of the men grabbed him by the throat and threw him against the wall, knocking the wind out of him, as the others closed in for the kill. Ranveer punched the man nearest him, and was satisfied to see him go down, but then a blow from a club to his leg brought him down to his knees. Another glancing blow to his head send him keeling over, blood streaming down his face.

Just as Ranveer thought he was about to meet his end at the hands of illiterate thugs in a dirty alleyway, he saw one of his attackers crash against the wall and fall down, grabbing his head in agony. As the others turned to see what had happened, Ranveer saw a solitary figure among the five remaining men, moving with impossible speed, balance and grace. A leg stuck out at an awkward angle, catching a man on the side of the head, bringing him down in one kick. Another man raised his cleaver to strike only to have a crushing open-fisted blow delivered to his throat. The man grabbed his shattered windpipe and fell down, never to get up again. The other men realized that they were in well over their heads and beat a hasty retreat.

When his saviour held out a hand to help Ranveer up, he looked up and saw a familiar face.

'Theo! My God, what did you do to those men?'

'A little thank you would be in order first, wouldn't it?'

Sheepishly, Ranveer thanked him.

'Don't mention it, we are even now. Though if you had just told them you were a Mussalman you would have spared yourself some pain and me some exertion.'

'I am not a coward.'

Theo looked at Ranveer and laughed, 'Well that you most certainly are not, I'll grant you that. Just remember that discretion is sometimes the better part of valour.'

Ranveer wanted to tell him that sounded like a coward's philosophy, but not wanting to insult the man who had just saved his life, asked another question that was on his mind.

'Where does a disgraced English teacher with a weakness for wine and women learn to fight like that?'

'China.'

'What on earth were you doing in China?'

Theo looked at Ranveer and winked.

'It's a long story.'

Theo ripped a measure of cloth from one of the fallen attacker's *lungis* and wiped Ranveer's face clean of blood.

'Hold the cloth there. It's not a deep wound, but letting it bleed can't help.'

As Ranveer started to mount his horse after thanking Theo again, the Englishman seemed to hesitate for a minute and then spoke as Ranveer as about to ride away.

'By the way, do you think you could spare some room for me to sleep for a night? I promise I'll be out of your way tomorrow morning.'

'Sure, I have no problem with that, but why do you need refuge?'

Theo spoke in a whisper.

'I got myself another job as a teacher to a noble, but you see his wife had a thing for Englishmen.'

Ranveer rolled his eyes.

'My God, man! What is it with you and women? Now climb aboard, it's getting dark.'

As Theo clambered onto the horse behind Ranveer, he said, 'My friend, you have much yet to learn about women. Doesn't your own poet Ghalib say to *take a new woman every returning spring, for last year's almanac is a useless thing*?'

Despite the pain in his head, Ranveer laughed so hard he thought his stomach would burst, and the two of them rode back to Ranveer's house.

***

When the two of them reached Ranveer's house it was already past nine in the evening, and even before Ranveer had dismounted, Qureshi rushed out to greet his son.

'Thank God you're fine.'

Then he caught himself as he saw Ranveer's bloodied face.

'What happened? Who did this to you?'

Ranveer had been consumed by worries about what had happened to his father, especially after what Ghantawala had told him. He knew his father was well known as a staunch supporter of the late Emperor and knew that if Abu Bakr was intent on creating a new regime based on his own agenda, then the most visible supporters of the old regime would be in a precarious position. So instead of answering his father, he leapt off the horse and into his father's arms.

'Abba-*jaan*! What is happening? I hope they are not going to cause you any harm.'

Despite the seriousness of the situation, Qureshi smiled to

himself, remembering how Ranveer would seek comfort from him when he was a small child in a similar way when he had been hurt or scared by something. Then he reminded himself that unlike then, he could not just make things better with soothing words or a treat of sweets.

'Come inside and we will talk.'

He glanced towards Theo, but when Ranveer said that he had saved his life, Qureshi clasped the Englishman's hands and welcomed him into his house.

The three of them sat around the dinner table and while none of them was in a mood to eat, Qureshi insisted that they have a full meal.

'You need to have all your energy for what lies ahead.'

When they had finished and all the servants been dismissed, Qureshi called Ranveer into his private study. Theo hesitated at the door but then Qureshi asked him to join them, saying that whether he liked it or not, he was now a part of the unfolding situation.

Before Qureshi could say anything, Ranveer began bombarding him with questions. Was it true that Abu Bakr had seized power? What was to happen with the other Princes? What exactly was Sarfaraz Ali's role in all this? Why was he creating disturbances between Hindus and Mussalmans?

Qureshi put up his hands to ask his son to stop.

'Enough, enough! I see that you are well up to date on the bazaar gossip. Unfortunately things are even worse than what you have heard.'

'It is true Mirza Abu Bakr is the new Emperor. As you have heard he proclaims that there was a Hindu conspiracy created by the Rajputs and Marathas to assassinate the Emperor and overthrow the Mughal Empire. He blames this on us going too soft on other religions and forgetting our Islamic roots- so that is where the Maulvi fits in. Sarfaraz Ali gives him the Islamic legitimacy he needs to back up his position.'

Ranveer asked why Abu Bakr would dig up Hindu-Mussalman tensions now. It was Theo who answered.

'Because, Ranveer, if he can blame everything on some external force, he can get the unwashed masses to focus outside, not look at how he is stealing the throne on the inside.'

'Absolutely, young man' said Qureshi, 'Ranveer, but things are much worse than that. Abu Bakr claims that the other Princes were part of this conspiracy. He has produced confessions of some of the supposed planners of the assassination implicating them. Both Mirza Mughal and Jawan Bakht are now in custody.'

'What about you?' asked Ranveer, suddenly very afraid for his father. Qureshi shrugged his shoulders and said in a matter of fact way.

'I was the loudest in proclaiming loyalty to Abu Bakr and saying that I believed he was the right choice for the Peacock Throne.'

'Why on earth would you do that?'

Qureshi took Ranveer's hand, 'Simple, my son, I sold myself out to buy a little bit of time- for you.'

'For me?'

'I haven't told you everything yet. Abu Bakr has also decreed that the Ahadis are also to blame, as he claims two of the assassins were retired Ahadi soldiers.'

'Nonsense!' exploded Ranveer.

Qureshi continued as if Ranveer had not said anything.

'Abu Bakr says that the Ahadis had become corrupted as many of them were Hindus. So he has decided to disband the Ahadis. All soldiers are to swear loyalty to Abu Bakr or be arrested. All officers must resign.'

Ranveer was stunned beyond words. 'What about the General?'

'Son, Zorawar Khan denounced Abu Bakr as a fraud and a thief.'

Ranveer felt pride surge into his chest only to be further shocked at his father's next words.

'General Zorawar Khan was arrested within an hour of the meeting beginning. An hour later, Abu Bakr announced that he had been killed while trying to escape.'

Ranveer sat down heavily on a couch, trying to take in everything that his father had just said.

'Listen, Ranveer, we do not have much time. They will be searching for all Ahadi officers and all Hindu officers in general. I hear that they are offering all Hindu officers a simple choice- convert to Islam or be convicted of being part of the conspiracy against the Empire.'

When Ranveer looked up at his father, Qureshi's heart almost broke on seeing the look of defiance on his son's face.

'I will fight them, father. They cannot get away with this.'

'My dear son, I had tried all my life to keep you sheltered from the harsh realities of life. I tried to create a life for you where you never had to worry about being stabbed in the back by your closest friend, or being at the mercy of a Prince's whims. Somewhere along the way, I think I also started believing in this world. Now I realize it was all makebelieve.'

Ranveer kept looking at his father, hoping in vain to hear some words of reassurance, but none was forthcoming.

'You cannot fight your way out of this. If you try and fight, you will die. It is as certain as that, and while I could not shelter you from this, at least I can try and save the life of my son.'

'But what will happen to you? I cannot run away, leaving you alone.'

Qureshi sat down next to Ranveer, placing his arms around his son's shoulders.

'Ranveer, don't worry about me. I have pledged my allegiance to Abu Bakr, and once you leave, I will say that I have sent you summons to come and join the new regime, and that you have accepted.'

'Summons? Where?'

Qureshi took out a *firman* with the seal of the Emperor.

'A summons that has just reached you outside Lucknow, where you had gone a week ago on orders from your Commanding Officer to carry out a patrol.'

Ranveer looked at the *firman* which was dated a week ago. When he tried to ask Qureshi how he had managed it, his father just said, 'It doesn't matter. This will buy us both time, and you can stay out of sight till things stabilize.'

'So what do I do now?'

'You leave immediately, Ranveer. We have some ancestral property west of Kanpur. Go straight there and wait for word from me. Here is a set of uniforms of ordinary Mughal soldiers. It should dissuade ordinary troublemakers from targeting you and also not give anyone a hint that you are a Hindu or an Ahadi officer.'

Ranveer took the coarse cloth in his hand, wondering if he should throw away his entire life in one stroke.

Theo had been listening to the exchange between father and son in silence. Seeing Ranveer's hesitation, he asked Qureshi for another set of uniforms.

'Sir, I will accompany your son. Once the new regime gets going after the infidels, being a white man in Dilli will be no safer than being a Hindu Ahadi officer.'

'Theo, you can just stay here with my father. He can protect you', said Ranveer.

'No my friend. I don't think I'll enjoy hiding in some attic waiting for them to find me, and besides, if they ever find me, it would be big trouble for your father. I'm coming with you- just get me a helmet with some chain mail covering the face. I don't think they have too many white *sowars* in the Mughal Army.'

The Englishman's words elicited a smile from both father and son, and Ranveer and Theo began changing into their clothes. When they were done, Qureshi opened the doors of the small armoury, telling them to arm themselves well, but not too ostentatiously. So the Ahadi shield was out as were big, showy lances. Both men picked a sword each, and then weapons that could be concealed yet would come in handy if they needed to fight. Each took two flintlock pistols, a knife and ample powder and balls.

When they were ready, Qureshi opened the back door. To his surprise, Ranveer found Iftiqar and five men waiting for them. They were all dressed similarly to Ranveer and Theo, and Ranveer recognized the five men as Ahadi cavalrymen, not of his unit, but men he had seen in parade grounds and trainings.

'Sir, these are my five most trusted men. They will not speak a word on pain of death.'

Qureshi acknowledged the men and asked Iftiqar if there was any more news.

'Sir, the only news I have is such that it should hasten our departure. Sarfaraz Ali has called for a *jihad* against all *kafirs*. It is expected that he will coerce the Imam of the Jama Masjid to back the call tomorrow morning, but I think the trouble will begin tonight.'

'Good God! Ranveer, go with Iftiqar and may the Almighty always watch over you.'

Ranveer hugged his father, not knowing what to say. He turned to Iftiqar and asked him if he was not taking a big chance.

'Master, I owe my life to your father a dozen times over. If he commands me to slit my wrist, I will do it. Now, let us leave quietly through the Northern Gate. That is lightly guarded, and then we can swing East for our destination.' As the eight horsemen left, Ranveer couldn't help but keep looking back at his home, seeing the solitary figure of his father framed against the light from the doorway.

'Ranveer, don't look back. It just makes any parting harder', said Theo as the small group of men headed out towards Kashmiri Gate. In several alleys around them, they could already hear the cries that signalled that Sarfaraz Ali's call for *jihad* had found an immediate response.

Allah ho Akbar

Naara e Takbeer

The mobs had started going about their business, and their cries sent a chill through Ranveer. When he heard the sounds of a woman screaming, he stopped his horse. 'Ranveer, I know it is difficult, but do not stop. We ride away tonight, even if makes us feel like cowards, because there is no shame in escaping to fight another day, when the odds are more in our favour.'

Ranveer thought about Iftiqar's words and what Theo had told him earlier about discretion being the better part of valour, and while he forced himself to keep riding, he found it impossible to screen out the sounds of slaughter and looting coming from the alleys around them. When they passed Kashmiri Gate, and out of the walls of Dilli, IftIqar asked them to step up the pace. After ten minutes of hard riding, Ranveer finally gathered the courage to look back. He saw several dozen columns of smoke rising above the Mughal capital.

***

Four

Iftiqar kept the group going at a relentless pace, without a break till it was almost dawn. Ranveer and Theo were thirsty, tired and on the verge of falling off their saddles out of exhaustion. However, if they were looking for any relief from Iftiqar, there was none to be found.

'Ranveer, we have to keep going. We must get to a safe distance away from Dilli. Abu Bakr's men will still be consolidating their hold over Dilli, but we cannot take the chance of being anywhere they may venture.'

Finally, to everyone's relief, Iftiqar ordered the men to halt. Ranveer thought about the fact that just a day before, he had been Iftiqar's superior officer, and the older man would have unquestioningly done his bidding in front of their men. Now, however, the balance of power had shifted so seamlessly he wondered whether he ever had really commanded Iftiqar's obedience or led him, or whether Iftiqar had just made a show of it out of deference to Qureshi. Ranveer would have felt angry had he not been so tired, and so when Iftiqar asked the men to take a short nap before they resumed their journey at daybreak, both Ranveer and Theo almost instantly fell into a deep slumber.

When they awoke, Ranveer found the five soldiers who had accompanied them gone. He found Iftiqar sitting near a tree, watching over him and Theo, a loaded pistol in each hand.

'Iftiqar *chacha*, where are the others?'

Iftiqar looked up at Ranveer with eyes bloodshot from lack of sleep or rest.

'They were all men with families. I had ordered them to escort us to a safe distance, but now their place is back home, so I asked them to leave. We will need to get going in ten minutes. We are still about thirty *kos* from Agra, and we will keep riding till we get there- and then take a day's break before we proceed.'

Ranveer was about to say that the three of them stood little chance if attacked by any sizeable force, and was about to question the wisdom of Iftiqar's decision when he realized that his opinion counted for very little. He walked away, pretending he was going to wake up Theo, but in reality just trying not to let his embarrassment show in front of Iftiqar.

Theo was also up by the time Ranveer approached him, and the three men set out shortly on the trip to Agra. When he had been growing up, Ranveer had carried a very romanticized image of the city, largely shaped by the legendary Taj Mahal.

He had learnt to leave those romantic notions behind early on in his career when he discovered that Agra was a tourist trap in more ways than one. Robbers and dacoits had long discovered that the roads leading into the city of the Taj Mahal made for rich pickings and many merchants and travellers had found themselves paying a heavy price for a trip to admire the beauty of the Taj Mahal.

As they entered the city's outskirts, Theo was the first to point out something peculiar.

'Ranveer, see those six men by the roadside? Don't you think it's a bit warm to be wrapped in shawls in this heat?'

Both Ranveer and Iftiqar noticed, and the three men quickly exchanged glances among themselves. The group of men Theo had spotted was squatting outside a mosque, and as they passed the group, they looked up casually at the men in Mughal Army uniforms, one of them even nodding in greeting.

'I bet those rogues have weapons under those shawls, and if the Maulvi inside hasn't already relayed Sarfaraz Ali's proclamation of Jihad, he will soon, and then they will begin their nasty business.'

Ranveer thought about Iftiqar's words and back to what a teacher had told him when he was a student. The cynical old man from Bengal had said that progress and development always trickled slowly through the nation, but when it came to pestilence or trouble, there was no more efficient a transmitter than the mob mentality of Hindustaan. Ranveer had dismissed the words at the time as the ravings of a disillusioned old man, but now he thought his old teacher had a point after all. The developments in Dilli were not yet one day old, yet it seemed certain that they were to soon engulf much of the nation.

Theo had been a man of few words in the journey so far, but now he ventured forth with a suggestion that both Ranveer and Iftiqar warmed up to.

'Look, it is not my place to suggest tactics, but having some experience in being on the run, I would say we should change into civilian clothes and blend in as best as we can.'

Theo had said the words with a wink and a smile, but Ranveer and Iftiqar acted immediately on his plan. They purchased plain tunics and trousers from a cloth merchant and with their weapons concealed in large sacks tied to the backs of their horses, continued their journey. Theo did attract a few glances, but on balance it was perhaps better to be seen as civilians accompanying a European trader or missionary than to be stopped by soldiers asking which unit they were from. They rented a room in a modest guest house for the night.

As they lay on the mattresses on the floor, Ranveer found it hard to sleep.

'I cannot believe I am on the run in my own country', he said to nobody in particular.

Neither of the other men responded, though Theo turned to him and said.

'You know, I always wanted to write. That was my childhood dream, and here I am lying on the floor with two men, wondering if I'll live to see the next day.'

'Englishman, if we live through this, then you will have a good story to write about', said Iftiqar, and all three of them laughed, trying to forget the stresses of the previous day. Soon, they succumbed to fatigue and fell asleep, only to be jolted awake by the sound of gunfire. The three of them sat huddled in a corner of their small room, backs to the wall, facing the door, swords and pistols beside them, as they listened to the sounds of carnage outside. The cries of *Allah ho Akbar* were interspersed with cries of *Har Har Mahadev*, as both Hindus and Mussalmans joined in an orgy of bloodletting that lasted till daybreak.

None of them spoke, as if evading the horrors they had listened to through the night would somehow make them less real. However, when they emerged from the guest house to continue their journey, the evidence of carnage was all around them. Several shops were gutted and burnt, and bodies lay strewn across the street.

Iftiqar was mumbling verses from the Holy Koran to himself, Ranveer closed his eyes in silent prayer, and Theo crossed himself, each man trying to seek some meaning behind the mindless violence that they saw unfolding around them.

They rode out in a South-East direction, planning to cross the Jumna river and then continue on to Kanpur. However after just a couple of hours of riding, Theo spoke what was on all their minds.

'I don't think we should try and ride any longer after it gets dark. The rioters will be back, and we will be prime targets for lunatics of all faiths'

When Iftiqar looked at him quizzically, Theo answered in his understated way, which Ranveer was fast coming to both recognize and enjoy.

'Think about it, there's a Hindu infidel for the Mussalmans to butcher, a Mussalman for the Hindu mobs to skewer and a white man whom both sides would probably kill. So whichever mob we run into, we can basically kiss our fugitive backsides goodbye.'

Ranveer laughed but agreed with the Englishman's assessment, and they quickly changed their plan. They would stick only to the main roads, and would stop at a *caravanserai* each night. That meant that the crossing of the Jumna, which Iftiqar had estimated could be done in a day's time now lay three days away, but if Iftiqar disagreed with the plan, he did not display it.

On the third day after they had left Agra, they got their first news of what was happening in the capital. Since their escape from Dilli, their primary focus had been to lie low and continue their journey undetected, so they had not even ventured to find out what had happened in the five days since they had left Dilli in the dead of night. The three of them had been sitting in the dining area of a *caravanserai* about fifty *kos* from Gwalior, eating a frugal meal of *chappatis* and *dal*. Two fat merchants soon sat down at the table next to theirs.

'Truly we have entered *kalyug*, Ram Kishan. Now the streets of Dilli are prowled by Afghan thugs, not raiders like in the past, but with the authority of the Emperor!'

The other man looked furtively around.

'Jitesh, watch what you say. Even the walls have ears, and I don't want to leave my wife a widow quite so soon.'

The man called Jitesh scoffed.

'What kind of life would we lead by staying alive? I had heard tales of how things used to be in the old days when the Afghans raided Hindustaan and then when Aurangzeb cut down Hindus for crossing his path. Now we have to live through such an age again.'

His friend did not respond, and instead tucked into the food in front of them. While both Ranveer and Iftiqar were curious to know what they had been referring to, they did not dare strike up a conversation. However to their shock and surprise, Theo got up and walked over to the two men, pulling up a chair and sitting down beside them.

The man called Ram Kishen looked at the sudden intrusion with irritation and on seeing the intruder was a European dressed in shabby Hindustaani clothes, asked Theo gruffly what he wanted.

'Sirs, I am sorry for intruding on your private conversation, but I must confess that I disagree with you.'

When the men asked what he was talking about, Theo launched into a diatribe, gesturing dramatically in the air, in the process sending a tumbler of water crashing to the ground.

'This country needs some order, and if it takes Afghans to make that happen, so be it.'

If they hadn't known better, Ranveer and Iftiqar would have sworn that Theo was drunk and as they watched in fascination, he soon entered into a heated argument with the two men.

'You say that because you are a foreigner. They are not looting your houses or carrying away your women.'

The second man spat on the floor.

'The Army of Kabul is in charge of Dilli now. Think about it, thirty thousand troops just happened to be waiting to march onto Dilli the moment Abu Bakr proclaimed himself Emperor, and they still think the poor old Emperor's death was caused by a Hindu conspiracy.'

'Yes, and I hear that half blind Maulvi he's got as a pet is proclaiming that they should reintroduce the *jizya* tax on us. If that were not enough, I hear Abu Bakr's dogs are already marching against any ruler who does not acknowledge his rule.'

When Ranveer saw that the other guests were beginning to whisper among themselves, he walked up to the table.

'Excuse my English friend, he is too fond of his wine and sometimes not fully the master of his tongue.'

As the three of them walked up the stairs to their room, Ranveer and Iftiqar were in splits.

'Englishman, you are too much! Where did you learn to act like that?' asked Iftiqar.

'Actually, I became acquainted with the stage at an early age, when I was performing the works of the Bard in London.'

'The Bard?' asked Ranveer.

'The man, who inspired my love for literature- William Shakespeare.'

'So Englishman, you are a teacher, a philanderer, a drunkard, an actor, and from what I hear from Ranveer, proficient in some Chinese martial arts. You are a man of many talents, or one big fraud.'

With a theatrical bow, Theo said to the men,

'I only follow the dictates of my heart, and yes, sometimes of an organ located somewhat below it.'

The three of them laughed and retired for the night, knowing they would be on the home stretch of their journey the next day.

***

They left early, hoping to cross the Jumna by sunset, and then depending on the weather and how safe they judged the countryside to be, to either make for their destination at night or break their journey at a *caravanserai* along the way. Iftiqar asked them to ride at a modest pace, since in the heat their horses would get tired and dehydrated if pushed too hard. They had barely ridden for an hour when Ranveer started noticing something peculiar. From the East, he started seeing small groups of villagers walking along the road. Some were accompanied by bullock carts piled high with their belongings while the less fortunate ones were carrying large sacks on their heads. Many of the women had a child, or even two, tied to their bodies with cloth while they balanced large bags on their heads.

All three of them noticed several groups pass and finally Ranveer could not contain his curiosity any longer. He rode up to an emaciated looking man near the rear of a group.

'*Ram Ram, chacha*. Where are all of you headed?'

The man looked at Ranveer and replied with a sigh before continuing down the road.

'Son, I have no idea what destination fate has in store for us. All I know is where we are fleeing from.'

'Iftiqar *chacha*, what is going on?'

The old soldier took one more look at the people passing them.

'I've seen this before- during famines or invasions. These are refugees fleeing from some catastrophe.'

'Refugees? From what, or whom?' Theo asked, and his question was soon answered when they came upon two black-clad riders about thirty minutes later. Both men were in full battle armour, a thick layer of chain-mail armour covering their bodies, armoured shoulder plates, and wearing black turbans on their heads. Each of them was carrying a curved blade in one hand and a round shield decorated with red and blue concentric circles in the other. When they had left Dilli, Ranveer and the others had ridden out in ordinary horses, not the specially bred and grown warhorses the Ahadis rode into battle. As a result, the two riders they now faced towered over them, since they were seated on armoured warhorses.

'Afghan heavy cavalry', whispered Iftiqar as the two riders approached them.

One of the riders said something in a language Ranveer could not understand. Iftiqar whispered again to Ranveer, 'They are speaking in Pashtun, let me handle this.'

Iftiqar rode up to the two men, deliberately keeping his head bowed low so as not to appear threatening. Ranveer and Theo watched him exchange some words with them, when one of them suddenly swatted Iftiqar on the back with the flat of his blade. Ranveer instinctively reached into the bundle behind him. The pistols were unloaded, and they would have a tough fight armed with swords against two fully armoured soldiers, but he was not going to let his old teacher be humiliated. Before he could do anything, Iftiqar signalled to him, frantically shaking his head. Theo also saw the cue and placed his hand on Ranveer's wrist.

'Relax. The old man knows what he's doing.'

A few more words were exchanged before the two Afghans rode ahead, leaving the three of them behind. Iftiqar rejoined them, wincing a bit in pain at the blow he had suffered.

'Those arrogant fools! Anyways, the news is that Abu Bakr has launched a punitive raid on Gwalior. The king, Jiyajirao Sindhia, had apparently not been enthusiastic enough in acknowledging the new Emperor so he's sent some of his Afghan dogs to make an example of him.'

'He's certainly moving fast', remarked Theo.

'This was all planned. There is no way he could have launched a raid this fast unless he had battle ready troops. Anyways, it seems Sindhia himself was not even in Gwalior at the time, but after a short battle in which the Afghans scattered the defenders, they are looting the fort.'

The three of them kept riding till in an hour's time, Ranveer could see Gwalior fort appear on the horizon to his right. They would have kept going had Ranveer not noticed something strange once they passed even closer to the fort.

'Iftiqar *chacha*, there are people jumping off the walls!'

They all stopped and looked in horror as one figure after another appeared over the fort's walls and jumped. As Ranveer looked closer, he noticed that every one jumping off the wall was a woman. Without thinking about it, Ranveer turned his horse towards the fort and was about to gallop in its direction when Iftiqar stopped him, holding his reins in one hand.

'Ranveer, our mission is to get to safety, not to interfere in matters like this.'

Ranveer turned on Iftiqar, his eyes bright with fury.

'You know what is going on, don't you? We have all read our history books. Those are the women of Gwalior jumping to their death to avoid dishonour. And those threatening them are doing so in the name of the Mughal Empire, the same Empire you and I are sworn to serve.'

'Ranveer, Iftiqar has a point. The three of us won't be able to change anything. If we try and intervene, all we'll succeed in doing is getting ourselves killed', Theo spoke, his voice soft, perhaps in acknowledgement of the dilemma Ranveer faced.

'I've had enough of running. I've had enough of putting my life above all else, and more than anything else, I've had enough of being treated like a child. I am not suicidal, I will not just ride in there like a hero, but perhaps if we meet the commanding officers, we can tell them to convince those in the fort that the women will not be harmed. Afghans or not, these are soldiers of the Mughal Army, and bound by the same rules we are.'

Any further debate was quickly ended when they saw at least a dozen black-clad horsemen ride in their direction. Flight was not an option and standing and fighting was certain suicide, so they just waited for the Afghans to reach them. As the riders fanned out to encircle Ranveer and his companions, a man, marked out as an Officer by his red and black turban, approached them, speaking in flawless Hindustani.

'Brothers, what business do you have here? There is a battle going on and you should know by now that no civilians are allowed within five *kos* of the fort. Let my men inspect your belongings to make sure of your intentions.'

Ranveer quickly ran through the options before them in his mind. Trying to lie their way out of this situation would quickly turn suicidal the moment the Afghans searched their bags and found their pistols, swords and knives. Staying as close as possible to the truth was their best bet, and to do that, Ranveer knew he had to take the lead as the Officer in the group.

He saw Iftiqar start to say something, but he spurred his horse forward till he was parallel to the Afghan Officer.

'My friend, greetings, from a fellow Officer in the Imperial Army. I hope the battle goes well.'

The man was taken aback at Ranveer's greeting and then he asked Ranveer for some identification. Ranveer calmly reached into his saddle bag and took out his *dastak*. The man took one look and saluted Ranveer, knowing he was talking to a *hazaari*.

'Sir, if you don't mind me asking, what are you and your companions doing here in civilian garb?'

'My friend, I was enjoying a holiday in our ancestral family home near Kanpur when I received word of the developments in Dilli. I was on my way to swear loyalty to the new Emperor when we heard about the battle you and your men have been a part of, one which I hear you have won quite handsomely.'

That seemed to please the Officer, and he saluted and asked them to go on their way. Ranveer heaved a sigh of relief, and was about to turn to his companions when the Afghan stopped him.

'Sir, since you are here, please do come and meet our Commanding Officer. Most of us are new to this terrain and I'm sure we could benefit from your knowledge of the land and the people as we continue our mission.'

There was no way Ranveer could refuse, and the three of them accompanied the Afghans as they rode towards the fort. As they came closer, they saw that they were on the crest of a small hill, below which the landscape was dotted with hundreds of tents marking the Afghan camp. There were a couple of light field cannons in view, firing desultory shots at the fort, but from the looks of it, there was no return fire from within. The battle seemed all but won and it was a matter of time before the Afghans stormed the fort, if in fact they had not already done so. Ranveer noticed that there were no more women jumping off the walls, and he hoped that was because someone had reassured them that the Mughal Army would not harm them.

As they came closer to the army camp, Ranveer was informed that the General in charge of the raid was inside the fort, leading his men from the front in mopping up the last elements of resistance and the Afghan Officer asked the three men to join him inside the fort. Not being able to refuse, and also curious to see what was in fact happening inside the fort, Ranveer readily agreed. As they dismounted and went inside, they saw several dozen men kneeling on the ground, their hands tied behind their backs. Just a short distance ahead, Ranveer saw a hulking figure, dressed in black, carrying a blood-stained sword in his right hand. As the man turned to speak to his men, Ranveer felt a jolt as he recognized the man. It was Abdali, the Afghan General he had once had an argument with in the Palace.

***

Abdali had still not noticed them, and while they waited to meet him, Ranveer took in his surroundings. He was surprised to see some strange beasts carved into the walls of the fort, and then remembered that Gwalior fort was the only fort in India to be influenced by Chinese designs, and creatures known as dragons adorned its walls. In a corner of the fort, there seemed to be a huge pile of musical instruments which the Afghans seemed to be taking great pleasure in hacking into pieces. As he watched, one of them set the pile on fire. He remembered then that the Raja of Gwalior was famous for being a great patron of music, and was credited with having created the Gwalior *gharaana*.

Since the Afghans had evidently not got their hands on him, they were trying to heap insult upon injury by destroying the most visible symbols of his love for music.

Other than a few holes in the walls where there had been direct impact of cannonballs, there did not seem to be very heavy damage and it looked as if the garrison had surrendered without much resistance, perhaps hoping that the civilians had little to fear from a Mughal Army contingent. What did not make sense was why the women were committing suicide by throwing themselves off the wall. Clearly they had something to fear. He got his answer when he got closer to Abdali.

The General was speaking in Hindustaani to one of his non-Afghan Officers.

'Irfan, I do not have the time to cart away all those prisoners outside. Ask them if they will convert. If they do so, they can join us, otherwise, kill them and leave their bodies for the vultures.'

'Sir, we have captured about fifty women. Before I could pass on your orders to capture them intact, some of the men had their way with a few women, and a handful jumped off the walls, but we have the others in our custody. They are in a room on the second floor. What do you want us to do with them?'

Abdali, spat on the ground. 'The men have had a long day. Let them have their sport.'

Ranveer couldn't believe what he was hearing, and as he looked at Iftiqar, the veins in the old soldier's neck looked ready to pop as he tried to maintain his composure. All three of them were unarmed, their weapons still tied to the backs of their horses, and trying to stop the massacre and rape by force was impossible, but Ranveer still held out hope that he could reason with Abdali as a fellow Officer. He stepped forward towards the Afghan General, bowing to show the appropriate courtesy.

'General, I am a *hazaari* in the Imperial Cavalry and was passing by the area on our way to Dilli to swear allegiance to the new Emperor. Do let us know if we may be of any assistance.'

Abdali looked at Ranveer and was about to say something when recognition flashed in his eyes.

'I've seen you before, young man. Oh, yes, the one who stumbled into me at the Palace.'

As Abdali smirked, Ranveer tried hard to maintain his composure.

'Sir, I heard your orders to your men, and as a fellow Officer in the Mughal Army I urge you to reconsider..'

Before Ranveer could finish, Abdali put his arm around his shoulder and took him aside. To the casual onlooker, it may have seemed like a gesture of affection, but the vice like grip that the big man had on his shoulder told him otherwise.

'You will *never* again question me in front of my men!' hissed Abdali.

Ranveer was about to say something back when Abdali turned him around till he was looking straight into Ranveer's eyes. He had a heavy, armoured hand on each of Ranveer's shoulders.

'My friend, my memory is as sharp as my sword, and I do hope for your sake that you are indeed headed to Dilli to bow before the new Emperor. Otherwise a Hindu Ahadi officer nowadays tends to have a pretty short lifespan.'

The threat was not lost on Ranveer, and as he tried to think of something to say, Abdali continued, almost as if he hoped to provoke Ranveer into doing something rash.

'And don't talk to me about what the Mughal Army does or does not do. I've seen many like you–young, spoilt brats of rich fathers, who earn their stripes without ever really fighting a real war, and think killing a few untrained bandits is combat. Welcome to the real face of war, and if this is too much for you, go and hide behind your father's desk. I and my men are here on the express command of the Emperor and do not need you to question what we are doing.'

Ranveer almost exploded with fury. As Abdali spoke, Ranveer saw the knife tucked into the General's belt. One stroke and he would slit his throat. But then Ranveer quickly calmed himself. And then, what? He and his friends would be cut to ribbons, and the men of Gwalior would still be massacred and the women would be raped. Their deaths would serve no purpose other than to quench Ranveer's bloodlust. Ranveer took a deep breath and asked himself–perhaps for the first time–what would his father do? What would Iftiqar do? What could he do other than give into his natural instinct to lash out? Then his father's parting words in Dilli came back to him. It was as simple as it was liberating.

Buy some time.

He gently stepped back and bowed before Abdali.

'Sir, I apologize for my outburst. You are my superior and

more experienced in these matters. I reacted in an emotional manner, and I am sorry. When I am in Dilli I will convey your greetings and pass on news of your famous victory.'

Abdali smiled. It was not a genuine smile born of warmth, but the sneer of a bully who knows that he can make you do his bidding.

'General, if you agree, I would like to spend a day with your Officers learning about how you took the fort, so I could also learn what you have taught them.'

Abdali just shrugged, having lost his interest now that it was clear to him that Ranveer was no threat. He had no time for flattery, and as he turned to rejoin his men, Ranveer ran back to Theo and Iftiqar.

'What was that all about?' Iftiqar asked. To his bewilderment, Ranveer turned to the Officer who had escorted them in.

'My friend, I hear you have some women up there. My friends and I have been on the road for days, and it's been a while before I had a warm body beneath me. Can we as guests ask that we visit your little Harem?'

The Officer chuckled and asked them to go on. Ignoring Theo and Iftiqar's glances, Ranveer asked them to accompany him. As they fetched their horses, Ranveer asked them to take out their weapons and load their pistols. They continued to wear their civilian clothes, but over them fastened their Army belts, into which they tucked their pistols and knives.

As they walked back inside the fort, both Theo and Iftiqar kept whispering to Ranveer, asking him what he was trying to do. Just as they were about to climb the stairs that led to the second level, Ranveer told them about his plan.

'You have bigger balls than I thought. I just hope that General doesn't chop them off. But I'm with you, friend', chuckled Theo.

When Ranveer looked towards Iftiqar to see if his old teacher was going to support him, he saw Iftiqar snap to attention, pride glistening in his eyes.

'Iftiqar reporting for duty. Just give the order, *Sir*'

Ranveer looked at each of his companions one by one, just nodding, trying to convey his gratitude and then simply said,

'Let's get it done.'

***

Five

At the top of the stairs was a large carved door, which was bolted from the outside, and had two armed Afghans standing guard outside it. Ranveer may have been wearing the clothes of a commoner, but he walked like a General inspecting his troops. He strode up the stairs, flashing his *dastak* in front of the two Afghans.

'Let us in. Your General has told me that we are to be the first to sample of what you have inside.'

The Afghans hesitated, not knowing what to do, but the identification looked proper and when they looked down for any assistance, they saw their Officer nod and wink at them before he turned away to join the General further inside the fort. When they entered the room, Ranveer saw a number of women huddled against the wall. Many of the younger ones started to wail at their entry, and an elderly and dignified looking woman stepped forward, as if she thought she could somehow shield the other women. Ranveer both pitied and envied her act of courage, when he heard another woman cry out.

'*Rajmata*, please come back. They will kill you!'

At those words, Ranveer stepped forward and, to the old woman's shock, kneeled before her.

'Your Highness, my men and I had nothing to do with the rogues outside. I am an Officer in the Imperial Cavalry and will try and get you to safety. We do not have much time so you need to trust me.'

The woman's look of defiance crumbled and she sank to the ground, tears in her eyes.

'They told us they came in peace with a message from the new Emperor. The Raja was away, and we let them in, and then they turned on us.'

Ranveer knew the women had been through a hellish experience, but he also knew he had little time, so he interrupted the Queen.

'*Rajmata*, is there another way out of this fort other than down the main stairs?'

Another woman stepped forward.

'There is a servant's quarter's behind the main Fort, and there are stairs to the left of this room leading to it, but they may have it guarded.'

Ranveer quickly conferred with his friends, and then they set their hastily improvised plan into action. Theo poked his head out of the door and whispered to the two guards outside.

'Guys, you have to see this to believe it! Come in!'

Their curiosity getting the better of them, the two guards peeped inside. As they did, two things happened in quick succession. Iftiqar plunged his knife into the neck of one guard and pulled him inside, and Theo stabbed the other in the stomach. Both guards resisted for a few seconds, but the first surprise blows had been fatal and both soon lay dead. Iftiqar and Theo quickly put on their black uniforms and stood guard outside the door, while Ranveer told the Queen that he was going to create a diversion to help them escape. As he was about to leave the room, she held his arm.

'Young man, God must have sent you today to save us. Thank you, but I need to ask one more favour of you. I have hidden my daughter in a secret closet behind the bed in the main bedchamber two doors to the right. Please help her escape.'

'What about you, Your Highness? Where will you go?'

The steely resolve was back in the old woman's voice.

'Once we are out of the Fort, the villagers around will shield us, and we will find our way to safety. Just in case my daughter and I are separated, tell her that I will be going to Lakshmi's house and that she should join me there.'

Ranveer climbed down the stairs and was glad that the Afghan soldiers seemed too busy in looting the fort to pay him much attention. He walked towards the entrance to the Fort where the captives were still kneeling, their hands bound behind them. Two Afghans stood guard just to their left. They had seen their General embrace him, and so they bowed when Ranveer approached.

'What is going to happen to these men?'

One of the guards shrugged as if he was discussing the fate of some livestock, not the lives of nearly a hundred men.

'We've been asked to make them an offer to convert, but I suspect we'll just have to cut their throats.'

Ranveer looked at the men kneeling on the ground. More than half were soldiers, still dressed in uniform, while the others seemed to be attendants and servants. Most of the men looked away when he scanned the group, but one man held his gaze. Ranveer took a step towards him.

'What are you looking at, dog?'

The man spat in Ranveer's direction. Before the guards could react, Ranveer had slapped him hard with the back of his hand. The man fell to the ground, and Ranveer was on top of him, holding his neck in a vice-like grip. He brought his face close to the man's ears and spoke in a whisper.

'The Rajmata and others are safe upstairs. I am going to help them escape. Create a diversion and take as many of these pigs as you can with you. I am sorry, my friend, I cannot do any more for you, but you can at least die a soldier's death.'

Ranveer cut the cords binding the bewildered man's hands and without the guards noticing it, slipped the knife into his hands. When he stood up, he spat at the man.

'That's for daring to look at me!'

He walked up to one of the smiling guards and said the

General had asked for Ranveer and his friends to be given three fresh warhorses to continue their journey. Without wasting much time, word was passed around and Ranveer soon saw attendants bring three armoured horses. In an attempt to please this seemingly favoured guest of their General, the Afghans had filled the saddle bags with food. Ranveer gratefully accepted and asked the attendants to keep the horses near the rear entrance to the Fort.

His heart pounding, Ranveer walked up the stairs, hoping that he still had enough time. He had barely reached the top of the stairs when he heard shouts and screams coming from the front of the Fort. It was only a matter of time before the prisoners were overpowered or slaughtered, but at least Ranveer could try and ensure that their deaths would not be in vain. He heard gunshots break out and when he reached Iftiqar and Theo, he shouted at them to escort the women to the rear gate while he searched for the Princess.

Iftiqar peered down the stairs leading to the rear gate.

'Men, the prisoners have revolted! The General is in danger! Every man to the front gate!'

When the dozen or so Afghan soldiers guarding the rear exit scampered to reach the front, he and Theo escorted the Queen and the other women down the stairs. Ranveer waited till they had all safely reached the stairs when he ran to the main bedroom. The door was open and when he walked in, the room looked as if a storm had passed through it. Every piece of furniture was either upturned or shattered, and many of the paintings adorning the wall had been slashed. He ran to the large bed and struggled to pull it from its resting place against the wall. It took all his strength to budge it even a couple of feet. He frantically looked at the wall, trying to see where the hidden closet could be, but could see no obvious sign. In frustration, he banged his fist on the wall, and was shocked to hear a hollow sound echoing back. He hit the wall a few feet to the left, and only heard the dull thud of his fist hitting bricks, but again towards the middle, in an area outlined by a carved rose, he heard the hollow noise. He knelt close to the wall and spoke.

'Princess, I know you are in there. Your mother sent me to fetch you. She and the other women are on the way out, and I will escort you to safety. Please open the door, we have very little time.'

When there was no response, he banged on the wall again.

'Please, you must trust me. If I wanted to harm you, I would have already broken the door down by now.'

Suddenly, the wall opened up and a young woman stepped out. She must have been Ranveer's age, or perhaps a bit younger, and was dressed in the ordinary clothes of a servant girl, perhaps a ruse to conceal her identity in case she was captured. Her long hair was untied and fell around her face, framing eyes shining bright with anger. In her right hand, she held a pistol pointed straight at Ranveer. Her face and eyes flashed defiance, but Ranveer could see that her hand was shaking slightly.

'Watch where you point that pistol!' Ranveer took a couple of steps back as the woman emerged from her hiding place. When she saw that Ranveer was alone and not dressed in the Afghan uniform, she lowered the gun.

'Who are you?'

'We will have plenty of time for introductions later. Now, we just need to get out of here in one piece. Just follow me and you will be fine.'

Ranveer ran towards the door but then stopped when he saw several Afghan soldiers climbing up the stairs. He turned to the girl.

'Is there any other way down?'

'The balcony!'

Ranveer bolted the door and they rushed to the back of the room and into a balcony overlooking the rear of the Fort. He could hear the soldiers start to break the door down. They did not have much time. When he looked down, he saw that Theo and Iftiqar were almost directly below them, and that the Queen and the other women were going down a trail that led into the forests behind the Fort, and to safety.

Ranveer could hear the door start to give way.

'What now? We can't just jump off- it must be a twenty foot drop from here.'

The girl pointed to the heavy curtains behind the balcony, and Ranveer understood what she meant. They pulled down one of the curtains and tied it securely to the railings around the balcony. The curtain still didn't reach the ground, but would allow them to climb more than halfway down. Then they would have to jump. Ranveer asked the Princess to go first, as he turned to face the bedroom door. The Princess had just jumped to the ground when the door gave way and four Afghans ran in. Ranveer was ready for them, a pistol in each hand, and at such close range, he did not miss. Two of his attackers went down, and as the others hesitated, Raveer climbed over the ledge and down the curtain, reaching the ground to find Theo and Iftiqar waiting with the Princess. As they mounted their horses, Iftiqar asked if they should follow the Queen and the others.

'No, we would just lead the Afghans to them. Here they come now!'

They looked to their right to see more than a dozen horsemen coming towards them.

'Princess, climb aboard!'

Ranveer held out a hand and hoisted the girl onto his horse, and they set off, with the Afghans in hot pursuit.

***

The pursuit had turned into a prolonged battle of attrition and will, one which Ranveer and his companions were steadily losing. The heat was taking a toll on their horses and after more than thirty minutes of riding, the Afghans were no more than a *kos* behind, clearly visible across the flat terrain. The Princess had said nothing since they left Gwalior, and had been sitting motionlessly in front of Ranveer, but he could see her occasionally steal glances at their pursuers, her eyes increasingly betraying her fear. Knowing that sooner or later they would have to face the Afghans in battle, Ranveer loaded both his pistols.

'Iftiqar, they seem to have fresher mounts, there is no way we can outrun them!'

What was left unsaid was that one of their horses was weighed down by two people, and they were going only as fast as their slowest member. Iftiqar just looked at Ranveer and nodded grimly. Theo too was looking back at the Afghans.

'The bastards must be really angry at us, or must want the lady really badly to keep at it for so long.'

Finally the Princess spoke, first to Theo and then tilting her head back towards Ranveer.

'The lady has a name, and it is Mayavati. As for them wanting me, you have done quite enough for me and my people. If leaving me behind helps you escape, do so.'

She had barely finished when Ranveer's horse lurched to a halt, its hind legs buckling under it. Ranveer struggled to control it as he and the Princess were thrown to the ground. As Ranveer looked at the horse, he saw that she had broken a leg. Iftiqar and Theo also stopped and dismounted, running back to where Ranveer was. The Afghans were now fast gaining on them.

Ranveer looked at his friends. 'I've had enough of running and if it is my destiny to die today, I will not meet it being hunted down like a dog. I will stare it in the face and take as many of those bastards with me as I can!'

Iftiqar smiled, and when Ranveer asked him why he was smiling, Iftiqar simply said.

'If I have to go today, it will be good to go remembering you like this.'

Ranveer saw that the Princess had her pistol in her hand and simply told her, 'Use it on them or yourself as you see fit'.

'Well gentlemen, it's been nice knowing you. I dare say we may not meet again, but since I am likely to be spending a lot of time with these Afghans in Hell, let me go and make their acquaintance.'

With those words, Theo began running towards the Afghans, screaming English obscenities at the top of his voice.

'The English truly are mad!' shouted Iftiqar as he and Ranveer ran after Theo.

The Afghans had stopped, perhaps shocked at being rushed by an enemy one fourth their number. However, when they saw Ranveer and Iftiqar take out their pistols, they began to fetch their own firearms. Some of the Afghans had flintlock rifles slung behind their backs and they started frantically loading them. That was a stroke of luck, thought Ranveer. In the chaos of the escape, the Afghans had not had time to load, and the few seconds they would take to do so could prove decisive. They were still at the edge of what would be considered acceptable range for their pistols, but they had no more time. Ranveer knelt and took careful aim with one pistol, and as he fired, he heard Iftiqar discharge a weapon as well. Ranveer took aim and fired with the other weapon, again closely followed by Iftiqar. When the smoke cleared, they saw that they had hit only two Afghans. That still left ten enemies to their three. Ranveer saw that Theo had not stopped running and was now barely a few dozen paces from the Afghans. He was about to shout out to the Englishman to fire when he saw Theo take out an unfamiliar looking pistol from his bag. As Ranveer and Iftiqar watched in fascination, Theo fired not once, but six times, without pausing to reload. They were not shots scattered at random, but aimed with deadly precision. Three brought down the Afghans who had their rifles ready to fire and three more slammed into two men who were loading their rifles. That left just five Afghans, and with the odds more evenly matched, Ranveer and Iftiqar rushed forward, swords in hand.

Ranveer watched Theo rush the Afghans, picking up a rifle from a fallen man just as another Afghan rode at him, sword flashing through the air. Theo parried the blow, but its force sent him falling to the ground. Ranver dove to the ground as an Afghan sword passed through the air where his head had been just seconds ago, and watched Iftiqar evade a similar blow. Outnumbered and with their adversaries in armour and on horses, the three of them clearly had the odds stacked against them. Ranveer parried another blow only to see an Afghan bearing down on him, sword slicing through the air at his head. Ranveer knew that he would not be able to move out of the way in time, and waited for the blow to fall.

Just then, he saw the Afghan's head explode in a mist of blood.

He looked to his right and saw Princess Mayavati standing there, smoking pistol in hand. Ranveer mounted the Afghan's horse and charged another enemy. The man was focused on attacking Theo, who was by now bleeding from a cut on his left arm, and never saw Ranveer streak in from his right, killing him with a cut below the lungs. Iftiqar had despatched another man, and the remaining two Afghans, seeing the balance of forces shift so dramatically against them, rode away.

They tended to their wounds, armed themselves with a rifle each, and gathered as much ammunition and food in waterproof bags as they could from the fallen Afghans, and then continued their flight. Iftiqar and Theo continued on their horses, and when Ranveer asked the Princess to join him on a fresh horse he had taken from a slain Afghan, she said she was quite comfortable riding on her own, and took a horse for herself. Not much was said as they rode- they knew they had to get as far away as possible from the Afghans before night fell. An hour later, it started raining, the monsoon more than making up for its late arrival with a ferocious downpour.

'We must take shelter somewhere', said Ranveer.

'But, where?' God alone knows where we are.'

Theo's question had been asked to nobody in particular but found a ready answer when the Princess suddenly spoke up.

'See those hills there to the South? Just keep riding in that direction and we will reach Haripur. Many of the nobles in our court come from there, and they will protect us.'

After a few minutes of hard riding, they were all wet and miserable, but soon enough saw the flickering of lights in the distance ahead. That gave them a fresh burst of energy and they rode into the village, to be encircled by a mob of curious villagers. Some of the men had knives and swords in their hands, and things looked on the verge of getting out of control when the

Princess stepped down from the horse and faced the crowd.

'People of Haripur. I am Mayavati, the Princess of Gwalior, daughter to the King Jiyajirao Sindhia. As you must have heard by know, our beloved kingdom is under attack and the Fort has been overrun. These men risked their lives to save me, and we request shelter till we can resume our journey.' Everyone before them bowed and an old man stepped forward.

'You will be safe here, daughter.'

Then turning to Ranveer, he added.

'I will ask some of my men to conceal your horses so they do not attract attention. Welcome to our village and please come inside and dry yourselves. Once you are fed and warm, we will talk more.'

Mayavati was led away by some women while Ranveer and the other two men were escorted to another hut. As they dried themselves, a villager came in with fresh clothes for all of them and another brought in plates heaped with food. One of the villagers cleaned and bandaged Theo's injured left hand. It was a superficial cut, but Ranveer insisted he get it tended to, since they could not risk any infections so far away from any medical care. When the villagers left, Theo looked at the food.

'Mango pickle! I love Mango pickles. It may well be the biggest contribution of Hindustaan to the world.'

After the tensions of the day, all of the men loosened up a bit and sat down, wolfing down the food. Theo belched loudly and winked at Ranveer but noticed that Ranveer did not smile back.

'Hey, what's wrong? We escaped, rescued a Princess, and a pretty one to boot, and took on God knows how many Afghans and lived to tell the tale. What could be better than that?'

'The truth.'

Iftiqar noticed the sudden hardening of Ranveer's tone and looked up.

'What do you mean?' asked Theo, already sensing where the conversation was headed.

'Theo, a vagrant English teacher does not carry a weapon like the one you used. The Mughal Army does not yet have such a weapon. Our lives now depend on each other, and I refuse to place my life in the hands of someone I cannot trust. Who are you?'

Theo walked to his bag, taking out the gun he had used on the Afghans and placing it before Ranveer. As he spoke, it was as if he had suddenly transformed. No longer was he the bumbling, good natured English teacher with a weakness for women. He spoke with the demeanour of a man used to commanding many others.

'It's a Colt revolver. Issued in the British Royal Army a few years ago. This particular one was gifted to me by my Commanding Officer as a reward for gallantry during a battle in China against their so called Boxer revolutionaries.'

Ranveer and Iftiqar did not say a word as Theo continued.

'My father is a senior officer in the Royal Army, and is currently, believe it or not, the Viceroy in China. He always wanted his only son to follow in his footsteps, and I did. Eton, Oxford, and then the Army. Fought and bled for Queen and country in all sorts of hellholes around the world, and you know what I learnt?'

When neither of the others said anything, he continued, shaking his head bitterly.

'That what I mistook for glory and adventure ultimately made us no better than the so called savages we were pretending to civilize. We got the native tribes in the New World drunk on fire water and turned them against each other to steal their lands; we got the Chinese addicted to opium. For what? So the traders could make more money and the Generals corner more favour in London. I guess I was never meant to be a soldier- should have just gone ahead and done what I wanted- write and act. So I quit, and tried to escape my past.'

Ranveer asked him what he was doing in Hindustaan.

'I sought employment as a teacher, hoping to earn enough to finish a book about my journeys in Hindustaan. And yes, I do have a weakness for women that sometimes borders on the suicidal.'

He winked, and in an instant, the Theo they had met in the deserts of Rajputana was back. Iftiqar was about to say something when Ranveer touched Theo on the shoulder.

'We all have pasts, and I thank you for sharing yours. Now nothing's hidden between us.'

He held out his hand which Theo clasped gratefully. All three of them were tired after the day's events, and soon fell asleep. When Ranveer woke the next morning, he found a villager at the door.

'The *Mukhia* requests your presence at the Panchayat.'

Ranveer roused the others and they set out to meet their hosts.

***

It seemed as if the whole village had gathered to meet them, since there seemed to be hundreds of people gathered around the village square. As Ranveer, Iftiqar and Theo walked through the crowd, it seemed like they had entered a carnival. Children were playing games or enjoying sweet treats, while their parents seemed to have donned their best clothes. They all seemed to be gawking at the three strange men in their midst, with most of their attention directed at the Englishman.

'*Firangi*' shouted a child gleefully, and then burst into laughter when Theo looked at him and patted his head. Ranveer saw that in the centre of the square was a huge Banyan tree, towering over the village, and beneath it were seated several men, among them the old man who had greeted them the previous night. He was wearing a bright red turban and smoking from a *hookah* set up in front of him. Ranveer assumed that he was the headman of the village. As the three of them approached the tree and greeted the men the *Mukhia* motioned for them to sit down on mats set up next to him. As they were sitting down, they heard a sudden commotion. Several women had emerged from the left, and in their midst was Princess Mayavati. She was dressed in the very best sari the women of the village had between them, and wore the best gold ornaments they had to share. It was a far cry from what she must have been used to in her Palace, but she looked every bit the Princess in their midst. As she walked towards them, Ranveer realized that in all the chaos of the previous day, he had never even noticed just how beautiful she was. Of course, Theo had no such issues. He nudged Ranveer and whispered, 'Quit gawking, I told you she was a beauty.' There were several cheers from the crowd as she walked through them and sat down on a mat next to Ranveer.

As the crowd started to settle down, she looked up at Ranveer and whispered.

'I never did thank you properly for saving my life nor did I even properly introduce myself. Running for one's life tends to make one forget one's manners, I suppose. Please call me Maya, everyone who is my friend does.'

She smiled, and Ranveer, looking at her up close properly for the first time, saw that Theo had been quite accurate in his assessment of the Princess' looks.

'Princess, my name is Ranveer Pratap and I am an officer in the Imperial Cavalry. As for giving thanks, I also owe you my life. Where did you learn to shoot like that?'

'I had a good teacher', replied Maya with a smile. 'And again, please call me Maya.'

Just then the *Mukhia* began speaking, first welcoming Maya in their midst and thanking the Gods that the Royal family had escaped unscathed after the attack on Gwalior. Then he addressed Ranveer.

'Young man, thank you for bringing the Princess to us. What is the news from Dilli? What madness is engulfing our nation?'

Ranveer told him the latest news that he had heard, and also what he knew about the usurping of power by Abu Bakr and his joining forces with a fanatic like Sarfaraz Ali. The *Mukhia* looked at Ranveer with sadness in his eyes.

'I do not know how it is in Dilli, but in a poor village like ours, we cannot afford to kill each other in the name of religion. That is because all of us, Hindu and Mussalman alike, are at the mercy of common vengeful gods. Gods called poverty, hunger and disease. So we share our burdens and get along, but when something like this happens, it could tear us apart like never before.'

Iftiqar asked if there had been any trouble in the neighbouring villages. Another man in the Panchayat spoke up.

'We keep hearing of how Hindus were massacred in one village by mobs heeding the Maulvi's call for Jihad, and how Mussalmans were butchered in another. We don't know how much of it is true, but even if they are rumours, they fan more mistrust and fear.'

The *Mukhia* carried the conversation forward.

'So far we have been left untouched, in part because the Hindus and Mussalmans here are used to living in peace. But it is the outsiders we fear- there are a lot of *Jihadis* on the rampage, seeking loot and plunder in the name of waging *Jihad* and then there are the *Bhumis*, some of whom are taking advantage of the weakening of central control to use their weapons to prey on the weak, again in the name of fighting for the Hindus.'

Ranveer had no idea that things had gotten so bad so fast, and was even more surprised to hear the fatalistic attitude of the headman when he asked him why the villagers did not seek assistance from anyone or even prepare for their own defence.

'It's all in the hands of Fate. We can but pray that things turn out well.'

When they retired back to their hut, Ranveer was surprised to see Maya join them. She thanked Iftiqar and Theo personally as well, and when the Englishman held her hand and bowed to kiss it, Ranveer felt himself feeling irrationally jealous, and silently chided himself.

'So what do we do now?' He asked his companions.

Iftiqar responded by saying that going to their original destination was out of the question as they would have to pass through the Afghan lines. Theo said that going back to Dilli was not an option either, especially as the Afghan General knew who Ranveer was. As he said that, something struck Ranveer and he sat up, ashen faced.

'My father! Once they know what I have done, he will be in great danger!'

Iftiqar sat down next to him.

'Ranveer, I have known your father for more than thirty years, and this much I can say with certainty. He would readily face whatever perils come his way as a consequence of our actions instead of having to live with the shame of being the father of a son who left innocents to be killed and ravaged. He would be proud of what you did. Also, he is an experienced player in the ways of the Court, and should be able to handle himself better than anything we could do for him.'

Maya could see how troubled Ranveer looked and knelt by his side.

'You have risked a lot for me and my people, and I cannot imagine how we could ever repay that. But perhaps I could suggest a place where we could find refuge and safety while you decide what to do next.'

''Where would that be?' asked Ranveer.

'The same place I am sure my mother is headed to.'

Just then, Ranveer remembered what the Queen's last words to him had been.

'Oh God, I totally forgot. She told me that she was going to the house of some Lakshmi, and that you should join her there.'

Maya smiled at the name.

'Yes, that's the place. Lakshmi, an old friend of my mothers, Queen of her kingdom, and the woman who taught me how to shoot and ride.'

'Sounds like quite a formidable woman' said Theo with a smile.

'Oh, that she most certainly is. And if in these troubled times, there is someone who will not lose her head or her faith, and someone who will not stray from what she believes in, it is her.'

Ranveer looked at Iftiqar to see what he had to say to Maya's offer, but he just shrugged, indicating that he would go with whatever Ranveer decided.

'Fine, Maya, we will go where you suggest. I do not see any better options for us and also, you could rejoin your mother.'

Maya got up, saying that they should leave soon, so that they could reach their destination by nightfall. When she had almost reached the door, Ranveer remembered something she had said, and asked, 'You said, this Lakshmi was a Queen- which kingdom is it that she rules over?'

Maya looked back at him and smiled.

'You may have heard of her formal title–Lakshmibai, the Rani of Jhansi.'

***

Six

They rode on for most the day, and on Ranveer's instructions, Iftiqar ventured ahead of the others, acting as a scout. Theo brought up the rear, and Ranveer and Maya rode together. It was clear that Maya needed no babysitting. She rode like a professional and had already established that she knew how to handle a gun. However, now that their immediate mission was delivering her to the safety of Jhansi, Ranveer wanted to take no chances. Having spent most of his adult life in the company of male soldiers, he was however a bit at sea on how to deal with the young woman in their midst, so he decided to err on the side of caution. Iftiqar seemed to take this protectiveness with his usual stoic silence, while Theo nudged Ranveer in the side, whispering, 'I would definitely want to guard her body, if you know what I mean.' A scowl from Ranveer had sent him scurrying back.

Maya took it all in good humour, but when Ranveer had them all halt when he mistook some mules on the horizon to be attacking Afghans, she burst out laughing.

'Ranveer, please remind me to never introduce you to my father!'

'Why do you say that?' asked Ranveer.

'Because if he knew how paranoid you are about guarding me, he'd appoint you my chaperone and I'd never meet any men!'

Ranveer blushed while the other two men laughed at his discomfiture. That also broke the ice a bit, and for the rest of their journey, Ranveer told Maya about himself and what had brought him to Gwalior. When he asked her about herself, she looked at him, with a naughty smile playing on the edge of her lips.

'A woman does not share so easily of her past, especially when she has just met a man. But if you really want to know, I was born in the Palace, lived there among servants who would not permit me enough space to breathe let along do anything for myself, and thought I'd die there without ever getting to see the real world. You're the first man outside the Royal family I've ever really had a conversation with.'

Ranveer again found himself tongue-tied, not really knowing what to make of this young Princess. He had not had much experience with women, and certainly had never met anyone with as sharp a tongue as Maya. Theo, observing the conversation, piped in, winking at Ranveer.

'Princess, my friend is much better at letting his sword do

the talking for him, if you know what I mean. However, if it is real conversation you want, rest assured that all men outside the Palace are not like him.'

Maya and Iftiqar laughed again, leaving Ranveer glowering at the Englishman.

The first sign, that they were near their destination came in the form of a guard tower that they passed. The guards within said nothing but Ranveer noticed the flashing of a mirror in the fading Sun, signaling the arrival of unfamiliar horsemen. Within minutes, Ranveer saw a dozen horsemen appear over the horizon. When they drew closer, Ranveer saw that they were dressed in white, with saffron headgear, and every single man was armed to the teeth. The leader pulled up in front of Ranveer.

'Halt and identify yourselves!'

Ranveer was about to say something when Maya rode up and introduced herself. The man bowed in greeting.

'We have been expecting you. The *Rajmata* arrived here a day earlier.'

They found Jhansi a city preparing for war. There seemed to be armed men everywhere and the ramparts of the Fort were ringed by cannon. A group of sappers was digging traps outside the Fort walls, placing sharpened stakes inside and then covering them with a thin layer of branches and leaves. They rode straight inside the Fort and to the Citadel, where word had already reached of their arrival. The *Rajmata* of Gwalior was there, waiting for them at the foot of the stairs. It was the first time Ranveer had seen her since the escape from Gwalior, and she looked unrecognizable. She was wearing an expensive silk saree, and enough gold ornaments to bankrupt a small King. When they drew close, Maya dismounted and ran forward into her mother's arms. When Ranveer and the others had dismounted, the Queen came towards him.

'Thank you for what you have done. I owe you a debt of gratitude.' Before Ranveer could respond, he heard a loud voice to his left. 'So these are the heroes I have to thank for my friend's life!'

Ranveer looked to see a woman approaching them. She was dressed unlike any woman Ranveer had seen. There was no saree or jewellery, instead she wore a military uniform like the men who had escorted them in. Her long hair was tied behind her head, and she had a long, curved sword hanging from a scabbard at her belt.

'Welcome to Jhansi. I am Lakshmibai, and you and your friends can stay as long as you want. Just let your attendants know anything you need and we will do our best to serve you.'

'Thank you, your Highness.'

Ranveer and his companions were escorted to a guest house near the Palace, while Maya went with her mother and the Rani into the Palace. After they had changed and bathed, the three of them met over dinner, brought in by attendants.

'Iftiqar *chacha*, what do we do now? We can't head back to Dilli.'

'Ranveer, I really don't know. I think the best course of action would be to lie low for a few days, and then depending on the situation in Dilli, plan our next step.'

Theo had been too busy tucking into the food to hear what was being said, and when Ranveer asked him what he wanted to do, he shrugged.

'Now that is a fine question. The Afghans will kill me if they see me since I sent a few of them to Hell. The Jihadi mobs will slaughter me for being an infidel. I ran away from home, so my father hates me, and even if I did lose my mind and decide to seek his forgiveness, China is a long way to travel on an empty purse. So, taking all that into account, I think I'll just tag along with you.'

Ranveer smiled at how Theo as usual had made a tough decision seem so very simple. But that smile disappeared when he heard the Englishman's next words.

'Moreover, I'd say you should stay here for some time. That Princess may well want to show her gratitude in, well, a more personal manner.'

'Theo, you are impossible!'

'And you my friend, are blushing again.'

When they retired for the night to their individual bedrooms, Theo remarked to Ranveer through the connecting wall.

'This is the first real bed I've slept in since we left Dilli. I will certainly not miss sleeping on the floor with the two of you, or Iftiqar's snoring.'

Iftiqar's spoke up as Ranveer laughed.

'Englishman, I can hear you. What about your foul smell? Do all the people of your land never take a bath?'

As they kept exchanging insults, Ranveer slipped into a dreamless sleep, finally sleeping well after many days. He was abruptly awakened by the noise of someone knocking on his window. When he looked outside, he saw that the Sun had not yet fully risen. Wondering if it was some mischievous child or a blundering thief who had awakened him, he flung open the window, ready to heap abuses upon whoever it was.

To his shock, he saw Maya standing outside, wrapped in a shawl to keep out the early morning chill. Seeing him speechless, she broke into a grin.

'I always get bored being cooped up in palaces with nobody to talk to or nothing to do, so I thought I could show you around town.'

Ranveer looked at her, not believing what she was doing.

'Come on, join me outside at least' she insisted. Ranveer realized that they would just be drawing more attention to themselves if they continued talking like this, so he came out to meet her.

'Are you out of your mind? You're a Princess, you shouldn't just be walking around town with anyone at odd hours like this. What have you told the Queen?'

Maya looked at him and whispered.

'Actually, she thinks I am fast asleep in my room.'

Ranveer clutched his head.

'My God! If they find you outside, won't you get in trouble?'

'Not at all, if they find me, I will just say that you abducted me.'

She said the words with such a straight face that Ranveer did not know if she was joking or not. Once again, seeing him speechless, she laughed.

'You blush more than any man I've ever seen.'

'That's because you are unlike any woman I have ever seen or heard of!'

Realizing that Maya was in no mood to go away, Ranveer relented and the two of them began a stroll around the surrounding areas. Maya seemed to have no shortage of things to talk about, and in less than ten minutes, Ranveer knew that her chambermaid was sleeping around with the doorman; that the Royal Cook was known to drink while on duty; and that she had once gotten into big trouble by letting her father's pet pigeon escape. Finally, she took a break.

'Ranveer, you don't say much, do you?'

Ranveer smiled, 'It's just that you have had more to say in the last ten minutes than you did in the entire two days we spent travelling together.'

Now it was Maya's turn to smile.

'I was just scared to death–being attacked by Afghans and then being in the company of strange men, whose intentions may or may not have been honourable.'

'Why do you say that? Did I ever indicate anything but the most honourable intentions?'

Maya smiled again as she realized she had once more got Ranveer on the wrong foot.

'Relax, it was a joke. Now, tell me, shouldn't a young

officer like you be up for marriage soon. Is there someone waiting back in Dilli?'

Ranveer was not accustomed to speaking so freely with a woman, but in the short time they had spent together, he had already realized that it was very difficult to do anything but play along with what Maya wanted.

'Actually, my father has brought up the subject more than once, and who knows what plans he had? With all the chaos in Dilli now, marriage is the last thing on my mind.'

'You men are lucky in that way. At least you can decide to postpone things like marriage or refuse if the girl does not strike your fancy. My father will one day marry me off to some Prince whose face I will have never seen.'

Ranveer glanced over at the woman next to him.

'But that is the way it is.'

'Perhaps it is, but that does not make it what I want. I realize I will marry one day, but what harm is there in dreaming that perhaps I will marry someone who wants to marry me for who I am, not what I am. But perhaps also, being a Princess is a curse in that your title defines you more than who you may be.'

Ranveer had initially dismissed Maya in his mind as a spoiled and headstrong Princess, but as she talked, he realized that there was much more substance to her than she let on. As they neared the Palace, Maya turned to him.

'Thank you for coming with me. I just needed someone to talk to. I do not know what your plans are, but if you came to visit before you left, I would like it.'

Ranveer wished her goodbye and was on his way back to the Guest House, thinking of the strange girl he had spent the morning with, when a man stepped in front of him.

'Are you the young man who brought the Princess of Gwalior in? I went to the Guest House to look for you and was told they did not know where you were. I was waiting for you to return.'

Ranveer looked up to see a thin man with a long, curved moustache. He was dressed in the fashion of the Marathas, wearing a white tunic and tight trousers and carrying a dagger and sword at his belt.

'Who do I have the pleasure of meeting?'

'I am a General in the Maratha Army, and as you well know from personal experience, we seem to be headed into a time of war. With your experience in the Mughal Army, we thought you could be of some assistance.' Ranveer wondered what he was being asked to be a part of, but knowing that he was addressing a General, he simply asked how he could help.

'Just be at the Palace at noon. We will be waiting for you.'

As the man turned to leave, Ranveer called out to him.

'Sir, if I may know your name.'

The man looked at Ranveer and smiled.

'My name is Tatya Tope.'

***

Ranveer arrived at the Palace with mixed feelings. He despised the thugs who had taken over the throne in Dilli, but he was still an officer in the Mughal Army. In his lifetime, the Mughals had enjoyed peaceful co-existance with the other kingdoms, but he knew that was largely due to the unspoken acknowledgement of the vast superiority of Mughal arms and Bahadur Shah Zafar's pragmatic policies. He had never tried to conquer and hold land in any of the kingdoms like the Marathas, an endeavour which had bled some of his predecessors dry. However, he ensured they acknowledged Mughal supremacy in Hindustaan by allowing free passage of trade and officials, and paid a share of their taxes to the Mughal treasury. It was a loose federation, but it had survived so far. Ranveer worried that if the Marathas and others were to take advantage of the chaos in Dilli, he would not find it easy to choose which side to take.

When he arrived at the Palace he was ushered into a huge meeting room. Rani Lakshmibai was seated at the table, as was Tatya Tope. Along with them were two men he had not met before. As he entered, they introduced themselves. The first was a hulking figure, with a flowing beard, and wearing an elaborate turban.

'I am Nana Sahib, Peshwa of the Marathas.'

The second man was Azimullah Khan, who was the Diwan to Nana Sahib. Ranveer wondered what Queens, Peshwas and Generals wanted with someone like him. Rani Lakshmibai spoke first, pointing to a map of Hindustaan spread out on a table before them.

'Ranveer, the reason you are here is that we fear that Abu Bakr will do what the last Emperor never did- return to the era of aggressive conquest.'

She must have read the expression on Ranveer's face, so she softened her tone as she continued.

'I realize you are an Officer sworn to be loyal to the Mughal throne, and I will not ask you to go against that oath. Indeed, we have no desire to provoke any conflict, since we know that would be catastrophic for our people. There is just one specific area where you may help us, only if you choose to.'

When Ranveer asked, what that was, Tatya Tope spoke.

'It is well known that the core of Abu Bakr's loyal force is the Army of Kabul. We have had long and friendly relations with the Mughal Army, and even if Abu Bakr does declare war, we will be forced to fight against people who are bonded to us, if not by friendship, than at least by mutual respect. At least we know they will obey the rules of civilized war.'

He pointed at the map, his finger on the borders of the Afghan lands.

'However, the Afghans are an unknown quantity, and as you yourself have seen in Gwalior, they behave more like looters and vandals than professional soldiers. You are in the unique position of being a Mughal Army Officer who has not just seen the Afghans up close, but has also fought against them. We request you to share what information you have about their leaders, their equipment and their capabilities- only if you choose to do so, of course.'

Ranveer was already feeling much relieved and was about to talk about the Afghan troops he had encountered, when a commotion broke out near the door. He could hear several voices shouting at once.

'A massacre in Dilli!'

'Imagine how they made it here!'

Rani Lakshmibai asked Ranveer to wait inside as she and the others went outside to see what was happening. In a few minutes, they had all returned, and accompanying them were three unexpected guests.

There was Zahir Dehlavi, the *Daroga* of the Mughal Court and Bahadur Shah Zafar's closest confidante; then there was Ghalib, the poet laureate of the Mughals; and finally there was a young man, actually more a boy still in his teens. Jawan Bakht, the young Prince, who was supposed to be the most likely to be appointed heir-apparent by his father. They were all dressed in the finery of the Court, but their clothes were filthy and they were caked with dust and sweat. Lakshmibai ordered refreshments brought in for them and for their family members who had accompanied them. She offered them rest, but Dehlavi insisted on pleading their case there and then.

'Respected Queen, we ask for refuge in your Kingdom.'

There was stunned silence in the room as Dehlavi continued his tale.

'Two nights ago, the killing started. It seems Abu Bakr felt confident enough of his position to start removing all possible threats. All the other Princes are dead- only Jawan Bakht lives to carry on his father's name.'

Ranveer was aghast. He had never heard of such barbarity in the Mughal Court before. Nana Sahib spoke what was on all their minds.

'How could he do this? All he has are his Afghan thugs so how did he presume to commit such an atrocity? What were all the Mansabdars doing?'

This time it was Ghalib who spoke.

'My Lord, every man can fall prey to three traps- fear, greed and desire. And Abu Bakr is skilled at using all three. The Mussalman Mansabdars are largely in his grip, driven by both fear and his promises that they will share in the riches when he conquers the other Kingdoms in Hindustaan, and the Hindu Mansabdars decided to live rather than throw away their lives. The few that opposed met their end that ghastly night.'

Ranveer's thoughts immediately went to his father.

'Ghalib-sahib, do you know what happened to my father, Amir-e-Azam Shamim Qureshi?'

Ghalib turned his eyes away, and this time it was Jawan Bakht himself who spoke. The bazaar gossip had him painted a spoilt brat, but either those had been exaggerations or he had just matured a lot in the last few days, since he spoke with the self-assurance of someone much older than his sixteen years.

'Sir, Qureshi sahib was a man among men. He is the reason we stand before you today.'

Then he told them of their daring escape from Dilli when much of the Harem, Dehlavi, Jawan Bakht, Ghalib, their families and some other nobles loyal to Bahadur Shah Zafar had slipped out. They were led and escorted by Qureshi and a hundred of his loyal soldiers. They had thought they were safe when they had suddenly crossed paths with a force of several thousand Afghan soldiers on their way back from Gwalior. Ranveer's stomach tightened as he sensed what was to follow.

'We were asked to surrender, and we knew we would all die if we were taken back to Dilli, but then Qureshi sahib told us that he would hold the Afghans long enough for us to get away. He told me that we must live so that the true Mughal Empire could rise again.'

There were tears in Jawan Bakht's eyes as he continued.

'Imagine, a hundred men against several thousand! We heard the sounds of battle for many hours as we rode away- they must have fought like lions.'

His head dropped as he ended his account.

'Then there was silence. The Afghans must have been badly bruised for they did not follow us, but one soldier from your father's detachment caught up with us- he was badly wounded and died just outside Jhansi. Your father died saving us. He died with a pile of Afghan dead at his feet.'

Ranveer could hear someone saying something to him, but none of the words seemed to be registering. His mind had gone blank. His father gone? He felt himself stagger against the table, a hand reached out to steady him, but he pushed it away. He strode out of the Palace, and by the time he reached the Guest House, tears were streaming down his face. Theo met him at the door and was about to ask him what he had been up to when he saw his face.

'My God, what happened, man? Come in.'

When Ranveer saw Iftiqar, he could no longer control

himself and collapsed into his arms, sobbing like a child. Iftiqar had heard from the Palace Guards about the refugees from Dilli and like Ranveer, he had also heard tales of the heroic last stand of their escorts against the Afghans. He had not known if Qureshi had been a part of the escape, but seeing Ranveer in this condition, he guessed what had happened. When Ranveer told him what he had learnt, Iftiqar let out a cry of anguish, and the two men sat together for a long time, saying nothing, just seeking some solace in each other's company. Theo watched them, not knowing what he could do to help. Finally Ranveer asked, to no one in particular.

'What is the point of my living now? My whole world is turned upside down, and my father is dead. What do I do now?' Theo sat down next to Ranveer, his arms around his shoulder.

'Ranveer, you need to choose what you want to do, but here's what I would do if I were in your place. I would hunt down and kill the bastards who brought all this upon me.'

Ranveer looked at Theo, anger slowly replacing the anguish in his eyes.

'Theo, you are right. You are so right. If I am a son of my father, grieving him like an old woman will bring no solace to his soul. The thing that may bring him some peace is the knowledge that he had a son who raised his sword to avenge him.'

Iftiqar reached out and held Ranveer's hand.

'Ranveer, you have been like a son to me, and your father was like my elder brother more than a master. I share your pain and your anger, but do not throw your life away in charging against Abu Bakr's men in haste.'

Ranveer stood up, facing his two companions.

'Iftiqar *chacha*, that is what the old Ranveer would have done. But if there is one thing that has come out of the last few days, it is my realizing that I was living in a fool's paradise.'

Iftiqar tried to say something, but Ranveer continued.

'All my life, I was shielded from life's harsh realities by you and my father, and all I did was think about myself and what I wanted from my life. When I blundered in my haste or hot-headedness, I never paid for it because you or my father fixed it. But now, it is time I grew up and acted not like an impulsive child but like the son my father deserved.'

'What will you do?' asked Theo.

'Use the few talents I do have. Despite my father's best efforts, being a man of learning and culture eluded me.'

Iftiqar smiled at last at memories of Ranveer playing truant from his classes. 'But there is one thing I am good at- and that is being a soldier. So I will use that, not in one suicidal dash against the enemy, but by bleeding him a thousand times, each a small cut, but together, making them pay a heavy debt in blood for what they have done.'

'Will you then join Nana-sahab and Lakshmibai in the coming war?' asked Iftiqar.

'Yes, Iftiqar *chacha*, I will place at their disposal every skill I have learned, and if I perish, I will do it after I have personally caused or helped cause, the death of as many of Abu Bakr's dogs as possible.'

'My boy, I am with you as always. From what we hear, your father sent many of those bastards to Hell, and we should hasten to send more of their friends their way.'

His despair replaced by a look of cold determination, Ranveer was about to walk out the door when he turned to Theo.

'My English friend, you have been through much with us, but we are about to enter a most perilous phase. This is not your fight, so if you walk away, please feel no shame.'

Theo looked Ranveer straight in the eyes.

'Ranveer, we met under strange circumstances, but if I had met you in any circumstance, I would be proud to call you my friend. I have wandered enough, and have philandered enough. I was trying to escape the life of a soldier, but perhaps it is my destiny to fight after all. But I have no regrets, for I know I am going to be fighting on the side of what is right. So, count me in.'

The three men clasped hands, and then Ranveer set out for the Palace.

***

Ranveer walked into the room where he had been earlier in the day. Everyone was gathered around the table and a hush fell over the room when Ranveer walked in. Suddenly conscious that he was the center of attention, Ranveer bowed to Rani Lakshmibai and the others and then sat down against the wall along with other aides and officers.

Jawan Bakht began speaking, and it was immediately apparent to Ranveer that there was much more substance to the young man than the bazaar gossip had made him out to be. Despite being in the presence of royalty and men more than twice his age, the young Prince was holding forth.

'I thank you for the refuge you have offered us, but neither do I want to become a burden on you nor do I wish to put you and your people in jeopardy, so I will let you know what my plans are. If after that, you do not wish to offer us further refuge, then we will leave.'

There was pin drop silence as he continued speaking.

'I will issue a Firman proclaiming that Abu Bakr is a usurper and that the throne should be restored to the rightful heirs to the Peacock Throne.'

'How will you do that? He sits on the throne and claims it to be his own' asked Nana-sahab.

This time it was Dehlavi who interjected.

'Peshwa sahib, sitting on a throne does not make a man the Emperor. Before we left, we brought with us all the ancestral symbols of the Mughal Throne and the official *mohur*. That is what will be the seal on the Firman we issue.'

'How in blazes did you manage that?' asked Tatya Tope.

'Greed and fear are not currencies that only Abu Bakr knows how to deal in', replied Jawan Bakht with a sly smile that once again reinforced among everyone present that this young man was not just a spoilt brat but a real contender to the throne.

'I assume you know what will happen next?' asked Lakshmibai.

'War. Abu Bakr will have no choice but to hunt us down and kill us.'

'And you still wish to provoke a war that means suicide? Or do you ask us to support you in this war?' asked Nana-sahab.

Jawan Bakht stood up and paced the room, so that he addressed not just those at the table but everyone in the room.

'Ghalib-sahib mentioned about fear, greed and desire as motivators. I can offer you no fortune, nor can I coerce you into doing anything, but I can appeal to your desire.'

Several of those present looked at the Prince questioningly as he finished.

'I can appeal to your desire to survive as a free people. Do you really think Abu Bakr is content sitting in Dilli? He will come after all of you sooner or later. See what he has already done in Gwalior. And all of you have a choice, either you fall one by one before his armies, or you join forces to oppose him in the struggle that comes.'

Rani Lakshmibai stood up, and nodded at Nana-sahab and the others to affirm that she was speaking for all of them.

'You have spoken well, young man. We have all been admirers and supporters of your father, and I think I speak for all of us when I say that he would be proud of you. Ghalib-sahib, I beg your pardon, but I think you are wrong on one count.'

A murmur spread across the room as the Rani continued.

'There is something that motivates us more than fear, greed or desire. That motivator is principle. So, yes there are all the pragmatic reasons you mentioned why we should support you, but there is also the matter of standing up for what is right, and we and our people will stand by you.'

Cheers went up across the room and Ranveer saw that Jawan Bakht was visibly relieved.

'If it is war Abu Bakr wants, it is war he will get. We will rally our armies and amass as large a force as we can' said Tatya Tope, his mind already thinking of the logistical details.

'I may be speaking totally out of place, but perhaps we should approach this differently.'

Every single person in the room turned to look at Ranveer when he said those words, causing him to almost instantly regret having said anything. He was about to say something by way of clarification when Rani Lakshmibai encouraged him to continue.

'Young man, your valour and your father's supreme sacrifice have more than earned you a place at this table. Speak your mind.'

Ranveer began, growing in confidence as he spoke.

'My father once compared the Mughal army to a massive elephant, and it is. With all due respect, in a straight contest of brute force, none of your armies can stand against it. Abu Bakr will have more cannon, more horses and more elephants than all your armies combined.'

'Yes, we know that, so should we just give up?' said Tatya Tope irritably, but when he saw that the others were listening intently, he kept quiet and let Ranveer continue.

'To bring down a massive elephant, there is no one killing

blow- but we need to cut it at its flanks, deliver a series of blows that weaken and bleed it, moving in and out so fast it cannot bring it's brute strength to bear.'

Tatya Tope smiled as he began to understand where Ranveer was headed.

'Guerilla warfare.'

'Yes Sir, the same sort your own Shivaji was such an expert at. And in doing so, we use the same levers that Ghalib sahib mentioned.'

As Ranveer looked around the table, he saw only smiles of encouragement.

'The Mansabdars we can strike fear into. I have been one of them, and I know how corrupt most of them are. Many of them have huge armies only on paper- they maintain fictional armies to draw state allowances, and those that have armies use them for little more than hunting parties.'

He looked anxiously at Jawan Bakht to make sure he was causing no offence with his candid remarks, but the Prince just laughed out loud.

'Most of them have never been in battle, and we can force them to rethink whether they are actually safer in siding with Abu Bakr.'

'What about the Afghans?' asked Rani Lakshmibai.

'Your Majesty, they may look like brutes, but they are fearsome warriors. Most of them have been fighting all their adult lives, and will not be done in by fear. Their undoing will be greed. Many of them are here dreaming of plunder and loot- and we can use that weakness against them and lure them to their death.'

'Young man, you may have heard that sometimes showing leadership can be a double edged sword.'

When Ranveer looked at Nana-sahab questioningly, he smiled and gestured to Rani Lakshmibai who nodded her assent.

'My friend Tatya Tope here is going to be the General of our combined forces, and he tells me that he needs an Officer to lead his cavalry. I am told that you know a thing or two about fighting on horseback. The job is yours if you want it.'

'I want nothing more than to send as many of the enemy to Hell as I can', said Ranveer almost without thinking. Then he quickly looked around to see if he had spoken too freely. All he saw were broad smiles and nods.

As the meeting wrapped up, Ranveer rushed back to meet Iftiqar and Theo.

They had a war to plan for.

***

Seven

Ranveer watched as the sowars and bandookchis emerged from their tents at dawn below him. He and his three hundred men had been waiting in utter silence for over eight hours. Their horses were muzzled so as to not cause any noise and were placed more than one *kos* behind them. He and his men were a filthy and bedraggled lot- not having bathed for over two days, surviving on little more than figs and dates and over the previous night, having relieved themselves where they lay.

'Let's attack the bastards. The stench and boredom will kill me before any enemy blade', whispered Iftiqar, lying just a couple of feet to Ranveer's right.

'Patience. Our time will come' said Ranveer as he continued watching the men below.

There were at least two thousand men in the camp, all soldiers in the pay of a Mansabdar named Ilyas Khan, one of the nobles who had thrown in his lot enthusiastically with Abu Bakr. His reasons for doing so had become apparent soon enough. Bolstered with Afghan troops, his men had begun a campaign of plunder in Rajputana, extracting what they claimed was the *jizya* tax that the new Emperor had entrusted him to collect. It mattered little that he was collecting more than twice even the extortionate rate prescribed by Abu Bakr, or that his men were happy to whisk away women and livestock by way of their 'tax collections'. When it came to deciding which Mansabdar would be the first to be made an example of, there had been an almost immediate consensus that Ilyas Khan was the man.

A month had passed since the fateful day in Jhansi when Ranveer's life had been turned upside down by the news of his father's death and his joining forces with Jawan Bakht and the coalition supporting him. That month had passed in a blur of training, exercise and planning. Tatya Tope had given him one thousand of his best cavalrymen to form the core of an elite cavalry unit, which at Ranveer's request was to be named the Ahadis. Ranveer was happy with the quality of the men he had been given, and Iftiqar had driven them hard. Whether all that training had been enough ,would be tested this day.

Ranveer saw a portly figure emerge from a tent that was larger than the others around it. That would have to Ilyas Khan. In the three days that Ranveer and his men had been stalking their prey, it was apparent that Ilyas was a terrible commander. His camp had no apparent sentry system, and he had marked himself out with his luxurious tent- elementary mistakes that any officer would have avoided. But then, Ilyas Khan was one of those Mansabdars who maintained an army that largely existed on paper. Ranveer guessed that many of his *bandookchis* would have never fired a gun in combat and his sowars probably rode for leisure, not training for war. The one concession Ilyas had made to the Mughal Army manuals was in placing his camp with its back to a hill, believing that the enemy would be best engaged on flat ground where his cannon and heavy cavalry could be brought to bear. Sound theory, but useless, when practiced against an enemy intent on using guerilla tactics.

The one thing Ranveer worried about was the inexperience of his own troops, They were all well trained and fit, but most of them had never been in battle before, He was sure that once they joined the fray, they would perform well, but uneasy that in their eagerness to join the battle, someone would make a mistake and lose the element of surprise. A young soldier to his left shifted in the grass to get a better view of the enemy below, and accidentally struck his sword against the side of his shield. Ranveer winced, anxious that the enemy would be alerted and held his breath, waiting to see the reaction of the men below. When they did little other than go about their business, he relaxed.

'Where is the damn Englishman? I hope he is as good an actor as he claims to be.'

Iftiqar was also losing his patience, and for all his outward composure, Ranveer was also straining at the leash. However, he knew that for all the enemy's failings his force was outnumbered almost ten to one. The only way they stood a chance was to count on the element of surprise, and hope that the diversionary tactic they had planned worked.

Just when Ranveer was beginning to wonder what had happened to Theo, he saw a solitary horseman appear on the horizon. The man was dressed in the red uniform of an officer of the British East India Company, and rode towards the Mansabdar's camp at a leisurely pace. When the men at the camp caught sight of him, the camp suddenly erupted into a frenzy of activity, like a beehive that has been disturbed with a stick. Men grabbed their weapons and formed a perimeter around the camp, and a dozen riders sallied out to meet the strange figure riding towards them. Ranveer watched as the men rode up to Theo, and briefly exchanged words with him before one of them galloped back to the camp. Ilyas Khan himself mounted a horse and rode out to meet the Englishman. The plan was as simple as it was bold, and while Ranveer admired Theo for having thought of it and volunteered for the mission, he prayed that his friend would get out in one piece.

As Ilyas Khan approached Theo, Ranveer involuntarily clutched the locket around his neck. All his life he had dismissed suggestions that he wear any lucky charms or amulets, branding them as superstitious trinkets. But this one was different- it had been given to him by Maya before he left on this mission. In the month since their walk together, he had met Maya only twice, with the entire Palace consumed in little other than preparations for war, and Maya being cloistered with the women in the inner chambers once her father arrived to join his family. Despite that, or perhaps because of that, Ranveer found himself thinking of Maya more and more frequently. Theo had told him that all he needed was to finally get in bed with a woman, but perhaps it went deeper than that. If all that existed between him and Maya was lust on his mind, why had Maya secretly come to meet him before he left and given him the locket, saying it would bring him luck? His mind was yanked back to reality when he heard Iftiqar whistle softly.

Ilyas Khan was alongside Theo, listening to a bogus story about how a whole regiment of English soldiers were waiting a few *kos* away, having been invited by the new Emperor to help keep the peace and how Ilyas Khan and his men were to join up with the English. In his hands was a Firman with the Imperial seal. It was a far-fetched story, and Theo's uniform, stitched by tailors in Jhansi based on what he remembered, would never have fooled an experienced Mughal Army officer, let alone a real English officer, but Ilyas Khan was neither. Ranveer watched as Theo rode away and Ilyas Khan began barking orders to his men to pack up their tents and follow the Englishman.

It was when the men were halfway through the packing that Ranveer attacked. One hundred and fifty men took aim below with their rifles and fired a devastating volley. Many of the Mansabdar's men fell, dead or wounded and as the others scrambled to gather their weapons and meet the threat behind them, the remaining half of Ranveer's men fired. There was a brief lull as Ilyas Khan and his men thought it was over, and then they saw the horsemen streaming down the hill towards them. Ranveer was at the head of the column, a pistol in each hand. Fifty paces from the enemy, he fired both, seeing one man go down, and then holstered them, bringing out his sword and shield. He made straight for Ilyas Khan, swatting away two men who tried to stand in his way. He could see the Mansabdar scream in fear and order his men to stand and fight, but this battle had been won even before the first shot had been fired. With total surprise, and fighting against poorly trained enemies, Ranveer's men cut a swath through the Mansabdar's men. A few of the more experienced men tried to make a stand, but the others began to run after offering token resistance.

Ranveer made straight for Ilyas Khan knowing that the fastest way to end the fighting was to strike down the enemy leader. Through his peripheral vision he saw a man charge at him from the right, and without turning he swung his sword, slashing his attacker. Another man brought a sword down with both hands from his left. Ranveer blocked the blow with his shield and then kicked the man, sending him sprawling to the ground. Before he could get up, Iftiqar, always watching Ranveer's back, had skewered him with a lance.

When Ranveer closed in on Ilyas Khan, he saw that the Mansabdar had taken out a pistol and was trying to load it, spilling most of the gunpowder in his panic. Ranveer spurred his horse on and blazed past the Mansabdar, his sword arm reaching out in a quick jab. When he wheeled his horse around, Ilyas Khan was lying dead, his neck nearly severed by the blow. Seeing him fall, the remainder of his men threw down their weapons, trying to surrender.

'Stop!'

Ranveer screamed out the order to prevent a massacre, and was gratified to see his men obey in an instant. Of the two thousand men Ilyas Khan had in his camp, perhaps a thousand were left standing, the others lying dead or wounded on the ground. As the prisoners were rounded up in a corner of the camp, Ranveer found Iftiqar.

'How many did we lose?'

Iftiqar took a look around, 'Perhaps fifty killed or wounded. There comes our actor.'

Ranveer watched Theo ride up, a grin plastered across his face.

'I told you I could act. What are you going to do with the prisoners?'

Ranveer knew well the orders he had been given.

'Hold them and if any one of them is found to be guilty of crimes against civilians, then try them as criminals. A larger back-up force is on the way to pick up prisoners. The rest we let go. Let them return to Dilli and tell them about how their force was wiped out. Let them spread the word that Abu Bakr's dogs are no longer safe even in their own camps.'

Ranveer dismounted, stretching his aching muscles and taking stock of the arms and ammunition they had captured. Outnumbered and outgunned by Abu Bakr's forces, a priority had been to recover as many captured firearms as possible. Ranveer took off his helmet, and was wiping the sweat off his brow when he noticed some commotion behind him. He turned to see four prisoners struggling with his men. One of the prisoners grabbed a knife and killed one of Ranveer's men, and the others started to make a run for it. Two of them were cut down immediately by the Marathas, and a third ran into Iftiqar, who struck him down with a blow to the head. The fourth however grabbed a pistol from Iftiqar's belt and struck him across the face with its butt, sending him staggering to the ground. Ranveer's men were closing in on the man when he raised the pistol and fired.

Ranveer felt a sharp prick of pain in his side as the bullet struck home, and he fell to the ground. He tried to raise himself, but the pain was overpowering.

Then there was darkness.

***

Ranveer thought he heard Iftiqar and Theo talking. One of them was calling out to him, asking him to wake up. Then the darkness took him again. He then saw himself back at his home in Dilli. His father was at the dining table, asking him how the war was progressing. Then his father recoiled in horror, screaming, 'You've been shot!' Ranveer tried to reassure him that he was okay, but his father was inconsolable, saying that it was not time yet. Once again, the darkness took him. Ranveer lost all track of time, flitting as he was between consciousness and unconsciousness. Through it all, one face kept appearing before him, a face that he had never thought would be the anchor that was keeping him from sinking under. The face that he so wanted to see once more.

Maya.

When he finally came to, he found himself inside a tent, thick bandages swaddling his torso. He tried to get up, but the effort was beyond him, and he collapsed back in pain.

'Shh. Lie down, you need rest.'

Ranveer wondered if it was all another dream, since he swore he had heard a woman speak. He looked closer and saw Maya sitting next to him.

'Where am I? What are you doing here?'

Maya smiled as she asked him to be quiet.

'There will be time to recount all that later. For now, let me go and tell the *hakim* and Iftiqar that you have awakened.'

She left and a few seconds later, Iftiqar and Theo burst into the tent. Iftiqar hugged him, causing him to wince in pain, while Theo stood there, grinning his lopsided grin.

'Our man has returned to the world of the living. Iftiqar, do you think it was to hear your snoring or to hear my amorous antics that he returned? Or do you reckon it was to spend some more time with his Princess?'

Ranveer learnt from Iftiqar that they were encamped about fifty *kos* from Jhansi, where they had finally found a *hakim* to tend to his wounds. He had spent two days slipping in and out of consciousness, kept alive by the crude bandaging Iftiqar and Theo had managed after he had been shot.

'So what's Maya doing here?'

'My boy, when word reached the Palace, she arrived that night and has been here ever since. The *hakim* may have provided the balms and medicines, but she's the one who has been sitting by your side every waking minute applying them and nursing you back to health.'

When Maya re-appeared a few minutes after Iftiqar and Theo had left, Ranveer asked her if her parents knew she was outside the Palace.

'My mother knows. As for my father, sometimes the less men know, the better it is' she said with a smile.

'Maya, thank you. Iftiqar told me what you've done.'

Maya was busy mixing some of the herbs the *hakim* had given, and smiled as she replied.

'He was scandalized when I came. Imagine a woman tending to you?'

Ranveer asked her how she managed to convince him.

'I told him the truth.'

'And that was?'

'The fact that I couldn't stay in the Palace knowing you were wounded and battling for your life.'

'Wouldn't your father go mad with anger when he hears you're here?'

Maya applied the mixture to Ranveer's side, making him wince in pain.

'In the state you're in, I think I'm quite safe, no matter how dishonourable your intentions may be?'

Ranveer just smiled and lay back, happy to be alive, and

happy to see Maya again. A couple of days later, he was strong enough to walk with someone's assistance, and the next day, they began their journey to Jhansi, with Ranveer sitting behind Iftiqar on his horse. Maya had gone ahead with her attendants, and Ranveer thought back to the few days they had spent together, wondering if he would get a chance to see her again once she disappeared into the cloistered interiors of the Palace.

His answer came rather surprisingly in the form of a totally unexpected visit from none other than Rani Lakshmibai, who sauntered into the Guest House one evening. Iftiqar and Theo were out preparing for the next raid, and Ranveer, still not fighting fit, was sitting alone, frustrated at not being able to get into the thick of action again.

'Ranveer, I am glad to see that you're recovering fast. Your raid was a huge success and similar raids across the Plains have broken the backs of most of the Mansabdars who were siding with Abu Bakr.'

Ranveer got up, bowing before the Queen.

'Raniji, you should have just called for me to come to the Palace. I'm sorry, but without any attendants here I cannot offer you much hospitality.'

Lakshmibai sat down on a divan near the door, motioning for Ranveer to sit down.

'Ranveer, I would have called you if I wanted to talk about official matters. As it were, I have come here on a personal matter.'

'I'm sorry, Raniji, I don't understand.'

'Maya.'

That one word made Ranveer freeze. He almost imagined Sindhia's men on the way, trying to wreak vengeance on the man who his daughter had gone to visit in secret, or of being banished by Lakshmibai for trying to seduce her protégé. Most of all, he dreaded the dishonour Maya would go through if knowledge of her visit to his tent became widespread.

'Raniji, she has done nothing wrong' he blurted out.

Lakshmibai smiled and continued as if Ranveer had not said anything.

'I have known Maya since she was a child and she is like a younger sister to me. If any man tries to play with her feelings, I will personally hunt him down.'

One look into her blazing eyes told Ranveer that she meant every word. Her features softened as she continued.

'You will not tell her this, but she has confided in me that she may have feelings for a young officer among us. She could have her pick of a Prince from any royal family, but one's heart is not subject to any royal *firman*, is it?'

Ranveer listened in silence as she continued.

'So, my friend, if this young officer wishes to reciprocate her feelings and do what is right, then I will make sure that I speak for them to her father.'

Lakshmibai left, leaving a speechless Ranveer in her wake. That evening, he ventured out of the guest house and spent a couple of hours loitering in front of the Palace, pretending to exercise to help his wounds heal fully. The guards all knew him and of his role in the raid, and as a result he was allowed to freely walk over the Palace grounds. He knew the ladies' quarters were to the rear of the Palace and his stroll gradually took him there, where he stood, hoping to catch a glimpse of Maya. He was about to give up and return when a servant girl came running to him.

'Sir, my mistress wishes to hear about your battle with the Mansabdar's army. She requests you to come in and meet her.'

A puzzled Ranveer followed her in, and was led into a waiting area. Then the door opened, and Maya walked in.

'Sneaking around the ladies' quarters is not behavior becoming of a noble officer like you, Sir.'

They both laughed and then Ranveer approached her, wondering where he should begin.

'Maya, I wanted to thank you...'

Maya giggled, 'You came all this way to thank me again?'

Ranveer walked even closer to her, and as he gently took hold of her arm, he felt her shudder under his grip.

'Not just that.'

Maya's voice was barely a whisper as she replied.

'What then?'

Looking into Maya's eyes, holding her so close to him, Ranveer realized that if he put aside the fact that she was a Princess and quite out of his league, she was also a woman. A woman, whom he was beginning to realize just how much he desired.

'Maya, what I wanted was...'

Ranveer did not get a chance to complete the sentence. Without making a seemingly conscious effort, his lips found Maya's and the two of them clasped each other in a passionate embrace. Ranveer winced as Maya's hand brushed one of his wounds.

'Are you alright?' Maya asked, pulling back, concern in her eyes.

'Better than I have ever been', was Ranveer's response as he pulled Maya close to him, and kissed her again. They kissed and caressed each other for what seemed like an eternity, reveling in each other, whispering all the desires that they had kept bottled up inside. When Ranveer's hand reached behind Maya's back to undo her blouse, she seemed to hesitate. Thinking that he was crossing his boundaries, Ranveer held up his hands apologetically. Maya seemed puzzled at this sudden rejection and then sensing his confusion, she smiled.

'Let me lock the door, silly.'

She was about to latch the door when there was a heavy knock on it. Ranveer froze, wondering what would happen if one of the Palace officials saw him there, alone with Maya. When the door swung open, he noticed with increasing dismay that the person who had just joined them was none other than Rani Lakshmibai. Maya also blanched as she saw the Rani enter, but Lakshmibai had neither the time nor the mood to question the two on their secret rendezvous. She ignored Maya's protests and strode up to Ranveer.

'I can understand the impulse of youth, but you are lucky nobody saw you enter here other than one of my trusted chambermaids.'

'Raniji, I was...'

Ranveer was half relieved when the Rani cut him off, sparing him the embarrassment of explaining what he was doing there. But any relief quickly gave way to concern when he heard the Rani's next words.

'I was looking for you, and would have sent for you at your quarters. When I heard you were here, I came straightaway. There has been a battle against the Afghans, and many of our finest have fallen.'

Ranveer could feel his pulse quicken as the Rani completed her sentence.

'Among them is your old friend Iftiqar.'

***

As the Rani mounted her horse and galloped towards the Palace, Ranveer ran as fast as he could. A Council of War was already in session and when he entered, breathless and flushed, he sensed that a thick pall of gloom hung over the room. Jawan Bakht was sitting in a corner, and while he was trying to maintain a look of self-assurance, Ranveer sensed that the young Prince felt very similar to what he himself felt–totally out of his depth. Tatya Tope and Nana Sahib were huddled in a corner with some Maratha generals and Jiyajirao Sindhia. There was only one person who did not look downcast, and that was the Rani of Jhansi. As Ranveer watched, she addressed all the men in the room.

'My friends, we have all known loss, and any loss of a dear one is to be mourned. But with any loss must come the resolve to continue the struggle with renewed determination, otherwise that loss would have been in vain.'

The Rani's words galvanized the men, as they were all too aware that she spoke not merely empty platitudes, but words born out of personal experience. Having lost her husband, she had taken on the mantle of ruling her people, and had done so with a vigour and honesty that would have put to shame any person who dared comment that the place of a woman was not at the throne.

Word was still filtering in of the nature of the loss, and as messenger after messenger trickled in, Ranveer learned the true extent of the catastrophe. Perhaps overconfident in their capabilities and strategies after routing Mansabdar after Mansadbar, the coalition that had rallied around Jawan Bakht had committed a fatal error. They had assumed that the Afghan troops would behave the same way as the poorly trained and led forces of the Mansabdars.

The battle had begun as many ambushes against the Mansabdars had–with a surprise attack at dawn to drive terror in the enemy camp, followed by a quick withdrawal. Then would come several probing attacks- the thousand cuts that Ranveer himself had recommended, serving to cause disarray in the enemy ranks. In this battle, the Afghans had played along, pretending to break rank and flee in disarray, and the coalition forces, perhaps carried away by their first battlefield triumph over the Afghans had given pursuit. That had been a fatal error. Far from fleeing in disarray the Afghans had led their opponents into a vicious trap, and with Afghan horsemen closing in on them from three sides, the coalition forces had been lucky to escape without being totally destroyed. But that escape had come at a heavy cost – more than one thousand men were known to have been killed.

Ranveer did not want to believe that Iftiqar could have finally fallen in battle. Iftiqar, his old teacher and mentor, the man who always seemed to know how to get Ranveer out of harm's way. Just then, word came that the commanders of the defeated force were about to reach Jhansi along with the remnants of their army. Ranveer rushed out of the Palace and within minutes was at the city gates. He watched as gradually men on horseback appeared over the horizon. When the army had left for battle, it had marched out in perfect formation. Now, Ranveer realized, the commanders were still trying to hold on to that pride. The horses were still arrayed in perfect battle order. The difference was that almost half the army was no longer there, and many of those that remained were walking wounded.

As the column came closer, Ranveer searched its ranks frantically for any sight of Iftiqar, but he could find no sign of his old mentor. Finally, he saw Theo ride up to the city walls. The Englishman had lost his usual grin, and his head was swathed in a bloody bandage. When Ranveer hailed him, he merely looked up and shook his head sadly.

'Theo, what in God's name happened? Where is Iftiqar?'

Theo dismounted and walked alongside Ranveer as more wounded men streamed into Jhansi.

'Ranveer, we made a big mistake.'

Ranveer waited for Theo to continue as the two men walked towards their quarters.

'We thought we had the upper hand in this battle as we had better trained troops and better tactics than the Mansabdars, and that was true enough. The problem is, Ranveer, for all their training, the Marathas and the Rani's troops are no more battle hardened than the Mansabdar's armies. Decades of peace, I fear, have softened all of Hindustaan.'

Ranveer continued listening in silence.

'Not so the Afghans. They may not have fancy tactics, but they are shrewd and they know what it is to kill and be killed. You must have heard of their deception. It was a good tactic, but what did us in was the simple fact that many of our troops did not hold ranks and fire discipline when the main Afghan force charged. They panicked, and that was our undoing. That is the simple and shameful truth.'

'What about Iftiqar?' asked Ranveer finally.

Theo pointed to his bloody head and smiled a sad smile.

'The Afghan who gave me this little gift would have taken my head cleanly off my shoulders had Iftiqar not blown his head off with a musket. He was one of the few who tried to rally the troops and make a stand of it. He fought like a man possessed and for a magical few minutes, we all believed that he could carry the day for us. He cut down every Afghan that crossed his path. But every time an Afghan fell by his blade or shot, he marked himself out as a target for the other Afghans. They must have known that to take him down would sap the rest of our army of whatever little resistance it could offer.'

As Ranveer listened, he kept hoping against hope that Iftiqar had somehow made it out alive, but in his heart he knew what was coming.

'Though he was not a General, Iftiqar had earned command of the troops by his actions, and when he sounded the order to retreat in good order so that we may live to fight another day, everyone instantly obeyed. As we were performing a fighting retreat, fresh Afghan troops rode in, I'm told under the personal command of General Abdali. They surrounded Iftiqar and the last I saw, he went down fighting under a crush of Afghans.'

Theo was silent after that, his head downcast at the shame both of defeat and of not being able to save his companion.

Ranveer had rushed ahead of Theo and ran more than walked into the quarters the two shared. He locked his bedroom door and sat down on the bed, trying to make sense of what had just happened. He had lost a good friend, a trusted mentor, and also the last remaining link he had to the father who had also been snatched away from him. Anger boiled within him as he remembered Abdali and the other Afghans he had encountered at Gwalior. As he sat there seething, he realized that with the will of the coalition severely shaken by this defeat, his ability to get a chance of avenging the deaths of his father and Iftiqar were also in grave doubt.

There was knock on the door and he asked Theo to go away. To his surprise, the voice that answered was Maya's. He opened the door to find her standing there, concern in her eyes.

Ranveer was about to say something, when Maya pressed her fingers to his lips and hugged him. Ranveer's emotions came bursting out like the waters of a flood, and he found himself sobbing like a child. Maya just held him and let him cry. When he was done, she sat him down on the bed and placed his head on her chest.

'Ranveer, I am so sorry. I can't begin to understand the loss you have endured in the last few days, but I wanted to be here for you.'

Ranveer looked up at her and as he saw her moist eyes, something changed in him. He had been wallowing in the anguish of being alone, of having nothing or no one to live for, while all along he had forgotten what he did have to live and fight for. Maya must have noticed the change in his expression.

'What is it?'

Ranveer held her close.

'Maya, I had been silly and selfish in just thinking about what I have lost. Now, more than ever, I need to think about what I still have left to live, and fight for.'

Maya smiled at the renewed confidence that she saw in Ranveer. 'And what would that be, my love?'

'The life we will lead together once all this is over.'

That evening, Ranveer went to the Palace and sought out Ghalib. He found the poet sitting at a desk composing stanzas on a parchment laid out before him.

'Ghalib sahib, I wish to ask your advice on a matter related to the campaign.' The poet smiled and looked up at Ranveer.

'Young man, what can a man of letters offer by way of advice to a fighting man?'

'Sir, this war will be won in the mind as much as on the battlefield, and with your experience both in the Court and as an observer of people, you know more about the mind of men in power than most of us do.'

Ghalib kept writing and then asked Ranveer to lean closer so that he could read what the poet had just scribbled. 'Faith may open one's eyes to the Almighty's grace, but blind faith makes the most intelligent man stumble and fall on his face.'

The poet was chuckling at his words, as Ranveer looked at him, wondering what he meant.

'Young man, there are whispers in Dilli that General Abdali has taken a force to plunder the most sought after target for many marauders like him before. He has a force depleted by the last battle, but it seems the desire to wage Jihad among him and his Afghans was too much to resist, so off they have gone. Abu Bakr covets power and the throne, but many of Abdali's men are just soldiers for hire and are here for the looting. He himself is reputed to be somewhat of a fanatic and is here not just for the money but also to wage holy war on what he sees as a still impure nation. Perhaps we can cause him to stumble.'

'Where are they headed, Ghalib sahib?'

The poet went back to his parchment as he replied.

'Somnath.'

***

Eight

Ranveer rode like a man possessed. The five hundred men behind him followed in stoic silence, though behind his back, many of them wondered what tearing hurry their commander was in that was leading him to wear them, and their horses out. Ranveer had established a crushing routine- ride for four hours non-stop, then rest for only thirty minutes during the day; and if his men were hoping for much sleep at night, all they were allowed was three hours sleep before they set off again.

Just two weeks earlier, after his meeting with Ghalib, Ranveer had approached Rani Lakshmibai and the other leaders of the coalition, arguing that a small force be sent to intercept and ambush the Afghans on their way to Somnath. By then, there was even more concrete intelligence that Abdali and up to two thousand of his men had embarked upon a raid on Somnath.

Given the crushing defeat the coalition had just suffered, under other circumstances the leaders would not have approved another confrontation with the Afghans so soon, unless they were assured of victory. However, they all knew that if they allowed the temple at Somnath to be sacked, it would be a vivid demonstration both of the Afghan's superiority and of their own impotence. So they had approved a force of their best cavalry under Ranveer's command.

As Ranveer rode, he kept thinking back to his last night in Jhansi. It had been the first time he had made love to Maya. He had gone to say goodbye, and when they had embraced, he had hesitated at going any further, worried that he not deepen their bond, lest he not come back from this mission. All Maya had said was that if one night together was all they had, she wanted to make the most of it. Thinking of how he could get back to Maya was the one thing that was tempering his rage and making him think rationally instead of just wading into the Afghans. He had dispatched spies, and in a day, they had caught sight of the Afghans. Though they were formidable opponents on the battlefield, it was apparent that they were certainly no disciplined army. Their spirits lifted by their recent victory and the prospect of loot at Somnath, they were cutting a swathe of destruction and pillage through the villages they passed. Ranveer and his men had passed three villages where most of the women had been ravaged and all the adult men put to the sword. Sights like that had only hardened his resolve and also aroused the desire to seek revenge among his men.

The fact that the Afghans were stopping to loot and plunder at leisure, confident that the coalition would not seek them out in battle so soon, also gave Ranveer's force an important advantage. They would reach Somnath well ahead of the Afghans.

Another day of hard riding brought them close enough so that they could see the tall grey spires on the horizon. Ranveer dispatched a couple of fast riders to go ahead of the rest of the force to inform the priests that they were not a hostile force. As he looked to his right, he saw Theo peel away with two hundred riders, riding North till they disappeared over the horizon. There had not been much time to plan this mission or to assemble a larger force. The element of surprise was the only thing on Ranveer's side and he knew that he would have to milk it for all it was worth.

As they rode closer to the temple complex, he saw at least fifty saffron clad priests assembled in front of the temple. To his surprise, each of them was armed, with a motley arsenal of swords, knives, and in a couple of cases, shovels. Ranveer dismounted and saw the priests move aside to give way to a man who approached him. The man was dressed like the other priests, but looked more like a wrestler than a priest, with enormous shoulders and a thick neck. The man folded his hands in greeting.

'Welcome to Somnath. My name is Acharya Gobind, the Mahant at the Someshwar Temple. I am glad to hear that you are here to help us against the raiders.'

Ranveer was surprised to learn that the priests already knew of the impending attack.

'Acharyaji, how do you already know about the coming attack?'

As the Mahant led Ranveer into the temple complex, he smiled wearily.

'When your temple has been destroyed six times by invaders and rebuilt stone by stone each time, you learn to keep your eyes and ears open. I had thought we would have to lay down our lives in vain, but with your men here, we may have hope.'

Ranveer knew well both the legend and the history of Somnath. It had long been a magnet for invaders. According to legend that was because it was rumoured to house portions of the idols originally kept in the Kabaa at Mecca, and secreted away to India when that shrine was occupied by the early Islamic converts, who destroyed all the pre-Islamic idols there. Ranveer suspected that was just a justification offered up as cover for pure greed. Somnath was also by far the richest temple in Hindustaan, its donations and grants enough to be the envy of most Kings, and thus made for a natural target for invaders. That, and the added symbolism of defiling the infidel's holiest shrine, made it an irresistible target for Islamic raiders like the Afghans. As Ranveer looked to his left, he saw living proof of that. Part of the original complex that had been converted into a mosque by Aurangzeb. Bahadur Shah Zafar had been more enlightened, or perhaps just a shrewder politician, and when he had seen after the Battle of Palashi that the only way to resist the British was to foil their divide and conquer policy of pitting one side and religion against another, he had refurbished the complex, including expanding the temple site. It made for great politics, but also made the complex a nightmare to defend.

There were no raised walls, and in rebuilding the complex, much of the high ground it had originally stood on had been leveled, robbing the defenders of any advantage of terrain.

Knowing that they had perhaps as little as a day to prepare their defenses, Ranveer got his men straight to work. Anyone who wanted to grumble about the lack of rest kept it to themselves, knowing that their commander was in no mood to entertain any such thoughts. As his men prepared for battle, loading their rifles, and taking up positions, Ranveer went to the Mahant to explain their plan. To his surprise, the Mahant readily agreed and the other priests joined in with enthusiasm.

Just after noon, a Maratha rider came galloping into the temple premises. He was shouting for Ranveer even before he had dismounted.

'Sir, Afghans just a few *kos* behind me. Their General Abdali is with them, but they seem to be riding in without any formation. They are coming fast, and should be here any minute!'

The scout's words electrified the defenders of Somnath, and even without Ranveer giving the order, his men rushed to their positions. Ranveer took a look at his men, and while he would have liked to have trained with them longer, he knew they would give a good account of themselves in battle. He knew that because from Somnath there was going to be no escape. They had neither the rations, nor the spare horses to have any hope of retreat while being pursued by the enemy. They would either prevail or die. Ranveer still had not heard anything from Theo, and that was the only thing that worried him. His plan had been approved enthusiastically by the Council of War, and Tatya Tope himself had proclaimed it as a stroke of genius. However, now with the enemy just minutes away, Ranveer wondered whether his plan, and his luck, would hold in the heat and confusion of battle. All around him, men prayed, many of them bowing to the idols inside the sanctum sanctorum or seeking blessings from the Mahant. Ranveer just thought about his father and Iftiqar, and then about Maya, reminding himself of all those that he had to avenge, and the one he had to live for.

When he looked up, he saw the first Afghans riding in over the horizon. The scout had been right- there was no semblance of any formation or order, and individual riders were streaming in as fast as they could. Either they felt that they would not face any worthwhile resistance and so were dispensing with basic tactics, or perhaps as Ghalib had said, faith had blinded them, and they wanted to be the first to strike a blow against the *kafir's* holiest shrine. Whatever it was, it was something that Ranveer would exploit to the full.

As Ranveer watched, the first Afghans closed within a *kos* of the shrine and started passing by a thinly wooded area. It was then that the first line of defence sprang into action. Twenty saffron clad priests emerged from their hiding places among the woods and unleashed a volley of spears and arrows at the Afghans. The Afghans reeled around to meet the unexpected threat, but when they saw that not one missile had hit its mark, many of them laughed out loud at the hapless priests. As more Afghans rode up, the priests scampered back among the woods, waiting to be run down and slaughtered. To Ranveer's relief, the Afghans decided that the bigger prize lay ahead in the shrine and they continued their race to the temple, now more confident than ever that there was no resistance to contend with here.

The Mahant had now come up next to Ranveer at his vantage point on a mound near the sanctum sanctorum, and he could see that the priest looked visibly relieved. The twenty priests who had volunteered for the first phase of Ranveer's plan had lots of courage but little by way of martial skill. So, using their ineffectual attack to make the Afghans more reckless and overconfident required little more than asking them to do their best. Both Ranveer and the Mahant had debated whether they should be sending these men to what may be a certain death, but ultimately the men themselves had asked to go out, and if nothing else, at least strike one blow at the raiders.

The first Afghans were now within a hundred paces of the temple, and close enough that Ranveer could make out their individual features. Ranveer's three hundred men were itching to fire, and he could feel hundreds of eyes looking at him, waiting for his order.

Ranveer sent up a silent prayer that his men would remember his instructions and then shouted one word.

'Fire!'

***

The deafening roar of more than a hundred rifles being fired at once shattered the calm of the temple complex. Several Afghan riders fell in the first volley, but much more than the number that fell, what counted more in the chaos that was to follow was the role played by those left alive. Ranveer had guessed correctly that the first Afghans to rush at the temple would likely be the youngest, most hot-blooded and least experienced of their warriors. So he had instructed his men not to shoot the first Afghans to reach the temple but to aim for the men staying behind. Men who were likely to be more experienced and wary of rushing blindly into a situation no matter how easy a picking it seemed.

The first line of Afghans to reach the temple panicked at the sudden attack and any exultation at having been missed gave way to more panic when they saw the men behind them fall. Their hopes of easy plunder dashed, the young Afghans turned their horses around and tried to fall back to regroup. They never had a chance. At Ranveer's signal, the remaining soldiers of his force fired, adding to the carnage in the Afghan ranks. When the few Afghan survivors rode away to join the main force, more than fifty Afghans lay dead or critically wounded around the Somnath temple.

The priests and soldiers let loose a cheer, but Ranveer was silent.

'My friend, you can at least smile after such a victory', the Mahant said.

'Acharyaji, this was no battle. It was a small skirmish, and if we have killed fifty Afghans, we need to worry about having twenty times that number bearing down on us soon.'

His words had a sobering effect on all the men around him, and Ranveer spoke loudly, addressing his men.

'Men, you have done very well in this first battle, but we will face many more of them. We have a plan, but remember, we have killed their weakest and most foolish warriors. The ones who will come next are no fools. But respect for an adversary's skills should not come in the way of our killing them as fast as we can. So happy hunting and good luck!'

His men cheered again, and Ranveer loaded his rifle, watching as the next wave of Afghans rode in. As he had feared, these men were not riding in blind. A *kos* from the temple, the five hundred Afghans split into two groups, enveloping the temple like a vice and then closing in at high speed. Unconsciously, Ranveer turned to his right, hoping to ask Iftiqar what he should do, and then realized that the old man would never again be at his side in battle. This was a battle he would have to win on his own.

He had a split second decision to make- should he divide his meagre forces to fire at both groups of the enemy or should he concentrate his firepower on one flank? As the Afghans closed in to within a hundred paces, he made his choice.

'Every man to fire a volley at the bastards on the right! Acharyaji, you have the left!'

His men scrambled to their positions and let loose a volley of fire. The Afghans weaved to avoid the incoming bullets, but several were hit. The others unslung their rifles and fired back.

Ranveer couldn't help but be impressed at their skill. Moving at speed, and under fire, they still managed to take down a dozen of the defenders and sent the others scampering for cover. To his left, Ranveer saw the second group of Afghans almost at the temple walls. That was when the priests sprang into action.

Ranveer had asked his men to arm each of the priests with a rifle and a handful of bullets. An hour's training would never transform them into soldiers, but packed tightly in a corner of the temple, they let loose a volley at the Afghans that made up for its lack of accuracy by its sheer concentrated volume of fire. Five or six Afghans fell, and the rest wheeled away, knowing now that this flank was also not an easy picking. The Afghans circled around the temple, like vultures around their prey, waiting for an opportunity to strike. Ranveer ordered his men not to fire, knowing that trying to hit such fast moving targets was likely to end up achieving little other than wasting their bullets. Instead, he waited for the Afghans to make their next move. For several minutes, the Afghans did little more than circle the temple, occasionally loosing off a shot to keep the defenders on edge, but made no move to enter the temple complex itself. When Ranveer looked over the horizon, he realized the Afghan plan. The main force was headed towards the temple, and with their overwhelming numerical superiority, they would crush the defenders in no time.

Ranveer had planned for this, and sprinted to his horse, mounting it and galloping out the temple door, followed by fifty of his horsemen. The Afghans circling the temple had never expected a counter-attack and were taken totally by surprise. Ranveer launched himself at the head of the Afghan force, firing one pistol and then another, seeing both shots hit home. Then he unsheathed his sword just in time to parry a spear strike from an Afghan. Ranveer turned his torso on his saddle and cut the Afghan just below the kidneys, sending the man down. His men were also now mixing it up with the Afghans, and Ranveer could barely hear anything above the din of battle. Another Afghan lunged at him, but Ranveer deflected his blow with his shield and slashed the Afghan across the neck with his sword. As suddenly as the attack had begun, it ended,as Ranveer bellowed an order to retreat, and he and his remaining men bolted back towards the temple. Any pursuing Afghans were kept at bay by rifle fire by the men inside the temple. Once inside, Ranveer took stock of his losses. His men had accounted for perhaps fifty of the enemy, but a dozen men had not returned from the attack. Ranveer just hoped that their strike had achieved its primary objective- allowing a scout to escape unnoticed, to try and reach Theo and his men, telling them that the time to strike was now.

The main Afghan force was now just a couple of *kos* away, and Ranveer could see the green standard of General Abdali. As he looked closer, he could see the General himself, seated on a huge charger. As memories of his father came back, Ranveer resolved that if nothing else, he would have the General's head today. Suddenly, all hell broke loose as the Afghans streamed in towards the temple all at one. Once again, Ranveer looked on with grudging admiration at their tactics. Abdali would have known by now that he had overwhelming numerical superiority and rather than fritter it away in small engagements as he had done so far, he had chosen to use it in one crushing blow. Seeing more than two thousand Afghans close in on the temple was a sight that caused even Ranveer to pause, as he wondered what he and his men could possibly do against such a force.

Just then, he heard a rifle being fired close to his ear, and saw an Afghan horseman fall from his saddle. Another shot brought down another Afghan, and a third shot a few seconds later accounted for yet another. Ranveer looked to his right, and was astonished to see the Mahant reloading the three rifles by his side. The priest saw the look of disbelief on Ranveer's face and smiled.

'I was not always a priest. Even Valmiki was a dacoit before he saw the Path, so a mere mortal like me is allowed a past, am I not? Now shall we kill these bastards or do you want to invite them in?'

Ranveer smiled back and ordered his men to fire at the on-coming Afghans. For a few minutes, the two sides traded rifle fire, but the outcome was a foregone conclusion- with their crushing weight of numbers, the Afghans closed in on the temple, and for the seventh time in history, raiders defiled the premises of the Somnath temple. The Western wall was the one to fall first as Afghans swept aside the men placed there and streamed into the main complex. Ranveer ordered his men to fall back to the sanctum sanctorum, forcing the Afghans to follow through the narrow breach in the walls. Ranveer stopped a few feet away from the central shrine and then turned around to see a dozen Afghans inside the complex, running towards him. The Mahant was by his side, rifle in hand, and he knelt and fired, shooting dead one Afghan. Ranveer shot another one before the others were within touching distance. One of the Afghans swung his sword at Ranveer, but he moved out of the way, slicing the Afghan's calf with his own sword. As the Afghan clutched at his foot, Ranveer stabbed him in the neck, killing him. Ranveer watched as the Mahant brought the butt of his rifle down on an Afghan's head, and then swung it like a club, sending another Afghan down. But the Afghans kept coming, and Ranveer knew it would be a matter of time before they were overwhelmed. As a tall Afghan grabbed his left hand and pulled him down, trying to stab him with a curved knife, Ranveer wondered if this was how it would all end. Ranveer rolled over, unbalancing the man and using the man's own weight and momentum to send him sprawling to the ground, and then crushed the Afghan's windpipe with his heavily armoured elbow. Another Afghan grabbed at his neck with one hand, while bringing down a dagger with the other. Ranveer kneed the man in the groin and as he doubled over in agony, he wrenched the man's knife from his hand and stabbed him in the stomach.

Just then, chaos erupted in the Afghan lines. Theo, along with the remaining three hundred riders, swept in behind the Afghans, who were too preoccupied with the assault on the temple to even contemplate an attack from behind. Ranveer stood up to witness a scene of utter bedlam. Theo was right at the front, whooping like a maniac, firing his pistol with deadly effect, and then taking out a British cavalry sabre in one hand and a small curved axe in the other, slashing and stabbing at abandon as he entered the Afghan lines. Emboldened by the antics of their leader, the other riders also rushed into the Afghans, dispatching their rifles, and then coming in close with their swords and lances. The plan was working! Ranveer watched as the Afghan lines began to crumble, and the few Afghans left inside the temple rushed outside to aid their comrades. Ranveer ran to his horse and rode out towards the Afghans, screaming for his men to follow him.

Through the narrow range of vision of his armoured helmet, Ranveer saw the Afghan core before him, the green standard of Abdali fluttering in the wind. An Afghan rider tried to cut him off, but one of Ranveer's men speared him. Ranveer was now close enough to see the Afghan General, still trying to maintain calm in his ranks and trying to marshal his troops. If only he had a loaded gun! He could have shot Abdali dead easily from this range, but he would just have to close in and finish this face to face. Abdali wheeled around at the sound of approaching horses and saw Ranveer homing in on him. The big Afghan General lowered the visor over his helmet and unsheathed his sword- a long, curved blade. He waited for the young Rajput, a sneer forming on the edges of his lips. Seeing the complacent expression on Abdali's face further enraged Ranveer and as he passed Abdali to his left, he drew his sword back, aiming for Abdali's chest. For a man his size, Abdali moved with surprising speed and blocked Ranveer's blow with his small shield, in turn bringing his blade down on Ranveer's back as he passed him. Ranveer saw the blow coming and blocked it with his own shield. As he circled around, his left arm felt like it was on fire from the pain of having blocked Abdali's powerful blow. Yet, it was nothing compared to the rage he felt at the man who had been responsible for his father's death.

Ranveer charged in again, and this time their swords rang against each other repeatedly as they traded blow after blow. There was a temporary lull in the fighting around them as men stopped to watch the Afghan General take on the Rajput officer, both sides knowing that if their leader fell, the battle was as good as lost. Abdali was stronger, and Ranveer could feel his arms tire with the pain of blocking the Afghan's blows, yet Ranveer was younger, fitter and had much more stamina. Ranveer watched the Afghan's blows get slower and more labored, and he prayed his arms would hold till the Afghan made a mistake out of tiredness. Abdali was also getting frustrated at this unexpected resistance and finally his anger got the better of him and he lunged forward without bringing his left hand up to block any counter with his shield. Ranveer parried the blow and swung his shield in an arc, connecting with the corner of the Afghan's helmet. The blow, delivered by his tired and battered left arm, was far from decisive, but sent the Afghan General tottering on his horse, struggling to keep his balance as blood streamed down his face. Ranveer was about to close in for the kill when to his dismay, Abdali bellowed an order whose meaning in words he did not understand, but whose meaning in deed was obvious. Four Afghan riders stepped in between him and Ranveer, shielding their injured General as he rode away and the Afghans began to retreat.

Ranveer rode after Abdali and hacked away at the four Afghans in his way. He cut down one man, but was on the verge of being stabbed from behind by another when two of his attackers fell from their horses, shot by a bullet each. The fourth Afghan turned and followed the rest of his fleeing comrades. Ranveer turned around to see Theo with a pistol in each hand, smiling at Ranveer.

'That was some battle, my friend! We decimated them!'

Many of Ranveer's men, caught up in the heat of battle wanted to pursue the Afghans, but even though in his heart, he ached to get a chance to kill Abdali, Ranveer ordered them to stand ground. While they had won a decisive victory, their numbers had been depleted and many of the remaining men and horses were wounded, or just plain too exhausted to pursue and fight an enemy that still would outnumber them.

That evening, Ranveer and his men went to say goodbye to the Mahant.

'Acharyaji, they may come back, and this time we may not be around. Just be careful.'

The Mahant, who had suffered a cut on his cheek in the fighting, smiled back.

'My friend, let them come and discover that Somnath will not be destroyed so easily.'

Then he added with a wink, as he pointed to the rifles and

ammunition that Ranveer had left behind for the priests.

'Plus, beyond divine providence, we have a little something to help us this time.'

Ranveer's force began the journey back to Jhansi. There was a palpable buzz among the men, many of whom had privately not believed they would prevail against a much larger Afghan force, especially after the defeat the Afghans had recently dealt to the coalition forces. Theo was riding next to Ranveer. He knew how hard Ranveer had taken the death of his father and then Iftiqar, and did not say much, but leaned over and handed Ranveer something.

'Ranveer, I know you wanted that bastard so badly. You will get another chance and next time he will not be able to run away like a coward. Till then, comfort yourself with the thought that you came damn close.'

Ranveer looked at the object Theo had handed him. It was an Afghan cavalry helmet studded with precious stones, with a jagged crack down the right side, and crusted over with dried blood. Ranveer looked at Theo questioningly, and the Englishman smiled.

'One of our men found it, seems like the good General lost his helmet as he was in such a hurry to get back to his harem.'

Ranveer looked at the helmet in his hands, and felt around the edges of the crack, feeling Abdali's dried blood.

Father, he thought, I will avenge you yet.

***

By the time Ranveer and Theo arrived back at Jhansi, they had expected to find an atmosphere of jubilation. Word of the victory at Somnath had spread like wildfire and every village they passed seemed to have heard of it, with the truth gradually magnified by every whisper into a victory against ten thousand rampaging Afghans. The fact was that some of these rumours were spread by his own soldiers, eager to impress the villagers along the way, but Ranveer did little to dispel them, knowing that they raised the morale of his men and also that of the civilians who had finally begun to believe that victory against the new regime in Dilli was indeed possible.

However, when they approached the gates of Jhansi, Ranveer began to sense that something was terribly wrong. What they saw were not the signs of a population that was ready to welcome it's conquering heroes. Instead, Jhansi resembled a ghost town. People seemed to have barred themselves inside their houses, and even the normally bustling market outside the gates was barren. There were many soldiers milling around, but they had a crestfallen look, as if they were fighting for a lost cause.

'What's wrong with these people? Don't they know we are finally winning?'

Theo's question was answered when Zahir Dehlavi himself came out on horseback to welcome them.

'Ranveer, we have all heard about your victory at Somnath.' Ranveer couldn't make out why the young courtier was looking so depressed if indeed word of the victory had reached the court.

'So then why does everyone look like someone has died?'

'Because many have died indeed, my friend. Come to the Palace and you will find out what has happened.'

While their men rested, Ranveer and Theo rushed straight to the Palace. The Englishman had no official title or rank, but by his deeds in battle and closeness to Ranveer had become the de facto second in command of Ranveer's force. When they entered the Palace, Ranveer saw all the leaders of the coalition in the War Room. To his surprise, even the Rani of Jhansi, normally the one bright spark in a room of dour old men, was also looking subdued. Jawan Bakht was sitting with Tatya Tope and Nana Sahib at the table, while Zahir Dehlavi was dictating a letter to a scribe in a corner. Ranveer knew better than to speak before he was addressed, so he waited for a few minutes before Rani Lakshmibai saw him standing in a corner. She walked up to Ranveer, grief writ large on her face. To his shock, Ranveer realized that the formidable lady was on the verge of tears.

'Raniji, what has happened?'

The Rani turned away, unable to speak, and Jawan Bakht stood up and came up to Ranveer.

'Ranveer, you have done what many would have considered impossible, yet we are unable to celebrate your victory, for the joy of your victory is clouded by a catastrophe that has befallen us.'

Ranveer had no idea what the young Prince was talking about, and looked around the room, hoping someone would finally tell him what had happened. The Prince continued.

'While you were away, Abu Bakr announced that in retribution for the resistance to his rule, he would annex Gwalior. His

Afghans had already sacked the Palace, but had left without trying to take any territory. Now he offered a simple choice, under the egging of that fanatic Sarfaraz Ali, that the people of Gwalior embrace Islam and his rule or perish by the sword.'

A knot formed in Ranveer's stomach as he recalled his own confrontation with the Afghans at Gwalior and the narrow escape they had had. Jawan Bakht continued.

'Raja Jiyajirao Sindhia was of course here, along with his family and the remnants of his army, but when he heard the order, he insisted on marching to Gwalior's defence.'

Ranveer sensed what was coming, and blurted out, not caring in whose presence he was speaking.

'Has something happened to him? Why did you allow him to march alone against them? Didn't you send your forces to help him?'

The Rani of Jhansi had composed herself and addressed Ranveer.

'Of course we did. We mobilized a force of ten thousand Marathas, under the personal command of Tatya Tope and sent them with the Raja. But it seems Abu Bakr had another plan after all.'

Ranveer looked at her, not understanding what she was referring to.

'The force Abu Bakr unleashed was not the Mughal Army or even forces of allied Mansabdars. Instead, he used Maulvi Sarfaraz Ali's army of hooligans and *jihadis*. They needed no mobilization, and had no heavy weapons or armour. As a result, they were at Gwalior before our army had even covered half the distance. They burnt and looted their way through villages, raping and slaughtering in the name of Jihad.'

Tatya Tope took up the story.

'My force was still about three days away from Gwalior and I kept advising Jiyajirao not to rush ahead without our main force, but when he heard about the atrocities being committed upon his people, he charged ahead with his elite guards.'

Ranveer knew what would have happened. Only in fairy tales do the brave hundred defeat thousands. The Rani of Jhansi confirmed his fears.

'The Jihadis ambushed him even before he reached Gwalior, and he is no more.'

The loss of one of the central leaders of the coalition was a catastrophe which made the victory at Somnath look like a trifle, and Ranveer understood the reason behind the gloom at the Palace. Also, as he digested the Rani's words, his mind immediately went to one person.

Maya.

The Rani must have read his mind, so she leaned forward and whispered.

'She is taking the loss of her father quite hard. I think you need to be with her.'

Ranveer would have left immediately to be with Maya had a thought not struck him.

'Raniji, now that Gwalior is lost, what next?'

Lakshmibai smiled a sad smile and looked away. Jawan

Bakht pointed at the map before him which showed the known positions of the Afghans forces in red and the Jihadis in green. They were all converging to one point on the map.

Jhansi.

'Abu Bakr has announced that after Gwalior, Jhansi must now pay the price for supporting the rebellion against his rule. The conditions are the same- surrender and convert or be destroyed.'

Ranveer's mind raced as he took in the map. Abu Bakr's force was even larger than it had been–apparently he had called in reserves from the Army of Kabul and emboldened by the victory at Gwalior, many of the Mansabdars who had been sitting on the fence, had thrown in their lot with him. Abu Bakr's army would have a large numerical edge, and if they marched on Jhansi in a frontal assault, the guerilla tactics that Ranveer and Tatya Tope had been using would be of little use. He wondered what the Rani was planning to do, and when he looked up at her, he saw that her grief had been replaced by a steely mask of determination.

'I will not give up my Jhansi.'

***

Nine

Ranveer lay on the bed, Maya's head on his chest. He would be marching out into battle the next morning, and they had clung to each other all evening, as if that could somehow make the inevitability of their separation go away. Four weeks earlier, Ranveer had returned from the battle at Somnath and on learning of Maya's father's death, had rushed straight to her from the Palace. Convention or protocol be damned, he had run straight to her quarters and to the shock of all the other women there, Maya had collapsed into his arms. In any other situation, their bringing their relationship into the open in such a brazen manner would have the stuff of Palace gossip and scandal. With Gwalior in flames and Jhansi next on the list of Abu Bakr's conquests, people had more pressing matters of survival to worry about. Ranveer knew that everyone was busy with the coming struggle, and did not want to create a distraction, yet he wanted to do the right thing.

So three weeks earlier, a small group had gathered at the Mahalakshmi Temple in Jhansi. All the leaders of the coalition were there, along with the *Rajmata* of Gwalior, finally managing to smile a bit after the loss of her husband. Theo was there as well, dressed in his finest coat, and still reeling a bit from the effect of the alcohol he had consumed the previous night to celebrate the event that was coming. The Rani of Jhansi had herself accompanied the group from her personal palace- the Rani Mahal, and as the Sun began to set over the horizon, Ranveer and Maya were married. In the week since then, they had immersed themselves in each other, trying to forget their recent losses.

'Maya, in case I don't come back…'

Maya silenced Ranveer by placing her fingers on his lips.

'You will, and you have to. For me. For us. And in case you don't, then we will meet in the next life.'

Ranveer took a second to comprehend what Maya was saying.

'Maya, you must not…'

Without responding, Maya walked to the large chest kept in the corner of their bedroom and took out her red and richly embroidered wedding sari. She placed it on a corner of their bed, and next to it she began placing all her wedding jewellery. Ranveer could hear his heart pounding as Maya finished laying the last piece, a gold necklace embedded with rubies that Rani Lakshmibai had given her as a wedding present.

'Ranveer, I am now the wife of a Rajput warrior. The battle you go to fight will determine whether all of Jhansi, and indeed all of Hindustaan as we know it, survives or not. If you fall, and our army fails, then I will not be waiting here to be ravaged or enslaved by the Afghans or Jihadis. I will commit Jauhar and wait for you in the next life.'

Ranveer tried to wish away the image of Maya setting herself aflame, dressed in her wedding finery–a final act of defiance and sacrifice that had long been part of the code of honour among Rajputs. But the more he looked at the fire in her eyes, the more he knew that she could, and would do just what she was describing.

In the time he had spent growing up in Dilli among the nobles of the Mughal court, Ranveer had almost come to forget what his origins were. He was a Mughal noble, like so many others, all cast in the same mould- Hindu and Mussalman alike- all seeking to navigate the corridors of power in Dilli and eke out a career serving the Emperor. The events of the last few months had shaken that easy conviction in him. As he thought of what he considered himself to be now, he realized that his only real connection with the Mughals had ended when his father had been killed. He was now a rebel and outlaw to the very system he had been trained to serve all his life, and with little else to fall back upon, he had started rediscovering his roots, much of it due to Maya.

'You are not a Mughal officer anymore, so why do you bother wearing their uniforms and their badges of rank?' she had asked him one evening, as he came to visit her in her quarters straight from the Palace. Her words had stung at the moment, but he had then asked her what she thought he was.

'Lakshmidi always says that a man is what his actions depict him to be and you my love are my own chivalrous Rajput warrior.'

It had been said playfully and half in jest, but had struck a chord in him somewhere. Ranveer's father had always told Ranveer that his hotheadedness in rushing into battle was due to his Rajput blood, and his iron discipline when in combat came from his Mughal training. Qureshi had often said that Ranveer had inherited the best of both worlds–and they would make for an unbeatable combination. Tonight, unknown to Maya, Ranveer had acquired one final symbol of his Rajput roots.

'Maya, if it all must come to an end tomorrow, then you will not be the only one who goes to the next life like a Rajput.'

Maya's eyes were moist with emotion as she nuzzled her head against Ranveer's arm. Ranveer pulled her to him, kissing her first lightly, and then with increasing intensity as the two of them lay down on the bed, enjoying what may well have been their last night together.

The next morning, the first person Ranveer sought out was Theo. The Englishman was getting ready for battle, going through a ritual of his own that Ranveer had long come to recognize. The Englishman was seated before a small idol of the one the Christians called the Son of God, praying. When Theo arose, Ranveer saw that the Englishman was carrying enough weapons to equip a small army. His repeating revolver was slung at his waist, along with a matchlock pistol. On the other side of his waistband were slung a long curved Gurkha knife and a short axe. At his thigh was fastened another long knife.

Ranveer smiled at Theo.

'You're pulling out your entire collection today, aren't you?'

'Yes my friend, this *khukri* came from a Gurkha chieftain I killed in a skirmish along the Chinese frontier, and this tomahawk, as the tribes there call it, was recovered from a fallen hero of the Iroquois people in the Americas. It was handed down from my grandfather to me.'

Ranveer looked at his friend, who seemed to be a totally different person from the lighthearted womanizer and drunkard he had first encountered in the deserts of Rajputana.

'Theo, you were an officer in the British Army. As an objective observer, what do you think our chances are?'

'Objective observer, my ass. I am riding to my death, and you expect me to be objective about it!'

'So it is as bad as I feared.'

Theo pulled out a bottle from his cupboard and took a deep swig.

'My man, it is so bad that I won't even bother to pretend that I'm sober. See, the problem is that people mistake fanaticism for incompetence, and that can be a fatal mistake. Somehow, Abu Bakr has gotten one step ahead of us, and has outmaneuvered us, and we're exactly where he would want us, and where we would least want to be.'

While none of the leaders of the coalition would ever say it quite so bluntly in public, Ranveer knew that they would have agreed with the gist of the Englishman's assessment in private. In the preceding weeks, the coalition had first expected the bands of marauding Jihadis to come straight to Jhansi from Gwalior, and hoping to repeat the success of their guerilla tactics against the Mansabdars' forces, had deployed small scouting parties to attack and demoralize small pockets of Jihadis. Instead, the Jihadis, almost as if knowing what was in store for them if they made a mad and disorganized dash for Jhansi, stayed put, waiting till regular Mughal Army troops and Afghans supplemented them. Then, Abu Bakr's juggernaut had set out on a steady march to Jhansi.

The coalition had employed its tried and tested guerilla tactics- in one instance sending a force led by Tatya Tope himself. But their enemy had either proved to be a very quick learner, or as the Palace rumours suggested, got some inside information. There were no more small forays that could be ambushed piecemeal, no more indisciplined marauding of neighbouring villages. Instead the army of nearly a lakh soldiers proceed *kos* by sure *kos* on a route to Jhansi, in perfect formation. The coalition had been left with no choice- either they could meet this force in frontal battle, or they could abandon Jhansi. The choice was an easy one to make, but a terrible one to see through.

'So how is Maya?'

When Ranveer told Theo about Maya's plans, Theo shook his head.

'That's one area where you Hindustaanis are truly incorrigible. I wouldn't have believed it had I not seen such rituals firsthand. You know something, Ranveer?'

'What?'

Theo took another drink from the bottle, and offered it to Ranveer, who declined it with a smile.

'I envy you. Here I am, having spent the best part of my youth chasing every woman I could find, and have nothing to show for my efforts except a couple of cases of venereal disease and a dozen angry fathers and husbands after my blood.'

Ranveer laughed, remembering the circumstances in which he had first met Theo.

'And here you are, married to a lovely Princess, one who loves you so much she is willing to kill herself. That would make for a heck of a story.'

Another swig.

'So, Ranveer, I have decided that if I escape out of all this with my sorry ass intact, I will finally write that book I had often dreamt of writing. A book about us, about you, about what we have all seen and experienced.'

'Theo, I just hope your book has a happy ending.'

***

Just after noon, the coalition army was arrayed in front of the walls of Jhansi. It was an awesome sight- more than fifty thousand infantry and twenty thousand cavalry, flanked by all the cannon that the combined armies of Jhansi and the Marathas could muster on such short notice. The troops were a motley bunch-Marathas in white with saffron headbands, troops from Gwalior in yellow, forces from Jhansi itself in cream with red waistbands, and scattered among them, deserters from the Mughal Army, Hindus and Mussalman alike–more than five thousand of them, men whose conscience had overridden blind obedience to the orders they were receiving from Dilli and who had rallied to Jawan Bakht's flag. If one added together the irregular militias and volunteers from the common citizens of Jhansi–cooks, butchers, tailors- who had taken up arms in its defence, the force rivaled Abu Bakr's army in sheer numbers.

The women had gathered along the ramparts of the fort, watching the men go out to battle. Wives, mothers, daughters, all saying goodbye to the men in their lives as they marched out, to fight for their very existence. All the women that is, with one notable exception. A hush fell over the gathered armies as a slim, armour clad rider emerged from the gates. She had a sword and shield strapped across her back, and a rifle across one shoulder. The plumage that topped her helmet swayed in the wind as she rode out to inspect her forces. A murmur ran through the men as the Rani of Jhansi emerged in full battle gear to ride against Abu Bakr's army.

Another rider emerged from the fort a few minutes later. His appearance had none of the dramatic impact on the assembled armies as the Rani's had, but for those in the know, what he chose to wear into battle said it all. Ranveer had put on his customary

Ahadi cavalry uniform, but today, as he had promised Maya, he would meet his enemies as a Rajput should. On top of his armour, he wore a saffron tunic–a *kesariya bana*, the colour that Rajput warriors wore into battle when they intended to either ride back victorious or die fighting. The colour they wore into battle when they knew that if they perished on the battlefield, their women would be committing *Jauhar*. Maya was looking on from the ramparts, dressed in her wedding dress, her gold jewellery glistening in the sunlight. Ranveer caught a glimpse of her and smiled as he saw her.

As trumpets blared, the army set forward. As most marches did, this one had begun with much pomp and splendor, with loud trumpets, the beating of drums and blood-curdling war cries. Again, as most marches went, the realities of boredom, fatigue and heat soon started taking their toll. Theo rode up to Ranveer, shaking his head in exasperation.

'See those buggers over there! They can't even keep in formation and half of them have decided on their own accord to take a drinks break. Fine army we have.'

Ranveer looked to where Theo was pointing and saw that the civilian militia from Jhansi had indeed for all intents and purposes broken ranks with the rest of the army. Their enthusiasm and brave proclamations to fight to the death had not been backed up by any real training or discipline and Ranveer knew that when battle was joined, they would break. The very strength of the coalition- its diversity of many rulers and territories combining to oppose Abu Bakr–was also the root of its weakness.

That diversity did not matter when their weapon was the guerilla attack, when small, cohesive units could go into battle, but in a set piece battle with a large army like this, that diversity meant that different units did not have common signals, formations or even codes. A recipe for chaos–and one, that somehow Abu Bakr had managed to exploit.

As the army camped for the night ten *kos* from Jhansi, Ranveer was summoned to the tent where the leaders were huddled. When he entered, he found all the leaders huddled around a map. Ranveer was surprised to see Jawan Bakht taking a leading role in the discussions on tactics. The Prince had so far never been so involved in running the campaign. Tatya Tope was standing in a corner, looking a bit bored. When he saw Ranveer enter, he pulled him aside.

'Ranveer, we are headed for a big defeat.'

Ranveer and Theo had talked in private about their misgivings but to hear a senior General say it so bluntly caught him by surprise. 'Politics has overridden military realities. The young Prince there sees this as his personal battle for the throne of Dilli, the Rani sees it as fighting for the survival of Jhansi, and the Gwalior army sees it as revenge for their King. All fair motivations, but the problem is that everybody now wants to run the campaign.'

'So what are our orders?'

Tatya Tope looked Ranveer in the eye.

'Jawan Bakht claims, perhaps justifiably, that he is the most trained in the Mughal style of warfare, and is leading the thinking on how to approach this battle. To use the analogy you once used, we are a small elephant trying to get into a pushing match with a much larger elephant. Guess who will win?'

'Tatya Sahib, I may be speaking out of turn, but with all respect, the Mughal artillery will cut us to ribbons and I suspect our militias will just panic and disperse when their elephants come to the field. We cannot just attack them head on.'

The General held Ranveer's arm in a vice like grip.

'Which is why, I am asking you to break ranks and desert.' Ranveer was shocked to hear the General's orders. He was about to protest when the Rani of Jhansi came up to them and motioned for the two of them to come outside the tent.

'Ranveer, the men of Gwalior are not going to listen to our orders–they just want revenge for the sack of their city and the killing of their Raja, and the throne of Dilli is now too close for Jawan Bakht to see reason. He is a fine young man, and the heir apparent to the throne, but he is also just a boy who wants to avenge his father's murder and take back what is his. But we cannot just march to a sure defeat–so here is a plan that I, Nana Sahib and Tatya Tope have agreed on.'

A few minutes later, Ranveer walked out of the tent and went straight to Theo. The two talked late into the night, and then got to work. Word was spread whisper by whisper, man to man, and when the Sun rose, the coalition army was without its finest cavalry. More than two thousand experienced riders, under Ranveer's command, had just disappeared.

Jawan Bakht was furious at this apparent desertion but declared that he would rather go into battle with a hundred loyal men than a thousand turncoats. As rumours go, the message that reached Abu Bakr's camp through spies was that more than five thousand riders had deserted. By noon, the Mughal army, sensing an easy victory, was on the roll.

History's pivotal battles sometimes occur in the unlikeliest of places, whose only claim to fame becomes the fact that they provided the soil on which men shed their blood. Dabra was to be no exception. Located almost midway between Gwalior and Jhansi, the non-descript village awoke to what would have sounded to a layman like thunder. It was in reality the sound of thousands of soldiers and horses marching in unison as Abu Bakr's army loomed ever closer to Jhansi.

Ranveer and his men were now well out of sight of the combatants, having taken position on a small hillock halfway to the Damrauli Hanuman temple which was located almost two *kos* from Dabra. Keeping the rest of his force well concealed, Ranveer, Theo and a few men were peering through the cover of foliage, watching the battle unfold before them. Ranveer instantly recognized the classical Mughal Army formation that Abu Bakr had employed. His cannon and war elephants were arrayed in the centre, ringed by heavy infantry. One of the elephants carried the Royal banner, and Ranveer wondered if Abu Bakr himself had taken to the field. The Afghan cavalry rode on the flanks, waiting to sweep down on any opening caused by the initial artillery barrage. Facing them was an almost equally large force of the coalition armies, except that it had no war elephants and was much weaker when it came to artillery. The Mughal forces came to an abrupt halt, and Ranveer saw a flurry of activity as they began deploying their heavy cannon. He could hear Theo muttering next to him.

'Poor, stupid bastards. I hope they can close fast.'

Theo was just echoing what must have been going through the minds of the Rani of Jhansi, Tatya Tope and the other coalition commanders who were still able to see through the weakness of a strategy that played straight into Abu Bakr's strengths. The Mughal Army would have an overwhelming superiority in artillery and standing their ground to slug it out at long range with cannon was suicidal. The only real option was to charge and close in, when the advantage in cannon would count for little. Only there, they would have to contend with the war elephants. So there really was no easy way out, and Ranveer saw several puffs of smoke emanate from the Mughal guns, followed by their sound a second later, as the first salvo was fired. The coalition gunners fired back, but they had neither the number, nor the range, to make a serious contest of it. Ranveer and Theo watched as cannonball after cannonball careened into the coalition ranks, sending men and horses flying. For all the spectacle, both of them knew that no amount of cannon would win the battle, it would come down to a good old fashioned contest of arms and swords, and Ranveer exhaled in relief as he saw the coalition deploy its forces on the offensive.

From the left flank, Maratha riders, dressed in white and led by Tatya Tope himself, swept across the arid fields, their battle cry of '*Har Har Mahadev*' echoing across the plains. A column of Afghan cavalry broke ranks to engage them, and just then, the Gwalior infantry launched an attack on the right flank. Ranveer watched in fascination as some of the finest military commanders in Hindustaan displayed their prowess. The Afghans and the Marathas crashed together in a crushing melee of men, horses and steel. As a fierce running battle raged around them, the men of Gwalior, still maintaining perfect ranks despite their two hundred yard sprint towards the enemy, began arranging themselves into firing ranks two rows deep. Many of the men had lost family members in the sack of Gwalior, and itched to finally get their revenge. Several hundred yards away, the Mughal *bandookchis* began bringing their rifles to bear.

'Come on, come on. Just a few more yards and you can let those bastards have it!', Theo muttered, willing the Gwalior gunners to close in and fire. Just then, something unexpected happened. Before the Gwalior troops had even come close enough to bring their rifles up to fire, the Mughals fired, one salvo after another. Several of the Gwalior troops fell, tumbling to the ground, as some of their comrades fired back, watching in frustration as their shots landed harmlessly short of the Mughals. Ranveer watched helplessly as they tried to close in, so they could get a shot at the enemy, but were massacred as the Mughals fired salvo after salvo with impunity.

'Theo, what just happened? The Mughal Army uses the same rifles we do! How did they just do that?'

To his left, he saw the Afghan cavalry disengage and ride

back to the main Mughal force. By now, most of the Maratha cavalry had been committed to battle, and Ranveer quickly saw that the Afghan counter-charge had just been a ruse to get as many Maratha riders in the open and within rifle range. Once again, he saw row upon row of *bandookchis* kneel and fire their rifles, secure in the knowledge that the coalition forces had nothing that could touch them at that range. Rider after rider fell as the Marathas regrouped and retreated. Lots of people, Ranveer included, had harboured misgivings about the upcoming battle, but nobody had imagined that it would turn out to be such a total rout.

Jawan Bakht's green banner was still flying high, though Ranveer could see no sign of the Prince himself. Theo must have read his mind. 'Looks like the young scoundrel finally found out that moving markers on a map and a real life battle are two quite different things. Should we ride in to help?'

Ranveer had been thinking that himself.

'No, Theo. Our only purpose in feigning desertion was to keep some element of surprise. If we ride out now, we will just get shot down like those Marathas did.'

'Since when did you start being a thinker, my friend?'

Ranveer didn't say anything, but he knew the answer. Since I realized that I have someone to live for. Just then, there was a commotion in the coalition ranks, and a single rider moved towards the enemy ranks. Even at this distance, Ranveer knew who it was.

The Rani of Jhansi had entered the fray.

***

Seeing the Rani charge at the enemy galvanized her men, and several thousand riders joined her, as they made straight for the Mughal riflemen who had caused such carnage. The Mughal *bandookchis* fired at the approaching riders, and several fell, but the Rani rode like one possessed, and seeing her remain unscathed despite the barrage of bullets aimed at her, her men followed. Ranveer watched in fascination as the seemingly impossible happened. Seeing the approaching cavalry charge, several of the *bandookchis*, now not feeling so secure after all, began to waver. That chaos in the ranks spread like dominos as the Mughals lost fire discipline. Despite their new and unexpected edge in rifles, the bottom line was that most of them had not seen pitched battle before, and now as the enemy closed, negating the edge their rifle range gave them, many of them began to move towards the rear.

'Cut them to pieces, Raniji.' Ranveer muttered through clenched teeth.

The riders crashed into the ranks of the massed riflemen, their sheer momentum sending many of the Mughal soldiers flying, with yet others being crushed by the horses. The Rani of Jhansi was hacking away with her sword, and a cordon of loyal men had surrounded her, warding off any attempt to attack their beloved Rani. The core of the Mughal infantry seemed on the verge of total collapse when the Afghan cavalry from both flanks converged, trying to box in the Rani and her men. As they closed in on her, the remaining Maratha cavalry under Tatya Tope rode out again, intercepting the left wing of the Afghans and Ranveer saw Jawan Bakht deploy his loyalist Mughal infantry on the right flank to cut off the Afghans there.

The Rani of Jhansi had fought her way deep into the enemy ranks, and Ranveer saw that she was now within striking distance of the six massive war elephants arrayed deep in the Mughal ranks. One of them had an elaborate *howdah* and was carrying the Imperial banner. The Rani's intentions were clear. She was trying to do the unthinkable. If she managed to kill Abu Bakr then not just this battle, but the whole war would end. A phalanx of Mughal infantry charged the Rani and her men and managed to buy some time for the war elephants to retreat a bit. While the Rani and her riders were trying to fight their way through, Ranveer saw a column of dust in the distance behind the Mughal ranks.

'Theo, they have reinforcements!'

As both of them looked closer, it was clear that Abu Bakr had not yet played all his cards. A large column of heavily armoured Afghan riders was headed straight for the Rani. With the rest of the coalition army still engaged in fierce combat with the Afghan cavalry and Mughal infantry, there would be no help for the Rani. She would be surrounded deep behind enemy lines. As Ranveer looked closer, he saw a banner he recognized. He spat more than said the name as recognition dawned.

'Abdali.'

Before Theo could say anything, Ranveer ordered his men to mount and ride out to intercept the Afghans. Before most of his men had even started, he was riding at full trot towards the

Afghans. He saw that Abdali and some of his men continued on to attack the Rani, but a large force of Afghans veered course to meet this new threat. Still riding as fast as his horse could carry him, Ranveer took out a loaded pistol from his belt and fired at the nearest Afghan, sending him careening to the ground. As the next Afghan approached him, he then reversed his grip on the pistol, and ducking to avoid an oncoming sword strike, swung his pistol butt with all his strength into the Afghan's head, shattering both the man's skull and his pistol's wooden grip. Discarding the weapon, he took out his other pistol and fired, felling another of the enemy. As he took out his sword, he heard shots fired in rapid succession as Theo joined the fray, killing two Afghans. By now the rest of his men had joined the battle, and Ranveer veered his horse to the left to go to the Rani's rescue. Theo and a handful of his men followed.

As he rode towards the centre of the Mughal ranks, Ranveer saw that the Rani had fought her way through the defenders, and as he looked on in awe, fired two shots at the Imperial elephant with her pistols. He saw the *mahout* fall to the ground. Without its *mahout* and driven half crazy by the sound around it, the elephant panicked and started to trample the Mughal soldiers around it. The *mahouts* of the other elephants dismounted and tried to calm the elephant and save their leader. One was trampled underfoot and another swatted aside like a mosquito by the beast's trunk.

In the middle of all this chaos, the Afghans reached the Rani and attacked her from behind. Three of her men turned their horses between her and the Afghans, but taken by surprise, were cut down. Ranveer was riding as hard as he could, and cursed the fact that he now had no pistols to attack the Afghans at long range. He saw the Rani cut down one Afghan and then engage in a fierce sword fight with another before she dispatched him with a strike to the head. But there were too many enemies, and while her men rushed to her aid, caught behind enemy lines and hopelessly outnumbered, time was fast running out for her.

Ranveer finally caught up with the Afghans and this time surprise was on his side. He stabbed the nearest man in the back, pulling his sword out as the man lurched in his saddle and fell. Theo was right beside him, and had flung his tomahawk with deadly accuracy, hitting an Afghan on the neck. Ranveer cut down another Afghan and then saw that Abdali himself was now leading the attack on the Rani. There were five Afghans who had surrounded the Rani, and despite the odds, she was more than holding her own. Her hands were moving like lightning, parrying blows and striking out at her enemies. Ranveer rode straight at Abdali, but just then two Afghans rode in front of him. One of them slashed Ranveer on his leg, causing him to scream in pain and drop his sword, clutching his wound in agony. The second man was about to deliver the killing blow when Theo beheaded him with his *khukri*. Ranveer regained control of his horse with his left hand, and with his right, took off his armoured helmet and smashed it into the Afghan's face, turning his nose into a bloody pulp. The man screamed in agony and before he could recover and counterattack, Ranveer swung his helmet again at the man's head, killing him and sending him to the ground.

Ranveer picked up his sword and began to ride to the Rani's assistance again, but saw that he was too late. She was bleeding from numerous wounds, her tunic stained bright red. Yet, she kept fighting. Of her five attackers, only three now remained alive, and they continued to strike out at her, like a pack of wolves trying to bring down a wounded lion. Ranveer swung his sword like a scythe as he rode up to the closest Afghan, almost beheading the man, and then turned to see Abdali stab the Rani in her back.

'No!'

His cry of anguish caught Abdali's attention and the General turned to face him. As recognition dawned, he turned the sword in the Rani's back, a twisted grin on his face. The remaining Afghan had meanwhile taken advantage of Ranveer's distraction by slashing him across the leg, but driven nearly mad by rage, he did not even notice. He rode straight at Abdali, his blood stained sword in hand.

Abdali tried to pull his sword out and meet this threat, but even in death, the Rani of Jhansi proved that not for nothing would she come to epitomize courage for a long time to come. She grabbed Abdali's blade with her right hand, preventing him from pulling it out. Helpless, the Afghan General watched Ranveer bear down on him, holding up his left hand to try and ward off the blow that he knew was coming. Ranveer swung his sword down as he rode past and when he turned his horse around, Abdali's left arm fell to the ground, severed just below the elbow. The Afghan General grabbed the bloody stump that was left and screamed in agony, a cry that for a moment drowned out even the din and chaos of battle around him.

Ranveer prepared to ride by again and finally do what he had dreamt of doing ever since he had heard of Abdali's role in his father's death. Just as he prepared to charge, he saw the Rani of Jhansi fall to the ground, Abdali's sword still embedded in her back. She was bleeding from countless wounds, but still she struggled to hoist herself up by grabbing onto the stirrups of her horse. Taking advantage of this distraction, an Afghan horseman rode up to Abdali, and securing his crippled General behind him on his horse, began riding away.

Ranveer would have given chase, but he remembered something his father had once told him. It takes a braver man to save a life than to take one. He dismounted and rushed to the Rani, and sat by her, cradling her head on his lap. Seeing their Rani go down, and that too after being attacked in such a cowardly manner had driven her men to a frenzy. With Abdali out of the action, and Abu Bakr having retreated far to the rear, with his elephant finally under control, the coalition forces finally began to get the upper hand. However, their initial losses to the *bandookchis* had been devastating, and they had nothing like the numbers needed to really press home the advantage. So while Theo and his men had a field day picking off stragglers and ensuring Abu Bakr's men left a thick trail of blood as they retreated, the Mughal forces were able to stage a fighting retreat.

Ranveer wondered what he could do. The Rani was beyond

saving, having lost way too much blood. By now the other coalition leaders had joined them, and Ranveer could see that in the desperate fighting of the last few hours, every single one of them had been blooded. Tatya Tope had a nasty gash on his left cheek, and was bleeding from a wound on his right shoulder where a bullet had grazed him; Nana-sahab had his right arm in a makeshift sling; even Jawan Bakht had apparently been involved in the action, as his sword arm was hanging limply to his side. But for now, all of them forgot their wounds and pain and looked upon the woman who lay before them.

Nana-sahab, an old friend of the Rani knelt beside her.

'Lakshmi, Jhansi will be safe. You have my word on that. Anand will be King, and I will ensure nothing comes in his way.'

Ranveer had heard about how the Rani had been ruling Jhansi after her husband's death four years ago, and her only wish was that she keep Jhansi free and strong till her adopted son, Anand Rao, was old enough to take over. The Rani looked at Nana-sahab and smiled, and then turned to Ranveer.

'Keep Maya happy. She is lucky to have you.'

Tears were streaming down Ranveer's cheeks and when he looked around himself, he saw that all the others gathered were crying. The Rani twitched in pain, asking for water, but before anyone could fetch any, she breathed her last.

The ride back to Jhansi was a somber one. The battle had been a stalemate, with both sides suffering terrible losses, yet everyone knew that the heroism of the Rani of Jhansi had helped them live to fight another day, despite the odds they had been up against. Ranveer rode in silence, his head bowed, trying to comprehend why God insisted on taking away the ones who perhaps had the most to offer. He had not realized it, but Tatya Tope had drawn up next to him.

'Ranveer, she was a remarkable woman. She had more courage than any of us, and she died in a way that will be sung in folklore for ages to come; but do you know the most remarkable fact of all?'

Ranveer looked at Tatya Tope, wondering what the General was referring to.

'She was only twenty two years old.'

***

Ten

Jhansi was in a state of mourning when the army returned. Ranveer went straight to his home. As he passed through the streets of Jhansi, he saw downcast faces everywhere. A part of him had hoped that, as with her army on the battlefield, the Rani's supreme sacrifice would have infused renewed resolve among the people of Jhansi. But any sign of resolve had evaporated with the crippling losses the state had suffered in the battle, in addition to the loss of their beloved Queen. It had taken the battered army a full week to make the journey back to Jhansi, and in that time, as often happens with bad news, rumours had magnified what had actually happened during the battle. So the Mughals now had a super rifle that could pick enemies off from many *kos* away, and that a new army of Afghans had joined Abu Bakr and were readying to march on Jhansi.

As soon as he entered his home, Maya came rushing into his arms. As he looked at her, he saw the conflicted emotions she was feeling- relief at the fact that Ranveer had come home when so many others had not, and also immense grief at the loss of her childhood friend and mentor. For his part, Ranveer's mind was numb. He had seen too much killing and experienced too much loss in the recent past.

'I heard you were with her at the end', Maya whispered.

'She fought like Durga herself. If it were not for her, it would be Abu Bakr, and not our army marching into Jhansi today.'

Ranveer sat down, wincing in pain as he did so.

'Are you okay? Were you hurt?'

Ranveer told Maya about his wounds but then told her not to worry.

'Maya, any wound I suffered stopped hurting the moment I realized that I would live to come home- to you.'

Maya sat down beside him, holding his hand.

'Ranveer, what will become of us? Will we ever live a normal life or did we just meet at the wrong time?'

Ranveer cupped her face in his hands and looked into Maya's eyes.

'My love, I don't know what will be in the future or what will happen tomorrow. If there is one thing that I have learnt from all that I have lost it is that I learn to cherish what I have today. So, as we have done, we will live every day together to the fullest, and if destiny has other plans in place for us, I will have no regrets, for I shall have loved and been loved in return.'

As they sat together, Ranveer told Maya about Rani's last moments, and felt her hand tighten in his as she learnt that the cause of the Rani's death had been the same nemesis that had plagued both their lives–Abdali. By afternoon, Ranveer was expected to report back to duty, and as he left he said to Maya.

'This war may last long or not, and we may prevail or not, but one thing I can promise you is that by the time this is over, Abdali will have died by my blade.'

All the coalition leaders were at the Palace except for Jawan Bakht, but without the Rani there, there seemed to be no spark or life in any of them. They had turned back a more powerful force, in the process inflicting terrible losses on Abu Bakr's army, yet they looked as if they had suffered a crushing defeat. In the past, whenever spirits or morale had flagged, the Rani of Jhansi had rallied all of them, some of them old enough to be her father, through her indefatigable spirit and sheer force of personality. Without her, it seemed as if the coalition was doomed to drift like a ship that has lost its sails. Ranveer stayed only a few minutes, and was about to leave when he crossed paths with Ghalib.

'Ranveer, you know the problem with all of them?'

'What, Ghalib sahib?'

'They loved Lakshmi–some as a daughter, some as a sister, and every one of them as a dear friend. And love, my son, is a dangerous thing, for love makes one lose one's mind and spirit when a dear one passes. One may say that when one loves and loses one wishes one had never experienced love at all.'

For once, Ranveer was in no mood for Ghalib's poetry, and

brusquely began to walk away, when Ghalib stopped him with a hand on his shoulder.

'Ranveer, when warriors lose their courage, sometimes fighting will not result in victory. In such cases, a whisper can be more devastating than any rifle fire.'

Ranveer was beginning to lose his patience with the old man's cryptic couplets.

'Ghalib sahib, everyone in there looks like we have already lost. What else can we do?'

'Follow me. While the old men fret, the young plot.'

With a smile, Ghalib led Ranveer to a side room and when he entered he was surprised to find a motley gathering sitting around a table. Jawan Bakht was there, as was his young courtier, Zahir Dehlavi, and along with them was seated Theo, drinking from his hip flask. When he saw Ranveer enter, Theo offered Ranveer a drink, which he refused.

'Theo, what are you doing here?'

Ranveer had been mortified to find his friend drinking openly in front of the Prince, but he soon realized that Jawan Bakht had other, more pressing matters on his mind than the impertinence of the Englishman. By way of reply to Ranveer's question, Theo just pointed to the table around which they were seated. Ranveer immediately grasped what was going on.

Lying on the table was a rifle. It was slightly longer than the muskets that Ranveer had grown up training with, and as he hefted it in his right hand, he realized that despite its length, it was considerably lighter than the rifles he had carried into battle.

'Enfield Pattern 1853 Rifle Musket. Brand new, by the looks of it. It's one of the few we captured from Abu Bakr's men during the battle. It can fire farther and more accurately than anything that any army in Hindustaan has–or rather had, till Abu Bakr's men used them against us', Theo spoke up, answering the question that was on Ranveer's mind.

'So this is the weapon that cost us so dearly. Where did Abu Bakr get such a rifle? If we find out, perhaps we can equip our own army and level the playing field.'

'No Ranveer, we cannot just buy these from a trader. These have only just been issued to the Royal Army just a couple of years ago during the Crimean War. I saw a few examples in China when these were being introduced there just before I left. This rifle is state of the art, and the only way anyone can get them is if the British Government wants them to.'

'And that, Ranveer, is what we were discussing just before you joined us', Jawan Bakht took over.

'I feel terrible about the battle since I feel it was perhaps my own doing- to insist that we follow Mughal tactics in meeting them head on.'

Ranveer had felt a lot of contempt for the young Prince during the battle but now he saw that the Prince was just another person trying to do the best he could under the circumstances.

'You need feel no shame. Abu Bakr had forced our hand- in marching on us with the full strength of his army, the only way we could have responded was through a frontal defense. And in doing that, your tactics were as good or as bad as that of anyone else.'

'What I do not understand is why the British would choose to arm Abu Bakr? Theo, since you understand the British mind better than any of us, what do you make of it?' Ghalib asked.

'Ghalib sahib, the key to understanding my people is to realize that we are part trader and part conqueror, and the lure of riches or empire is what drives our leaders. In this case, Abu Bakr must have offered a fortune–and he may as well, he now controls the richest empire in the world. Also, with the chaos in Hindustaan, I think our leaders fancy their chances of getting a foothold in this nation again after their last failed attempts.'

Ranveer was pacing up and down the room, so Theo asked him what was on his mind.

'Look, it's not relevant how Abu Bakr got these rifles or what the British want. The fact is that with these rifles, his forces have a huge edge over ours, and with the morale already so low, the moment he recovers from his own losses and marches upon us once more, all is indeed lost.'

'Ranveer, that is where the power of whispers may save us', Ghalib interjected with a smile.

Theo got up and took out a cartridge from his pocket, placing it next to the rifle on the table.

'The moment I saw this rifle, my mind went back to a conversation I had with my Commanding Officer in Peking. Mind you, the man was very drunk at that time, as was I, so my recollection of that evening are far from perfect, but this one fact I remember well.'

Theo paused for dramatic effect, and took another swig from

his flask. Despite all the tension, Ranveer could not help but smile at how his friend always seemed to lighten up proceedings.

'He told me, and I quote, *Theo, the Enfield 53 is a beauty that in the right hands could win any war for us, but my blasted luck is that my best troops cannot use them.*'

Ranveer began to wonder if Theo had just had too much to drink and shook his head slightly, muttering to himself that this was all a waste of time. Ghalib noticed and chuckled.

'Young man, controlling one's patience and one's lust can be the most difficult things a man does. However, as I can well attest, controlling the former is far easier, so just listen a little bit longer to your friend.'

Theo smiled and said, 'As the old man said in his own words, *those damn Gurkhees won't touch this.*'

As Theo explained, his Officer had a select group of Nepalese mercenaries whom he relied on to do his hardest fighting, so Theo was left puzzled as to why these loyal soldiers would not use the newest weapon in their armoury. 'He said no more, primarily because he soon passed out drunk, but to borrow a turn of phrase from Ghalib sahib here, when my lust and curiosity are aroused, I will not rest till I satisfy them.'

Delivered with Theo's trademark lopsided grin, the remark sent everyone in the room breaking out into laughter.

'I asked around, and I found out why. There were rumours that the grease on this cartridge here is made of beef or perhaps pig fat, and so the Gurkhas, being devout Hindus would not touch it.'

Ranveer couldn't see the point of this meandering story any longer.

'So what does all this have to do with us?'

'A whisper, Ranveer, a mere whisper in the right places could turn the tide for us.'

Jawan Bakht had spoken, and his eyes were twinkling, like that of a child who has dreamt up some new mischief.

'Ranveer, if word got around that Abu Bakr and his Afghan Generals knew of this and had still made their soldiers use this rifle, what do you think would happen? Their officers may know better, but the semi-educated *bandookchis* would take this as an affront to their religion. With the right whispers in the right places, we could even convince some of the Hindus that this is a ploy to convert them.'

The power of Jawan Bakht's words struck Ranveer like a bolt of lightning. Ghalib smiled, placing a hand on Jawan Bakht's shoulder.

'When the Prince heard Theo's story and came up with this idea, I reacted the same way. It would be a stroke of genius- we use the enemy's strength against him. My Prince, you will one day make a damned fine Emperor if you keep thinking like this.'

Ranveeer smiled as he thought through the ramifications. The reputation and visibility of the Afghans aside, the reality was that the backbone of the Mughal Army lay in the men its *mansabdars* could provide- common infantry and riflemen who bore the brunt of any fighting. And fully a third or more of them at any given time were Hindus, who would likely be more susceptible to such a rumour. A rumour like this would spread like wildfire and many of the Hindu soldiers, already chafing under the extreme policies of Sarfaraz Ali and other Mullahs who had come to the forefront under Abu Bakr would rebel. Chances were that some of the Mussalman soldiers would also start having doubts. The civilian population of Dilli had remained rather impassive so far, simply trading one master for another- but something like this could incite serious civil disorder that would force Abu Bakr to use some of his forces to just maintain law and order. Then, the most obvious question came into Ranveer's mind.

'But how on earth would we ever get such a rumour into the Imperial Army in a way that they would believe it? And even if we got it across, how would we ensure the men react to it? Their officers may just tell them it's a lie.' Ghalib was pressing his hands in glee. 'Young men, there is one more piece of wisdom I have accumulated in my many years, and it is that a man is most roused to action when his breeches are off and his manhood mocked. I could start a whole revolution with a rumour like this one.'

Jawan Bakht looked at the old poet, wondering what he had in mind. 'Ghalib sahib, which unit will you start this revolution in? Perhaps we could ask our intelligence which *mansabdar's* army is least loyal to Abu Bakr?'

Ghalib tut-tutted and began to leave the room.

'I need to write a few letters to some ladies whom I once knew well. Gentlemen, this revolution will not be started by soldiers. This one will be started by whores.'

***

Over the next week, the news spread like wildfire. Ranveer would later be unsure how much of it had happened in fact, and how much had just been truth magnified into mythical proportions. Either way, the impact was immediate and undeniable. The spark for the revolt, or so the story went, was a prostitute in Meerut remarking to her client, a *bandookchi* in the Imperial Army that she would not kiss him because he had eaten beef. The incensed man slapped her, only to be told that she had heard from other clients, officers in the Army no less, that the new rifle cartridge was made of beef tallow. One thing led to another, till a *bandookchi* in Meerut, a man called Mangal Pandey, staggered onto the Parade Ground one morning, fuelled by religious indignation, and some said, copious quantities of alcohol, and refused to use the new cartridge. His *mansabdar*, an Abu Bakr loyalist called Mohamed Ismail, ordered him arrested, upon which Pandey grabbed the *mansabdar*'s pistol and shot him dead. Pandey was hung the very next day, which further incensed his mates and started a daisy chain of events.

Several other acts of insubordination followed, till it was apparent within a week that the Mughal Army was dealing with whole scale mutiny among its soldiers. At first, Abu Bakr crushed any insubordination with an iron fist, but soon realized that for every soldier he had executed, several friends or family members joined the mutiny against the Mughal Army. Realizing that the tide was turning against him, he tried to ask his Officers to try and dispel the rumours and reason with the men, but by then the damage had been done.

The coalition was quick to capitalize on the near paralysis that had gripped the Mughal Army. Galvanized by the sudden turn of events, the leaders had shed their pessimism and embarked on a vigorous new campaign. This time, however, their targets were not the *mansabdars*, nor even the Afghans. To capitalize on the rising tide of discontent against the alleged violation of the religious beliefs of Hindus, the target was to be the group most loathed by the common Hindu- the large army of fanatics maintained by Mullahs like Sarfaraz Ali. These were the men who provided Abu Bakr with the muscle to do his dirty work like taking care of inconvenient rivals or sacking captured cities like Gwalior. Under Bahadur Shah Zafar, Sarfaraz Ali had remained no more than a member of the lunatic fringe, always breathing fire and brimstone, but unable to do anything with the Emperor having told him that any act of violence against members of other faiths would be crushed. Now, with Abu Bakr and his Afghans at the helm, Sarfaraz Ali had emerged as the self-styled spiritual leader of the new regime, and was using his men, whom he called *Ghazis*, to carry out his Jihad.

Ranveer and Theo had just four hand-picked Marathas with them, but they would be more than enough for the mission that night. This was not the kind of mission Ranveer liked, but it seemed that this was how this phase of the war would be waged- in the shadows. There were to be no cavalry charges, no armoured horses, no armour at all, in fact. They were all wearing civilian clothes with their swords and pistols in bags tied to the sides of their horses. Each of them carried a long knife concealed in the folds of their clothes. The six of them had been riding for several days and could now see the walls of Dilli in the distance. Being so close to Dilli, after months made Ranveer pause. This was the city he had grown up in and learnt to call his home- yet it was also the city where he had lost everything. Their plan was not to enter Dilli–it was too heavily guarded for any such attempt, but to strike near a mosque on the outskirts, near Ghaziabad.

As they rode to the mosque it was late in the evening, and much of the small village was enveloped in darkness. They saw the outline of the mosque before them. Four *ghazis* were sitting outside a small house near the mosque, armed with rifles and swords. With the revolt among the Hindu soldiers spreading, there had already been a backlash against the *ghazis* and they were taking no chances. Ranveer rode up to the mosque and dismounted, walking up to the nearest man.

'*Salaam alekum*, brother. We are traders who have lost our way. Can we seek refuge for the night?'

The man snorted, spitting out a thick wad of *paan*.

'This is not a *seraikhana*. Go on your way.'

'But, *bhaisaab*, where will we go in the dark? There may be robbers around.'

The man did not even deign to look at Ranveer and waved him off. That was the moment Ranveer plunged a knife into the man's throat. There was a flurry of activity around him as Theo and the others struck. Within seconds, all four men were dead, without a shot having been fired. Ranveer and the others took out their swords and loaded pistols and entered the building. Two *ghazis* saw them and rushed at Ranveer, swords in hand. Ranveer shot one dead and Theo dispatched the other. With the shots being fired, the *ghazis* sleeping in the house erupted into action like bees in a hive. Four more came running down the stairs leading to the second floor. All four were gunned down by the Marathas before they could raise their own weapons. Ranveer and Theo kicked open a locked door and entered the inner rooms. A large *ghazi* with a cleaver in hand leapt at Ranveer, but Theo intercepted him, slashing his jugular with his *khukri*. The man went down, bleeding to death from the fatal wound. Ranveer found his target cowering in a corner behind a *charpoy*. The man's name was Ghulam Beg, and after Abu Bakr's ascendance to power and the growing clout of Sarfaraz Ali, he had been transformed overnight from an illiterate village Maulvi to a leader of a notorious band of *ghazis*, which had been blamed for the worst of the rape and slaughter in Gwalior.

'Please have mercy. I am a man of God', he pleaded in a quivering voice when Ranveer came close.

Ranveer did not relish killing an unarmed man, but then thought of the tales of slaughter he had heard; of pregnant women being raped and killed; of whole families being butchered.

'No God would accept a devil like you as their servant.'

The man fell at Ranveer's feet.

'Please. Please let me go.'

As Ranveer hesitated to bring down the knife in his hand, Ghulam Beg took out a small knife hidden behind his back and brought it up towards Ranveer's stomach. Ranveer caught his hand at the wrist, and jerked it back, sending the knife clattering to the floor. Ghulam Beg cried out in agony as Ranveer's battle-hardened grip bent his hand back so much that he could hear bones snap. A knife strike to the heart and it was all over.

Ranveer and the others rode out silently into the night.

All across Hindustaan, similar attacks ripped apart the *ghazis*, and emboldened by these attacks, the rebellious *bandookchis* and common people, often joined and armed by rebelling *bhumis*, turned on the *ghazis*. Within a week, the irregular force of *ghazis* that Abu Bakr had come to rely on so much ceased to exist as a fighting force, other than the core that remained with Sarfaraz Ali.

With the armies of the *mansabdars* in open revolt and the *ghazis* crushed, that left the coalition with one last target.

Dilli.

***

'Are you sure we should be attacking Dilli?'

Maya asked the question in a tentative voice, yet the certainty in her eyes was clear to Ranveer. He rolled over to his side of the bed and lay on his back.

'Maya, there does not seem to be any other way of breaking the stalemate. Abu Bakr and his forces have concentrated in and around Dilli, and no matter how much of the countryside we control, as long as he has Dilli, he is the ruler of Hindustaan.'

'Ranveer, do you think we have enough forces to take Dilli?'

Ranveer did not answer that question. Instead he just turned to look at Maya, and she saw the doubt and uncertainty writ large on his face. Maya knew that the decision had been taken at a much higher level, and that whatever his misgivings, Ranveer would have little choice but to follow his orders. As he reached out for her hand, she took it in her own and smiled.

'I am lucky to be with you.'

Ranveer smiled back and leaned over to kiss her. Maya had meant every word, and in a sense beyond what Ranveer may have realized. In a society where women were expected to do little more than cook and rear children, she found Ranveer a breath of fresh air, someone she could speak her mind to, and be respected for it. She kissed him back and they lay together, savouring their moments together, for they both knew that the next morning Ranveer would leave for Dilli.

'I don't fancy clambering up those walls to be skewered on an Afghan's sword.'

Theo was the only one who spoke his mind aloud, but every rider around, Ranveer included, echoed his thoughts. It had been a week since their army had encamped outside Dilli, laying siege to the capital. However, apart for a few probing raids, there had been no order to attack yet. Abu Bakr had used the lull to strengthen his defences and Dilli, always a formidable target to besiege, was now bristling with defenders armed to the teeth- the Afghans, the remaining *ghazis* along with Sarfaraz Ali and also the still considerable number of troops of *mansabdars* loyal to Abu Bakr. The coalition forces had been joined by a number of rebelling *bandookchis* but they were of limited utility in a siege like this.

Ranveer had heard that there had been considerable debate on the tactics. Tatya Tope had argued that they should close all supply lines and starve the city. Jawan Bakht had vehemently opposed it, saying that any hardship to the common people would just turn them against the coalition and strengthen Abu Bakr. Ranveer suspected that the decision had as much to do with altruistic intentions towards the people of Dilli as with Jawan Bakht's desire to not let anything spoil his smooth ascendance to the throne once Dilli was taken. Theo and Ranveer were sitting at their encampment, with their men already asleep in their tents around them. Ranveer had just re-read the letter Maya had given him when he was leaving. It had ended with the words.

'Come back or I will come looking for you myself. Even an army of Afghans will not keep me from having you.'

He smiled at Maya's spirit, despite all she had endured, and at the twists and turns his life had taken for him to be with her. Theo was sitting with his hip flask, sipping some hooch he had managed to secure from nearby villagers. Ranveer looked at him and smiled wearily.

'Theo, how can you drink so much and still fight?'

'My friend, I can fight only because I drink so much. The alcohol cleanses my mind and body of all impurities so I can focus.'

Ranveer laughed and asked Theo what he thought about the siege.

'I think that our leaders want us to bore them to death by just sitting here and doing nothing. The men grow lazy and impatient and the enemy fortifies their positions. This is not how we fought.'

'What else can we do with Abu Bakr closeted in Dilli? But yes, I fear we are waiting too long.'

Their conversation was interrupted by the sudden sound of gunshots nearby, followed by loud screams. Ranveer and Theo picked up their loaded pistols and rushed to the North side of their camp where the commotion seemed to be coming from..

'Must be some damn drunk fool. I'll have his hide for this', shouted Ranveer as he sprinted towards the gunshots. When they reached the scene, they saw something they had never expected. Five of their men lay dead and three more were on the ground, clutching their wounds. 'What happened here?'

A badly shaken guard answered Ranveer.

'Afghans! They attacked in the dark and caught us by surprise, and disappeared before we could even fire back.'

Later that night, after ensuring more guards had been posted at the perimeters of their camp, Ranveer rode up to the encampment that the coalition leaders were using, located a few *kos* away. He was half expecting that he would wake up Tatya Tope and the others to tell them about the attack, but he was surprised to find all the leaders wide awake, huddled in Jawan Bakht's tent.

'So, you too, Ranveer?'

Ranveer was caught off guard by Tatya Tope's question.

'There have been attacks all across our lines. Some are still continuing, but from what we already know, we've lost about a hundred men dead. Pinpricks if you look at each attack by itself, but the psychological impact could be huge. My men are already whispering that if they aren't safe in their own tents, where are they safe?'

Nana-sahab and Jawan Bakht were silent but nodding in agreement. Ranveer, already upset at the loss of his men and impatience at what he had seen as a long delayed attack, decided to speak his mind.

'It looks like we are fighting like them, and they are fighting like us.'

Jawan Bakht leaned across, as if making sure nobody was standing outside the tent, and addressed Ranveer.

'What we were talking about just now was something even more serious. There were whispers before the battle at Dabra that Abu Bakr somehow knew all about our tactics and how to exploit them. Now there are whispers that he has a spy in our camp, which is why he did not march out to meet us like we would have expected, but sat tight and waited for us to sit outside the gates before hitting us with these sudden night attacks.'

'Does he have a spy?'

Nana-sahab was still sitting, and his eyes looked bloodshot, as if he had been woken up to attend this meeting. He stretched his arms over his head and addressed Jawan Bakht.

'Who really knows? There may well be someone, but whether there is a spy or not, we cannot wait for the next surprise to do something about it. Our men are getting restless and will soon lose their appetite for battle. Before Abu Bakr strengthens his position, we must move.'

Two days later, early morning brought with it a sustained barrage of artillery fire concentrated on Ajmeri Gate. Over the early hours of the morning most of the coalition field artillery had been moved to the forested area overlooking Ajmeri Gate and at the crack of dawn began firing. Shot after shot slammed into the large fortified walls. There were a few cannon shots fired in return, but by and large the defenders seemed to either be taken by surprise or to be waiting to play their hand.

The next logical step in any siege would be for the attackers to try and breach the walls, but for once, the coalition had surprise on its side. Tatya Tope had spent three sleepless hours overnight personally modifying the plans and in the early hours of the morning, the plans had been passed on from one unit to another.

Ranveer and Theo were part of a caravan of traders who were entering Dilli through Kashmiri Gate. The real traders were guests of the coalition several *kos* away, having been bribed with an exorbitant amount of money to let the troops take their place. With the extra security at all the gates, neither Ranveer nor the forty soldiers with him were carrying any weapons. With the city under siege, caravans of traders like these were the lifeline for the population and the government was paying almost triple the market rate for grain and vegetables. They passed through three rings of heavily armed soldiers who searched every inch of their carts but with their permits in order and nothing to arouse the suspicion of the guards, they were waved through. As always happens in such cases, there was a thriving black market and one of the first men Ranveer met at the entrance to the city was an official who ambled up to the caravan.

'Pay your tax and be on your way.'

Ranveer looked at the man with scarcely disguised contempt. The man must have been a lowly clerk in the Treasury but had taken advantage of the current chaos to enrich himself in the name of collecting 'taxes'. He handed over the demanded amount of money and the caravan was waved into the city with only a cursory security check. Ranveer led the group of horse drawn carts deeper into the city. In the distance they could still hear the sounds of cannon fire, and all around them, they saw soldiers rushing to reinforce Ajmeri Gate, anticipating that to be the focal point of the coming assault.

Ranveer led his men straight to his home. It was an eerie feeling to return to the house he had grown up in after so many months. Ranveer had been worried that his home would have been confiscated by the government, in which case his back-up plan was to turn to some of older Ahadi officers who had sworn loyalty to Abu Bakr for their families' survival but had sent out feelers to spies that they would support any uprising against the new regime. He was pleasantly surprised to see that their loyal servants were still there, keeping the house clean despite the fact that their master had long died and been branded a traitor by the new regime. When the group drew up to the building, Ranveer disembarked from his cart and walked up to the main gate, taking off the shawl that had been covering his head. The watchman, an old man he had always known as Ramu *Chacha* was startled to see him. The old man, who had once served in the Army under Qureshi, soon replaced his look of bewilderment with a smile.

'Ranveer *baba*, I hope you avenge your father. We have kept everything as it was.'

The men quickly entered the armoury, which was always kept fully stocked with enough arms and ammunition to equip a small army. Ranveer saw that the room was now bare, and guessed correctly that the government would have confiscated Qureshi's armoury. What they had not bargained for was the fact that Qureshi always believed in having a back-up plan. A small panel on the floor, known only to Qureshi and Ranveer, was opened up, revealing an underground chamber full of weapons and ammunition. Ranveer and his men descended into the chamber and began picking up their weapons of choice. As discreetly as they had come, the men left in their carts, heading straight for Qila Mubarak on the banks of the Jumna river. By now, the sounds of firing near Ajmeri Gate had intensified, and Ranveer knew that Tatya Tope would have launched his first diversionary attack, with Maratha sappers trying to breach the walls. Ranveer knew many good men would die in the ploy, and hoped that he and his men would not let their sacrifice go in vain.

With most of the defending troops deployed at the walls

of Dilli to fight off the attackers, there was only a thin security screen at the fort. They did not pay too much attention to the group of traders till it was too late. Huddled among the sacks of grain were Ranveer's troops who began firing at the guards around the fort. Taken completely by surprise, a dozen men died in the first volley. The remaining half dozen guards began to bring their weapons to bear when the second volley rang out, dropping them to the ground. While his men paused to reload, Ranveer and Theo raced into the fort. Two surprised guards crossed their paths. Ranveer cut one down with his sword while Theo shot the other. The two continued running straight towards the inner chambers.

They heard shots behind them as their men cut off guards who were attempting to follow them. Bullets zinged past their ears, some bouncing off the walls mere inches away as Abu Bakr's guards began firing at them. Ranveer and Theo dove behind a large metal table, overturning it for cover, before pausing to reload. Their men were engaged in a fierce firefight outside and from the sounds of chaos and confusion they heard, they gathered that at least one part of their plan had worked. News of the attack on the Qila Mubarak would have spread like wildfire and some of the soldiers defending the walls of Dilli would be diverted to deal with this new threat, while even the ones who remained would wonder how large an enemy force was already inside the city. The attackers would take full advantage of this to press home their attack, with Tatya Tope leading his Marathas on a frontal assault on the city walls.

'Theo, how many are there?'

Theo peeked around the corner of the table.

'Must be three or four of them. You get out, I'll keep them occupied.'

Before Ranveer could say anything, Theo leapt out from behind their cover towards their attackers. He fired one pistol, then the other, dropping two of their attackers, before tackling a third man with both of them falling to the ground in a heap. Ranveer followed a split second later, shooting dead the fourth man before he could attack Theo. While Theo grappled with the guard, Ranveer raced towards the exit.

Their plan did not call for them to either occupy the fort for any period of time nor did they realistically hope to get Abu Bakr. Tatya Tope had been explicit that he did not want this to be a suicide mission, and had ordered them to melt into the city once the initial attack had been accomplished and then link up with the attacking forces once the walls were breached. Ranveer turned a corner, coming to a door that was guarded by two heavily armed Afghans. He had the advantage of surprise and felled the first man with his second pistol. The second Afghan lunged at Ranveer with his sword, but Ranveer swung out of the way, and brought his own sword to bear. The two men circled each other, looking for the right moment to strike. The Afghan's sword shot out again, but Ranveer blocked the strike. The Afghan raised his sword again, but Ranveer stepped close to the Afghan and brought the butt of his sword up in a blow that crushed the man's jaw. As the Afghan staggered back,

Ranveer killed him with a blow to the chest.

'We're out, come on!'

Ranveer heard Theo's cry and was about to follow him out when he contemplated the room the Afghans had been guarding. The door was bolted from the outside, and for two elite Afghans to have been guarding it, it must have been occupied by an important member of the regime. Curiosity got the better of Ranveer and he loaded his pistol before unlocking the door, ready to shoot whoever was inside.

The room was dimly lit by a couple of candles placed on a table near the door, and a man was sitting on a *divan* to one side. When he saw Ranveer enter, the man stood up, holding the palms of his hands up, to show that he was unarmed.

'What do you want? I have done everything you wanted.'

Ranveer was about to shoot when he paused. The man's voice sounded familiar. He held up one of the candles and approached the man. As he came closer, Ranveer found himself looking into Iftiqar's face.

***

Eleven

Iftiqar looked like he had aged twenty years. His cheeks were sunken, his eyes puffed and swollen and the once ramrod straight back was bent as if he were unable to even carry his own weight.

'Iftiqar *chacha*! Thank God that you are alive! We all heard that you had died.'

Ranveer clasped his old mentor in a bear hug.

'Come on, we need to get out of here. Our forces should be entering Dilli any moment now.'

As Ranveer tugged at Iftiqar's shoulder, to his shock the older man shook Ranveer's arm off.

'Ranveer, please go now. Leave me here and save yourself!'

'No! You are coming with me.'

Ranveer realized that he may have already waited too long.

Theo and the others must have got cleanly away, and there was no more firing outside. Knowing that he might have to fight his way out, he loaded both his pistols and got ready to take Iftiqar with him. When he tried to pull Iftiqar with him he suddenly heard the door open behind him. He whirled around, pulling a pistol from his waistband. Two Afghans rushed into the room, swords at the ready. Ranveer shot the first dead but before he could take out his second pistol, the Afghan lunged at him. The Afghan swung his sword at Ranveer, who escaped death by no more than a few inches as he ducked out of the way. Before the Afghan could strike again, Ranveer had his sword drawn.

The Afghan drove his sword in a thrust at Ranveer's stomach and when Ranveer tried to block by bringing his own sword down in an arc from the left, the Afghan pulled back. The feint unbalanced Ranveer, and he almost lost his footing. The Afghan sliced at Ranveer's legs, but Ranveer blocked the blow, moving back to buy some time. The Afghan moved in again, relentless in his attack. The man stood more than a head taller than Ranveer, and was using his height and strength to his advantage, hammering away at Ranveer. As Ranveer blocked yet another strike, he noticed that his remaining loaded pistol had fallen out of his waistband in the melee and now lay just a foot from where Iftiqar stood. As the Afghan bore down again, a powerful blow sent Ranveer's sword flying out of his grasp, but before the Afghan could strike again, Ranveer grabbed his hand.

The two men scrambled around the room, locked in a life and death struggle. Ranveer screamed to Iftiqar.

'Shoot him!'

To his astonishment, Iftiqar did nothing. The Afghan's strength was now telling, and Ranveer found himself being bent backwards as the man's sword came ever closer to his neck.

'Shoot him, for God's sake!'

Iftiqar did not even move, but just stood there, watching and weeping.

'Have you lost your mind, *chacha*?'

No response.

The Afghan's blade was now just inches away from Ranveer's jugular vein. In desperation, Ranveer drove his knee up and connected with the man's stomach. As the Afghan reeled back in pain, Ranveer drove an elbow into his face, sending him to the ground. Before he could get up again, Ranveer picked up his pistol and shot his dead. Out of breath and furious, he turned on Iftiqar.

'What were you thinking?'

Before Iftiqar could answer, the door opened again behind Ranveer and he found himself facing four Afghans, each of whom had a rifle pointed at him. With his pistols empty and his sword lying in a corner of the room, Ranveer was defenceless. So this is how it all had to end, thought Ranveer, readying himself as the Afghans raised their rifles to fire.

'Don't shoot, I want this one alive', a voice boomed from outside the door. The Afghans kept their rifles pointed at Ranveer but moved aside as the speaker walked into the room. It was the first time Ranveer had seen Abdali outside of the battlefield since he had bumped into the General in the *diwan-i-khaas* many months, and a seeming lifetime ago. Abdali stood there, looking at Ranveer, a smile playing at the edges of his lips.

'So, it is my brave Rajput mongrel who has come among us again. I found out all about you since our paths seem to cross so often, and am glad to have you as a guest.'

Ranveer did not rise to the taunt, but noted with satisfaction how mangled Abdali was. There was a big scar running down the side of his face where Ranveer had struck him, and his left hand ended abruptly just below the elbow.

'General, I thought you may need a helping hand' Ranveer replied, spitting in Abdali's direction.

The smile was replaced by a look of fury as Abdali strode towards Ranveer.

'You fool. You have cost me my arm, but I have taken everything from you- your name, your father, and soon I will destroy you and your pathetic army.'

Ranveer was certain he would be killed, but tried hard not to show any sign of weakness.

'General, as you waste your time here taunting me, our army is breaching your walls.'

Abdali motioned to one of his men to pull up a chair and sat down, looking calm.

'You still do not fully understand what is happening, do you? As we speak, some of the rebelling Mughal units who had pretended to turn over to your side are now shooting your men in the back. Their commanders were sent by us, pretending to defect, while operating under our command all the time. In the confusion, my elite cavalry will ride out and sweep the attackers, while the Enfield, with which you are already acquainted, is being used by my sharpshooters to take down your men as they struggle with this betrayal.'

'You're bluffing. I don't believe you.'

Abdali smiled smugly.

'Their families are all hostage here- and any disobedience on their part will result in the instant slaughter of their families. And now your so called assault is being scattered to the wind. We handpicked them, based on very close intelligence about which ones would likely break and also which ones would be susceptible to bribery.'

Ranveer did not want to believe Abdali, but as time ticked by, he realized that there was no sound of shooting in the streets, no sign at all that the walls had been breached. To confirm his worst fears, a guard came up to the room and addressed Abdali.

'Sir, the enemy is in retreat. The Mughal officers and men who were inserted in their ranks are trying to seek refuge into Dilli. Should we let them in?'

Abdali dismissed the man with a wave of his left hand.

'Ask our men to shoot them. They've played their role and if they've betrayed their old masters, they can betray us just as easily.'

As the man left, Abdali rose and addressed Ranveer.

'I need to go and get some rest. In the meanwhile, you can catch up with your old friend here. He has been most helpful- he's been telling us all about your tactics and weaknesses before each battle, and also helped us handpick the officers whom we would bribe and threaten to cross over.'

As Abdali left and the door was locked, Ranveer sat down, the wind totally taken out of him. The prospect of being killed paled beside the realization of the betrayals the coalition, and he personally had faced. He turned to look at Iftiqar, who had been standing quietly in a corner.

'Iftiqar *chacha*, how could you?'

Iftiqar sat down next to Ranveer on the cot.

'My son..'

Ranveer turned on Iftiqar savagely.

'Don't call me your son. You have betrayed everything we have always believed in.'

Iftiqar smiled sadly.

'Ranveer, things are not as black and white as they seem. I fought as long as I could, and then I begged to be killed.'

Ranveer listened as Iftiqar continued speaking, and held up his hands, which till now had been concealed behind long sleeves. Ranveer caught his breath as he saw the mangled stumps that remained in place of Iftiqar's hands.

'Ranveer, every man has a breaking point, and the shame will go with me to my grave, but I too reached mine. They took out each fingernail, and then broke each finger with a hammer. But that was not my breaking point. Not yet.'

Ranveer wondered what else could have caused the once strong soldier to break. Iftiqar looked at Ranveer now, his eyes welling up with tears.

'I had thought my family was safe with our relatives, but they must have been betrayed. One day, they brought in the severed head of my youngest son. He was only fifteen.' Ranveer felt tears stream down his cheeks as Iftiqar continued.

'They threatened to kill the others unless I co-operated. I should have said no. I should have been brave, but I was also a father and a husband, and I gave into my weakness.'

Iftiqar broke down, and Ranveer just held onto his old mentor, not knowing what to say or do. Iftiqar looked at Ranveer again.

'My son, rest and prepare yourself. Soon they will come for you.'

The door opened even before the Sun had risen. Ranveer had tried to force himself to rest, but could not seem to keep his mind still. He kept thinking of the catastrophe that had befallen the coalition, what Iftiqar had gone through, and most of all, what Maya would go through when word got back that he was missing. As the door opened, and four Afghans rushed in, he though for a fleeting moment of resisting, but when the Afghans grabbed him, Iftiqar shouted to Ranveer.

'Don't fight! Conserve your energy and be brave.'

Ranveer was roughly pushed through the corridor outside, and his hands were bound with rope. The Afghans bundled him outside, where Ranveer saw Abdali and another man standing on the lawn. The second man was wearing a Maulvi's robes and had a long, flowing beard. Ranveer was forced to the ground on his knees before the two men.

'Ranveer, I thought you could start the morning with some entertainment. Maulvi sahib, begin your work.'

Ranveer guessed that the second man was Maulvi Sarfaraz Ali. One of the Afghans grabbed his head and jerked it up, forcing him to look at a wall nearby. There were more than a dozen men kneeling on the ground, their hands bound behind their backs. From the tattered remains of their uniforms, Ranveer realized that they were Maratha prisoners of war. The Maulvi clapped his hands and several *ghazis* appeared, each wearing a green headband and carrying a large knife.

'The General here said that you should witness this slaughter of the *kafirs*.'

As he clapped his hands again, his men went about their brutal work. Each prisoner was grabbed by one man while another jerked his head back and cut his throat. Ranveer wanted to turn away, to not have to see this bestiality, but the Afghans held him in a vice like grip, with one of them forcing his eyes open so he could see the prisoners get slaughtered one by one. Abdali motioned to his men to bring Ranveer to his feet.

'For good reason people have come to call this wall as *khooni darwaaza* and now, my friend, we have a lot of catching up to do. Bring him to the dungeons!'

***

Try and focus your mind somewhere else. Sing a song. Think about the last woman you bedded.

When his trainer had told him, that while sitting in a comfortable room teaching him about how to cope with possible torture, if he were ever to be captured in battle, it had sounded funny enough. Now there was nothing funny about it.

Ranveer could not remember when it happened, but after a point in time, he started reciting the *Hanuman Chalisa* as loudly as he could. It was a memory long buried in his childhood, when his mother would recite it every day with him sitting next to her. Growing up in Qureshi's home, a Hindu *aayah* who had taken care of him had done the same. He never remembered having memorized it, but now somehow it came back to him in bits and pieces.

Jai hanuman gyan gun sagar

Thwack!

He tried to block out the pain by concentrating on trying to remember the next stanza.

Jai kapis tehu lok ujaagar.

Thwack!

Each stanza he recited was instantly answered by another blow to his face. He paused, blood and broken teeth filling his mouth. He no longer knew how many men were around him or how long the beating had gone on for. His head was pounding in agony and his right eye was already swollen shut from the repeated blows. All he saw was the fat *ghazi* in front of him, who was rubbing his knuckles and preparing to hit Ranveer again. As the man cocked back his fist, Ranveer garnered every last reserve of strength he had and spat in the man's face. The man reeled back, his face covered in blood and spit. Snarling in rage, he slammed his fist into Ranveer's head again, causing him to pass out.

Ranveer had lost count of the days that he had spent in his tiny cell in the dungeons underneath the *Qila Mubarak*. For the first few days, they had left him alone, but had not fed him anything, instead just slipping in one saucer of watery *dal* every day. Enough to ensure that he did not die, but also enough to ensure that he kept losing his strength. Then one morning, the beating began, and never ended.

Ranveer came to when a bucket of cold water was thrown on his face. Sputtering, disoriented and with his head in excruciating pain, he struggled to get his bearings. When he looked up, he saw Abdali seated on a chair in front of him.

'The Maulvi's *ghazis* are itching to cut your head off. Another *kafir* to add to their tally, but I asked them to hold back.'

Abdali stroked his beard with his right hand.

'When I saw you again, my instinct was to slaughter you, considering all the pain you have caused me.'

Abdali held up the stump that was his left hand, and continued.

'But then, I thought, we are different from the *ghazis*. We are soldiers, after all, and such losses in battle are part of our life. You and I are much the same.'

Despite his weakened state, Ranveer itched to launch himself at the man he had come to hate so much, but found that his hands were still bound behind his back.

'We are nothing like each other', he spat out.

'Ranveer, I have found out a lot about you, and it would be a waste if someone like you threw their life away. A trained *Ahadi* officer, a well-educated young man with his life ahead of him, a beautiful wife who would probably be taken for Abu Bakr's harem after you died.'

Ranveer strained against the ropes again in vain.

'So I have a deal for you. I hear you have the trust of Jawan Bakht, Nana-sahab and the other leaders. They must have trusted you a lot to send you on their most dangerous missions–Somnath, and now the raid here. So, here is something you can do for me.'

As Abdali signaled to his men, three Aghans came in. Two of them undid the ropes binding Ranveer's arms and held him tight while another laid out a small table in front of Ranveer, placing on it a blank parchment together with an inkpot and a quill.

'Write down where your units are deployed and who the commanders are. Also, draw a map of what the next stage of your war plan is. I'm sure someone like Tatya Tope would have thought of a contingency that he would have told his officers. Where are they retreating to? When and how will they regroup?'

Ranveer kept his head down, not reacting to anything Abdali said.

'It is a simple request, my friend. Just do it and I will let you go.' Ranveer closed his eyes, as if weighing the choice before him.

'Fine, I'll do it.'

Abdali seemed surprised at how easily Ranveer had given in, and nodded to his men pinning Ranveer down. They dragged him forward to the parchment and one of them placed both of Ranveer's hands on the table. Ranveer found that his hands were shaking uncontrollably, and tried hard to still them. He picked the quill up and dipped it in the ink. Abdali was smirking at him, but speaking in a soothing voice.

'I think you have made a smart choice.'

Ranveer took the quill in his right hand, holding onto his wrist with his left hand to try and still it. He bent over the parchment and began to scribble. Abdali leaned forward to see what he was writing. That was the moment Ranveer struck. Still holding his right wrist with his left hand for balance, he drove the pointed edge of the quill up at Abdali. If he had his full strength and balance, he would have gouged Abdali's left eye out cleanly, but after hours of beating with no water or food, Ranveer was weak and sluggish. Abdali moved out of the way, though the quill left a nasty scar on his left cheek.

Ranveer felt everything go black for a second as one of the Afghans brought down an armoured elbow guard on his neck. As he tried to get up, Abdali kicked him in the face, sending him down again.

'Son of a whore! I have wasted enough time on you. Let the *ghazis* work on you some more and I'll give you one more day. Tomorrow morning you give me what I want or I'll let them cut your throat.'

Maya.

Maya when he first kissed her. Maya on their wedding night. Maya riding with them out of Gwalior. Maya....

Ranveer tried to keep thinking of Maya as a way to block out the pain, as a way to retain his desire to live. But by midnight, when he was dragged along the corridor, resembling a bloody slab of meat more than a man, and dumped into a cell, he wished and prayed that he would die. He prayed that he be spared any more suffering. His left shoulder felt like it was on fire, and several ribs seemed to be cracked from the way they hurt every time he coughed. He had no idea how many teeth he had lost and for a while amused himself by trying to count the gaps with his tongue. As he lay with his back against the cold wall, drenched in his blood and piss, for the first time, Ranveer began to doubt himself. Would he just write what Abdali wanted? Could he take any more pain?

When his cell door swung open the next morning, Ranveer was dragged out to the *khooni darwaaza* by two *ghazis*. Maulvi Sarfaraz Ali was there and from the looks of it, the slaughter for the day had already begun. A dozen or more corpses lay before the wall, with *ghazis* holding blood-stained knives standing beside them. As the *ghazis* pushed Ranveer to the ground before the Maulvi, he began to panic. Where was Abdali? Had he not promised Ranveer another chance? As soon as those thought came, they were replaced by a feeling of shame. No, he would not sell himself out to the man who had killed his father. All night, he had prayed for the strength to endure what was to come. Now he just prayed that he die a good death.

The Maulvi looked at him curiously.

'A *kafir* brought up in a Mussalman noble's house? Your father clearly was not a true believer.'

Ranveer looked up and answered, defiance burning in his eyes.

'He was a better Mussalman and a better man that you or your dogs will ever be. If killing me is what you want, get it over with.'

Sarfaraz Ali laughed, knowing that he held all the cards and motioned towards his men. As Ranveer looked up, he saw two men push Iftiqar onto the field next to him. Sarfaraz Ali spoke again.

'I am hoping your old friend here can talk some sense into you. Abdali insists I give you another chance, so I am obliging.'

Iftiqar shuffled close to Ranveer and reached out with his crippled right arm to hug Ranveer. He leant over and whispered to Ranveer.

'They will kill me today. With you in their custody, they have no more use for me. In any case, I have given them everything they wanted to know. Since the *Ghazis* are here and not Abdali, I assume that after they get what they want, they will butcher you as well.'

Ranveer looked at Iftiqar, somehow hoping his old mentor was wrong.

'Ranveer, just listen to me carefully. In the last stages of my life, I have let a lot of people down, but in my death, I hope I can teach you one last lesson.'

Ranveer was looking at Iftiqar, tears welling in his eyes.

'That lesson, my boy, is simple. It's something your father embodied, and I perhaps forgot in my weakness. We all have to die, but if we die at the hands of pigs such as these, then we sell ourselves as dearly as possible.'

Ranveer wondered what Iftiqar had in mind as he continued whispering.

'I once swore an oath to your father that if anyone tried to harm you, I would drink his blood. Today that oath needs to be fulfilled. Goodbye my son. Tell that English rogue that my acting today will be better than even his.'

Iftiqar got up and faced Sarfaraz Ali. 'He will do what you want. What do you want of me now?'

Safaraz Ali dismissed Iftiqar with a wave of his hand.

'Someone take him away and kill him.'

As two *ghazis* approached, Iftiqar fell to his knees before the Maulvi.

'Maulvi sahib, I have no fear of death now, as I feel I have finally discovered the true calling of my faith and helped our cause. But before I die, I would like to seek your blessing.'

Sarfaraz Ali looked bored but waved Iftiqar on as he approached him. As Iftiqar came closer, he fell at the Maulvi's feet, sobbing uncontrollably. Sarfaraz Ali took him by the shoulders and raised him up, seeming uncomfortable at this drama. Iftiqar looked back at Ranveer and winked before he fell into the Maulvi's arms, hugging the man, and still weeping, asking for forgiveness and salvation. The *ghazis* gathered around were sniggering at the old man's fear. One of them laughed, 'The old man must have pissed his pants as well'.

That was till they saw the Maulvi utter a primal cry of agony and his arms suddenly stiffen. The Maulvi was clawing at Iftiqar's back, trying to get away, but even in his weakened state, the hardened soldier was too much for the overweight Maulvi to shrug off. Safaraz Ali kept screaming, his voice now shrill like that of a little girl.

Realizing that something was terribly wrong, two *Ghazis* rushed forward and tried to pull Iftiqar away. When they managed to pry open his grip on Sarfaraz Ali, Ranveer realized what Iftiqar had done as his last act of defiance. His last act of repentance for his betrayal. Iftiqars jaw was clenched around Sarfaraz Ali's neck, biting deep, as blood flowed down, soaking Safaraz Ali's white *sherwani*. The Maulvi was now no longer screaming, but whimpering in pain, his hands hanging by his side, his eyes half closed as his life, and his blood flowed out of him. Unable to force loose Iftiqar's grip on his neck, the *Ghazis* began stabbing him. Finally, covered in blood, Iftiqar's grip on Sarfaraz Ali gave way, and both men slumped to the ground.

The *Ghazis* just stood where they were for several minutes, unable to believe that their leader had just been killed by a crippled old man. Ranveer's eyes filled with tears as he saw his old friend and mentor die before his eyes, but his heart swelled with pride. When one of the *Ghazis* walked up to him, blood-soaked knife in hand, Ranveer looked the man squarely in the eye.

'Kill me, you coward!'

Enraged, the *Ghazi* raised his knife but before he could bring it down, a voice cried out.

'Stop, you idiot!'

The *Ghazi* turned around in anger, only to bow deferentially when he saw Abdali stride into the courtyard, accompanied by a dozen fully armed Afghans. Abdali looked at the Maulvi's corpse, and then addressed the *Ghazis*.

'Looks like your job is finished. There will be no more killing of prisoners for now.'

The *Ghazis* were baying for blood after the Maulvi's death, but a dozen Afghan rifles pointed at them proved to be quite persuasive and they shuffled out of the courtyard, carrying Sarfaraz Ali's corpse with them. Not sure what was going on, Ranveer looked up at Abdali, who was shaking his head.

'Looks like it's your lucky day. I would have loved to have those *badmashes* beautify your face a bit more, but the Emperor has ordered that we keep all of you alive and well for now, since we may need you in negotiations.'

'Negotiations?'

Abdali smiled.

'Oh yes, you would not have heard. Jawan Bakht and his cronies have decided to surrender.'

***

Ranveer spent the next few days in captivity thinking of only two things. Elation at knowing that he had a chance of getting back to Maya and at the same time, despair that the coalition had capitulated so easily. Had all the sacrifices been for nothing? He was kept in a small room with no windows but compared to the tiny dank cell where he had been placed, it was downright luxurious. He was also fed well and his wounds tended to. Ranveer did not think that had anything to do with Abdali suddenly developing a humanitarian streak, but because he wanted the captive officers to be in good shape when the negotiations began.

What was there to negotiate anyways? Ranveer doubted that, having tasted victory, Abu Bakr would be in the mood for too many concessions. Perhaps what the coalition was looking for was just an assurance of continued survival. He found it hard to believe that leaders like Tatya Tope would have given in after one defeat, but then, he had come to realize over the last few months that things seldom went as one expected.

To keep his mind off such worries, Ranveer focused on regaining his strength. Painful as it was at first, he started exercising and by the end of a week, he found that while not quite ready to leap into battle yet, he had regained much of his old stamina. His looks were quite another matter- crude stitches on his head and four missing teeth made him look like a *rakshash* from fairy tales, but it was better than having his throat slit.

A full ten days passed before Ranveer saw Abdali again, and when he did, the General was in a foul mood. Ranveer had been summoned to Abdali's quarters and was marched there, his hands once again bound behind his back. Abdali was sitting at a table, mulling over a *firman* in his hands, a scowl on his face. When he saw Ranveer, he motioned for him to sit down.

'I could untie your hands, but then you may decide to try and kill me again.'

'I probably would.'

Abdali smiled as Ranveer was forced down on a chair.

'You must think that I'm a monster. All I am is a soldier, trying to do my duty. One day the politicians ask me to kill someone, the next they want me to babysit him.'

Ranveer was in no mood to chat with Abdali.

'Soldiers do not massacre innocents or stand by while prisoners of war are slaughtered.'

Abdali spat at Ranveer, who winced as the hot spit rolled down his cheeks where it struck him.

'You do everything to make me want to cut you to pieces. Perhaps one day I will just do that, but for now, I need to get you nice clothes and make sure you eat *biryani* every day so you look presentable when your brothers come to fetch you.'

Ranveer had no idea what Abdali was talking about, so the General waved the *firman* in his hand.

'The final deal, that they've struck with the Emperor. Jawan Bakht is to go into exile and relinquish all claims on the throne, and the Maratha dogs will accept the Emperor as the legitimate ruler of Hindustaan. In return, we agree to not attack their lands and to release all prisoners of war whose lives will be spared but who will be sent away to the Eastern marshlands so they may not threaten us again.'

Ranveer's defiance crumbled as he realized that his worst fears had come true. He would live, but as an exile, a veritable servant to the likes of Abu Bakr and Abdali. He walked back slowly to his room, wondering if he too should sacrifice himself like Iftiqar had done if he got a chance to strike at Abdali. Then he thought of Maya. Who would stand by her if he died? How would she cope with being transformed from a Princess to a refugee?

He thought about all those he had come to admire and lost. The Rani of Jhansi, Iftiqar and above all, his father. But for once, more than a sense of regret or loss, he began to realize the meaning of their lives. They had fought and given their lives so others could live.

The next morning brought with it a sudden flurry of activity outside his room. He could hear the Afghan guards chatter incessantly in their own tongue, and while the meaning of their words may have eluded Ranveer, their tone hinted at something big about to happen. In the late afternoon, the door to his room was opened and an Afghan deposited a finely embroidered *sherwani*.

'Wear it. Your fellow dogs are coming to beg at our feet tonight.'

Ranveer put on the clothes and just after sunset, his hands were bound again and he was escorted out of his room and led by two Afghans to the main fort complex. As he walked through the corridors, he remembered the last time he had been here- with his father, on the day of his promotion. That was a day when he knew he had made his father proud. He wondered what his father would have thought if he had seen his son being paraded like a common criminal through those same corridors? He was pushed into the *Diwan-i-khaas*, where he saw that a number of armed Afghans lined the walls, with more than three dozen other captured prisoners of war arrayed in front of them. Ranveer recognized many of them- all officers, from the army of the Marathas, Gwalior and Jhansi. All of them seem to have received at least as brutal a beating as he had, and many of them still had their faces swathed in bandages.

Ranveer and the other prisoners stood for what seemed like an eternity, and when one or two of them tried to whisper to each other, they were slapped by the Afghans and told to keep shut. Ranveer did not say anything or react to what was going on around him. He was already preparing for a worst case scenario- one in which they had been dressed up and marched here as part of an elaborate charade- to be massacred by the Afghans. It was something he certainly did not put beyond Abdali. His thoughts were interrupted by the incessant banging of a gong announcing the arrival of visitors. When the visitors did troop into the vast chamber, Ranveer's jaw literally fell open in surprise.

The procession was headed by none other than Jawan Bakht, who was dressed as a commoner and walked with his head bowed, like a supplicant, not a Prince of the Mughal Empire and a contender for the Peacock Throne. Behind him walked Nana-sahab and Zahir Dehlavi, both carrying large plates that were covered in silk cloth. Right behind them, to his surprise, Ranveer saw Tatya Tope, and next to him Theo, dressed in the full regalia of a British Army officer–with his gleaming medals, polished boots, a British cavalry sabre by his side and his immaculately fitted uniform. Ranveer guessed that this one had not been patched together overnight by a local tailor as had been done when Theo had used this as a ruse in the early battles with the *mansabdars*. None of them looked around, and when Ranveer did manage to catch Theo's eye, the Englishman refused to acknowledge him. Even more peculiar was the procession behind them. Six exquisitely carved wooden *palkis*, which would not have looked out of place in a Royal wedding, carried aloft by four men each. Ranveer had never seen one in the flesh before, but seeing the short stature, wiry muscle, a uniform that included a slanted *topi* and tan shorts, complete with fearsome *khukris* by their side, he knew that he was looking at Gurkhas.

The Afghans guards behind them were now themselves chattering in excitement and anticipation, and one of the captives next to Ranveer who knew something of their tongue leaned over to him.

'They say Jawan Bakht has come with innumerable riches to buy his life and peace.'

The Afghans were too preoccupied in their own gossip to notice, so the man continued.

'They also say that rumours are that the *palkis* contain diamonds, precious stones and also Princesses being offered to Abu Bakr for his harem as both proof of their genuine intentions to sue for peace and also to serve as hostages to ensure they never act against Abu Bakr again.'

Ranveer just shook his head in disbelief. Surrender to Abu Bakr and his thugs was in itself something that he had not believed men like Nana-sahab and Tatya Tope capable of. To debase and dishonor themselves and their people with terms like this was inconceivable to Ranveer. The man would have said more, but the guard behind him kicked him in the back, forcing him to kneel down. The Afghan hissed at all the prisoners around him.

'Your bastard brothers are here to sell themselves like the whores they are and the Emperor is about to arrive so kneel before him and stay down.'

Ranveer did as he was told to, his mind still unwilling to believe what he was seeing play out before his eyes.

Then he saw something that took the wind out him, and he sagged to the ground, finally defeated and deflated in a manner that even the worst torture he had faced had been unable to achieve.

The embroidered curtain covering the lead *palki* swung open in the wind for just an instant. But that was enough for Ranveer to catch a glimpse of the face the curtain hid.

That face belonged to Maya.

***

Twelve

Ranveer kept looking on at the proceedings, seething with impotent rage. His Maya was being bartered away to achieve a peace that was peace only in name, and servitude in fact. How could things ever have come to this? The gong sounded again, and this time, Abu Bakr entered, dressed in the full regalia of the Mughal Emperor, surrounded by pages and attendants and with Abdali walking just a step behind. Everyone in the chamber bowed and Abu Bakr took his place on the throne. He looked at Jawan Bakht, amusement twinkling in his eyes.

'So I see you finally found time to come and meet this brother of yours.' Several of his courtiers chuckled, and despite the insult and the fact that he was standing like a common petitioner and had not even been offered a seat, Jawan Bakht simply kept his head bowed and replied.

'I have merely come to make my peace and ensure that the people of Hindustaan suffer no more.'

Abu Bakr sniggered.

'And what makes you presume you speak for the people of Hindustaan when you are in the presence of the Emperor of Hindustaan?'

Jawan Bakht looked Abu Bakr straight in the eye.

'I have lost, and let us end the bloodshed today.'

'Okay, what do you want in return for my letting you live and your devious supporters keep their so-called kingdoms?'

Ranveer saw Nana-sahab stiffen at the insult, but the Peshwa of the Marathas said nothing. Jawan Bakht motioned for Nana-sahab and Dehlavi to come forward, and they placed the plates they were carrying in front of Abu Bakr. When they took off the covering cloths, a collective gasp went up in the chamber. Each plate was laden with the largest and most exquisite precious stones any of the men present had ever seen.

'This is just a small offering by way of tribute. As for the terms and why we are doing this, I would ask the one who has framed this whole arrangement to share the details.'

To Ranveer's shock, the man who stepped forward was not Dehlavi or Nana-sahab, but Theo. The Englishman took off his hat and stood at attention before Abu Bakr.

'*Jahapanah*, I would first like to present my credentials. I am Theophilius Metcalfe, son of the Governor General of China, and an officer in the service of Her Majesty, the Queen of England.'

Theo stepped forward, bowing as he handed over a sealed document to one of Abu Bakr's courtiers. The man opened it, nodding as he scanned it, and whispered to Abu Bakr that it looked to be in order. Ranveer wondered if this was all some new scheme cooked up by Theo, when Abdali stepped forward.

'Englishman, you are the one my men call the *Gora Shaitaan*. After slaying so many of our men, you come as a man of peace?'

Theo addressed Abdali with a nod of his head.

'General, we are both professional soldiers, and you know that we follow our orders.'

He then turned to face Abu Bakr.

'Your Majesty, the British Empire has long been wary of the instability that may follow any change in regime in Dilli, especially since our possessions in China are already under threat. As you well know, we rely on Hindustaan for reliable and profitable trade routes that were opened under the auspices of the late Emperor, peace be upon him.'

Abu Bakr motioned for Abdali to back down and the Afghan General sat down, his face still a mask of rage. Theo continued his account.

'I was inserted into Hindustaan with a mission of getting close to someone in the inner circles of the Court and report back on what was happening. All was going according to plan, when the Emperor was assassinated and in the ensuing chaos, I found myself on the side of those opposed to your rule.'

'And Englishman, you assisted them in fighting us and now

you come to talk of peace? Perhaps General Abdali is right in not trusting you.'

'*Jahapanah*, I will be honest with you. This has nothing to do with my personal preferences or alliances. I am an agent of Her Majesty's government, and my superiors sometimes play both sides. It is not that you have not been the recipient of their assistance. Or do you think some rogue traders showing up in your Court to sell you the latest Enfield rifles was a mere co-incidence? I hated my own superiors for it, since I knew nothing of it at the time, and it cost me many good men and friends, but that's the way the great game of politics works, does it not?'

There was a stunned silence in the chamber, and Ranveer, who till now had been sure that Theo was bluffing, was suddenly not so sure any more. He watched the Englishman and suddenly saw not someone he had come to count on as a dear friend, but a total stranger who had abused his trust.

'So *Jahapanah*, my superiors have concluded that the only lasting peace can be under your regime, and we are brokering this peace and trying to bring all of you together. The terms are on this paper, but I gather that you may have already heard about them through the usually reliable *bazaar* gossip.'

Abu Bakr took the paper Theo had handed him and studied it in silence. Finally, when he looked up, it was with a smile.

'Fine. I accept the terms.'

The normally reserved courtiers and nobles gathered around him smiled, knowing that their power and wealth was now secure. Only Abdali looked uncomfortable, and Abu Bakr addressed him. 'General, is there something on your mind?'

'Your Majesty, I do not like leaving sworn enemies alive to fight another day.'

Abu Bakr smiled and then looked at Jawan Bakht and the others, a hard glint in his eyes.

'I accept the terms, but remember that even the smallest infringement of the terms of surrender will mean that my friend Abdali will be let loose, and this time, I will show no mercy. So Englishman, what more do you want?'

Theo motioned for one of the Gurkhas to come forward. The man was carrying a large wooden case.

'*Jahapanah*, this is an offering from My Queen to you- from the ruler of one mighty empire to another.'

Abu Bakr opened the case and took out a packet.

'What are these?'

'*Jahapanah*, these are called cigars. These particular examples are among the finest quality in the world, savoured by the cream of royalty in Europe and containing tobacco from the finest plantations in islands near the Americas.'

Abu Bakr took one out and brought it close, smelling it, and grinning in approval.

'*Jahapanah*, we had been told that you perhaps enjoy the occasional smoke of the *hookah* and wanted to gift you this as you may appreciate its quality.'

Abu Bakr called an attendant and had the cigar lit. When he took a long drag and exhaled, he seemed to positively beam with pleasure.

'Englishman, this is indeed something that perhaps awaits mere mortals only in Paradise. Come on, my friends, you must try this.'

Abu Bakr passed on the cigars to his courtiers and they too began to smoke them. Only Abdali refused politely. Abu Bakr asked Theo to have one, and he took a cigar from his pocket and lit it up. The mood in the room relaxed visibly, and Abu Bakr called Theo forward, shaking his hand. He then turned to Jawan Bakht. 'Brother, we agree to the terms. Now that you are among friends, sit down and enjoy the gift your English friend has for us.'

Jawan Bakht and the others sat down on the floor, but did not seem to mind the implicit insult, as they too took cigars from Theo and lit them up. Ranveer, who had never particularly liked *hookahs* or tobacco found the smell nauseating, but nothing compared to what he was witnessing before him. Theo addressed Abu Bakr deferentially again and asked that the prisoners have their hands unbound. Abu Bakr, by now on his second cigar, agreed with a lazy wave of his hand. Ranveer saw Abdali's gaze harden, but the General was powerless to do anything about it. The guards began undoing the ropes binding the prisoners and when Ranveer's hands were freed, he had to restrain himself from launching himself. The question, he reminded himself, was whom should he attack first- Abdali or Theo? One thing he was already sure of was the fact that he would not want to live in the so-called peace that would follow this agreement, knowing that Maya was to be a part of Abu Bakr's *harem*. It was now just a question of seizing the right opportunity to attack and of taking as many of the bastards with him as he could.

He did not have to wait too long. Abu Bakr called on Theo. 'Ask your men to deposit the tribute with my *Diwan* and have the women escorted to my Harem. Mahabat Ali, where are you?'

The question was answered when a huge man, standing a head taller than even the Afghans, walked into the chamber. He had a curved scimitar dangling from his waistband, but the most incongruous thing about him was not his size or fearsome appearance, but the fact that his face was daubed with make-up. *Kohl* lined his eyes, and his brown cheeks glowed an unnatural pink, as did his lips. Mahabat Ali was the Chief Eunuch in charge of guarding the Royal *Harem*, and while Ranveer had never seen him in person before, he well knew that he had a fearsome reputation for cruelty. Mahabat Ali stood near the *palkis* and spoke with an unnervingly effeminate voice.

'*Begums*, please come with me to the *harem.* I shall prepare you for the *Jahapanah's* visit later when he may choose one of you to be his consort tonight.'

The curtains on the *palkis* parted and four women stepped out, wearing the finest of saris and bedecked in gold jewellery. Though their faces were veiled, Ranveer did not have to guess which one Maya was. She had chosen to wear her wedding sari. Abu Bakr was by now chuckling like a silly schoolboy and his courtiers were joining in as one of them made a remark about how the Emperor would feel when he was in bed with all four at one time. Ranveer felt his temple throb with rage. There was no way he would stand by and see Maya dishonoured like this. When Mahabat Ali stepped forward and took Maya's arm, pulling her none too gently towards the door, she resisted, and her veil fell off her head. She looked straight at Ranveer and smiled. As the eunuch tried to drag her aside, Maya clawed at his eyes. The giant eunuch caught her hands and laughed out loud. That was when Ranveer snapped.

Before any of the guards could react, he lunged across the room towards the eunuch, and put all his strength into delivering a blow to the side of his face. Ranveer was much weaker than he once had been, and was out of practice, but the element of surprise he had, and perhaps the sheer rage that went behind the blow, sent Mahabat Ali sprawling to the ground. At once, Afghan guards rushed forward, swords at the ready. Ranveer, realizing he perhaps had only moments left, gathered Maya in his arms.

'My love, if this is where it all ends, let us die together.'

As Maya clutched Ranveer tight, he saw Mahabat Ali get up, wipe the blood away from the side of his face and then raise his scimitar as he charged towards Ranveer, motioning for the Afghans to stop.

'This swine is mine!'

What happened next took Ranveer by utter surprise. There was a blur of red and Ranveer felt more than saw a sword flash through the air. With a howl of agony, Mahabat Ali staggered back, his arm severed at the wrist. Then there was Theo in front of Ranveer, his lopsided grin back, a bloody sabre in his hands.

'My impulsive old friend, you started it all a bit earlier than

I had planned, but what the hell, let's get it done.'

'Get what done?' asked Ranveer.

'Sending these bastards to hell!'

***

The room erupted in sudden and vicious violence as many things happened at once. Several Afghan guards charged at Theo and Ranveer, the Gurkhas who had been carrying the *palkis* unsheathed their *khukris* and waded into the Afghans and then the prisoners who had been watching from the sidelines turned on their Afghan guards. Ranveer pushed Maya to a corner and returned to the fray. He saw that Theo needed no help whatsoever. The Englishman was in his element in such a crazy free for all. On the one hand, he was wielding his sabre with the deadly precision that must have come from hours of formal military training, on the other, he was dealing out killing blows to his opponents with his bare fist and legs, using the martial arts he had learnt in China. Ranveer looked to see that three or four of the unarmed prisoners already lay dead, but a few of them had grabbed swords from their guards and had joined in the melee.

Some of the Afghan guards had rifles, and one or two fired when the fighting began. However, at such close quarters where combatants of both sides were locked in hand to hand combat, they realized that firing their rifles would just as likely hit their comrades as the enemy, and they waded in with their swords drawn.

An Afghan guard reared above Ranveer, his sword raised

above his head. Ranveer rolled away from the blow and picked up Mahabat Ali's scimitar, plunging it into the Afghan's stomach. Mahabat Ali was still groaning in agony, so Ranveer put him out of his misery by hitting him in the head with the scimitar's handle, knocking him out cold. He had not paid attention so far to what was happening in the rest of the chamber, and now that he did, he was shocked.

Despite the carnage going on around them, Abu Bakr and his courtiers were sitting still, most with silly grins on their faces. Abu Bakr was still smoking and babbling incoherently. With his remaining hand, Abdali was trying to shake some sense into the Emperor, but finally giving up, the Afghan General screamed to his men.

'These bastards have drugged them! Call for reinforcements and cut them to pieces!'

As the Afghans bore down on the unarmed Jawan Bakht, Gurkhas rushed forward to form a protective phalanx around the Prince, Zahir Dehlavi and Nana-sahab. Ranveer had never seen the little men from Nepal in action before, and began to understand why they had such a fearsome reputation. Any Afghan who came close was cut down by lightning fast strikes of their *khukris*, but Ranveer knew that if they just stayed and fought in the chamber, they would lose, as reinforcements would surely be on the way.

He asked two Marathas to follow him and rushed to the main door. Peering out, he saw a dozen Afghans rushing down the corridor, carrying rifles in their hands.

'Close the door!'

The three of them heaved the heavy doors shut just as bullets tore into the other side. Ranveer asked the two men to try and hold the door as he rushed to Theo.

'Theo, what is your plan?'

His face smeared in blood, the Englishman grinned.

'We need to get Abu Bakr!'

As Theo whirled to meet an oncoming Afghan, Ranveer saw that a stalemate had quickly developed in the *diwan-i-khaas*. Corpses of both sides littered the floor, but each Prince was now flanked by armed guards–Gurkhas in Jawan Bakht's case, and the remaining Afghans in Abu Bakr's case. Four Gurkhas screamed and rushed the Afghans, and while they took down a couple of the guards, they found themselves facing Abdali himself. The Afghan General was carrying a huge sword in his right hand, and as a Gurkha approached, he swatted him away like a fly, his brute force sending the Gurkha flying against the wall, his neck almost severed by the force of the blow. The three remaining Gurkhas were overpowered and cut down by the other Afghans.

As Ranveer watched, Abdali marshalled his remaining men and sheathed his own sword, dragging Abu Bakr with him as they made their way towards the side door that led to the inner chambers and the *Harem*. The other courtiers were just left lying on the cushions, some of them unconscious, others babbling nonsense, all totally oblivious to the carnage around them. Tatya Tope had grabbed a sword and was leading the Maratha prisoners of war in a charge at Abu Bakr. The Maratha General cut down an Afghan, but now fighting for their very survival, the Afghans fought with frenzy, and soon the Marathas backed away, having lost three of their number.

Theo raced to Ranveer's side.

'Ranveer, those Afghans outside the door will get in sooner or later- and we have to hold them till our reinforcements come.'

'Reinforcements?' asked Ranveer.

'My friend, we did not come here to commit suicide. There are a thousand crack Maratha troops whom we have been inserting into Dilli over the last few days and there are many more Mughal troops loyal to Jawan Bakht who are preparing to strike as we speak. They will be storming the Palace any minute now. Hold the Afghans while I get a plan to cut off Abu Bakr's escape.'

As Ranveer rushed to the door, he caught a glimpse of Maya. While the other three women were huddled against a wall, Maya had picked up a sword and was standing guard over them. A dead Afghan lay at her feet. Ranveer smiled at her and then reached the door just as the Afghans on the other side began to force it open.

'Men, help me here!'

Four Marathas rushed to his aid, and struggled to hold the door in place. They had all been prisoners like Ranveer and none of them was anywhere near the peak of their strength, so bit by agonizing bit, the door began to give way under the crushing weight of the Afghans outside. Ranveer ducked as a bullet tore through the door, leaving a gaping hole where his head had been seconds earlier. Suddenly there was a repeated barrage of firing outside, and then the guns went silent. As the door was forced open, Ranveer saw who was on the other side, and a huge grin of relief spread on his face as he moved to the side as the doors swung open.

Ranveer saw Abdali's expression change from one of triumph to one of horror as he realized that the ones coming through the door were not his reinforcements but more Marathas, and this time troops armed with rifles. Abdali barked some orders to his men, and to Ranveer's astonishment, the remaining Afghans charged at their enemy in what was doomed to be certain suicide. The Marathas who had just entered knelt and fired a volley at the Afghans, dropping several of them. The three or four who remained managed to cut down a Maratha before they too were shot down.

The *diwan-i-khaas* resembled a slaughterhouse more than the opulent chamber where the Mughal Emperor would grant an audience. There were corpses everywhere, and the stench of death and gunpowder filled everyone's nostrils. But Abdali's final gambit had played off. In the chaos of the last charge, he and Abu Bakr had disappeared. Tatya Tope took charge of the remaining soldiers and rushed out to secure the Palace, as Jawan Bakht told him that Mughal soldiers loyal to him would also be at the Palace any minute to help secure it. Ranveer took advantage of the first real lull in the action to check on Maya. She rushed into his arms, and he asked her angrily,

'Maya, if this was all a deception, why did you take the risk of coming here?'

Maya looked at him and smiled.

'Because I wanted to see you for myself. At first when you went missing, I nearly went mad and killed myself. Theo stopped me, saying that we should wait for news. Then our spies began to report that you were a prisoner here. We all knew this mission was very risky- there was no way I was going to risk losing you without getting a chance to see you again.'

Ranveer looked at Theo angrily.

'Theo, you should have known better than to bring her here.'

The Englishman shrugged.

'When's the last time she listened to anyone? Look, we can figure out who gets angry with whom later. What matters now is that we have to get Abu Bakr. As long as he is loose, we haven't won anything. His men will not surrender if they think he can come back to exact his vengeance. Where could he have gone?'

Zahir Dehlavi spoke up.

'Theo, there are numerous inner chambers- leading to the *Harem* and inner living quarters. Abdali could be anywhere in there with Abu Bakr. There are no more troops there, but Mahabat Ali would have armed eunuchs who would cut down any intruder. I doubt Abdali would know the inner rooms, and Abu Bakr seemed quite senseless, so I don't think they would be too far ahead of us.'

As Theo and the others prepared to give pursuit, Ranveer took two loaded pistols from the Marathas who had just arrived, tucked a sword into his waistband and said goodbye to Maya.

Despite Maya and Theo's protests that he was in no shape to get into such a dangerous situation, he rushed into one of the inner chambers, saying to Theo.

'Do what you want with Abu Bakr, but Abdali is mine.'

***

As Ranveer entered one of the passages, the first thing that struck him was how utterly dark it was. Perhaps in the chaos, the servants had forgotten to light the lamps along the corridors. Or perhaps, he reminded himself that Abdali had snuffed the lamps to throw off any pursuers. He stopped for a moment, catching his breath, aware that the worst thing he could do would be to rush ahead blinded by anger. He was up against a shrewd and experienced adversary and he would need to use his brains as well as his weapons. He could hear Theo and the others just behind him, and he restarted his pursuit. He did not want anyone else to get to Abdali before he did.

After walking for a few minutes he came upon a small courtyard. There were two passages before him. One of them still seemed to be lit by lamps along the sides of the corridors, while the other was engulfed in darkness. Ranveer's mind raced. Where would Abdali have gone? He looked at the darkened passage and saw a few drops of blood near its entrance. As he began to run into the passage, he stopped himself. Abdali had seen more battles than Ranveer's years, and the General would have made sure that he could not be tracked so easily. Ranveer did not know for sure, but he had to make a decision, and clutching a pistol in one hand and a sword in the other, he ran into the lit passageway.

Ranveer walked a few more steps, beginning to wonder if he had taken the wrong passage after all. The voices behind him had trailed off, and he suspected Theo and the others must have chosen the other passage. He began to slow down, debating in his mind whether he should just retrace his steps when a figure leapt out at him from a hiding place behind a large vase in a corner of the passage. Ranveer barely had time to deflect the blow from the man's sword and then backed away, taking stock of his adversary. The man facing him, he realized, was not a man at all, but one of the eunuch guards he had been told of. He had a strong, lean build, but was adorned by the same garish make-up as Mahabat Ali had been wearing. The eunuch brought his sword up and swung at Ranveer again, who this time parried the blow easily. The eunuch looked at Ranveer through eyes filled with a mixture of hate and fear. As he readied for another strike, Ranveer realized that the eunuch, while fit and strong, probably did not have much by way of military training, and as he swung his sword at Ranveer with his right hand, he left his left flank unguarded. A fatal mistake, and one that someone as experienced as Ranveer took instant advantage of. Ranveer brought up his own sword, slicing through the eunuch's stomach. As he doubled up in pain, grabbing at his cut stomach, Ranveer delivered a killing blow to the neck and proceeded down the passage.

A few steps later, another eunuch charged at him with a spear.

Realizing that his own sword would put him at a big reach disadvantage, Ranveer instinctively brought up his pistol and shot his attacker dead. No sooner had he fired than he cursed himself.

Now Abdali would know for sure that he was being followed.

Ranveer discarded his spent pistol, taking his second loaded pistol in his left hand and walked on for a few steps, finally arriving at a wide pavilion that was filled with beds, each covered by satin curtains. As far as he could make out, there were at least twenty large beds, arranged in five rows of four. There was only one lit torch on a far wall, and as a gentle wind blew in from a small window near the torch, the curtains moved ever so slightly, casting eerie shadows on the walls.

When Ranveer walked into the room, he realized where he was–the Royal *Harem*. He looked around frantically–Abdali could be hiding behind the curtains on any of the beds. In the near pitch black darkness, with shadows playing on the walls and pin drop silence, Ranveer realized that Abdali held all the cards. Every step he took seemed to echo loudly through the room. He had totally lost any element of surprise he had hoped to have.

When one the curtains stirred, he pulled it open, ready to shoot. He stopped himself in the nick of time when he saw a middle-aged woman sitting on the bed, cowering in fright. Ranveer exhaled loudly in relief that he had managed to hold his fire in time. He did not know who the woman was, but by her bedraggled looks, she seemed to be an attendant. He whispered to her.

'*Bibi*, have you seen any men come through here?'

The woman just shook her head and began sobbing. Ranveer put a finger to his lip, pleading with her to shut up and then looked around at the other beds. It was a perfect place for Abdali to lay an ambush. Ranveer did not even entertain the thought of hacking through the curtains for more than a second-he was after all in the Royal *Harem* and moreover, he was not a mass murderer like Abdali. He tried to steady his breathing and forced himself to focus his thinking. A jingling noise to his right caught his attention and he whirled around to see a hand extend out of one of the curtains. The hand clearly belonged to one of the Emperor's favoured courtesans. The fingers were adorned with massive jewelled rings and the wrist had gold bangles studded with diamonds. Clearly not a hand that could belong to Abu Bakr or Abdali, thought Ranveer with a smile, and he was about to turn towards another bed when he noticed something strange.

The hand had not just slipped out by mistake. It was pointing at something.

To be specific, it was pointing at the bed right in front of it.

Ranveer tiptoed over to the bed, which was covered in a pink curtain. As far as he knew, Abdali did not have a gun, so he stood back with his pistol at the ready in his left hand and gently parted the curtain with the sword in his right hand. In front of him was sprawled the Emperor of Hindustaan, quite drugged and as Ranveer inched closer, snoring ever so gently. Ranveer wondered for a moment if he should just end the matter there and then by killing Abu Bakr, but killing a sleeping man did not strike him as right. He ripped the curtains and gagged Abu Bakr's mouth and bound his hands and feet securely. Abu Bakr did not even move a muscle. Ranveer then got up and spoke loudly, moving among the beds.

'Abdali, your master is now trussed like a chicken, so why is his dog hiding among the women? Come out!'

No response. He tried again.

'Soon the others will be here, and if it comes to it, we will go through each and every bed. There is no escape from here, so show yourself and at least die like a man.'

Nothing again.

Suddenly, Ranveer heard the rustling of curtains behind him and turned around. A woman's body was flung at him. He caught her just before she fell to the ground, only to see that her throat had been cut from ear to ear. As he dropped the body and stood up, Abdali struck, slicing at Ranveer's neck with his sword. Ranveer managed to move out of the way just in time, but the blade caught the edge of his left shoulder, leaving him wincing in pain. He brought up his pistol to fire, but Abdali struck out with a kick, sending the pistol careening under one of the beds.

Finally, the two were face to face.

Abdali was bleeding from his right thigh, presumably from the battle in the *diwan-i-khaas,* but moved with a speed that belied his size. He stabbed forward with his sword, catching Ranveer off guard as he barely parried the blow in time.

Don't be careless just because he has only one arm, Ranveer reminded himself as he grabbed his sword with both hands and prepared for Abdali's next strike.

'Ranveer, my time has come, and I shall be executed by the new regime. But before I go, I am glad that I get to cut you up, like I did your father.'

Blinded by rage, Ranveer lunged forward, his sword extended towards Abdali's stomach. The Afghan sidestepped, blocking Ranveer's thrust with his sword and catching Ranveer in the side with an armoured elbow. Ranveer was sent crashing against one of the beds, and as he scrambled to get up, he saw Abdali grinning.

'You know, boy, I think I'll be telling stories about how I needed just one hand to kill you.'

Abdali feinted, his sword coming in fast at Ranveer's face. Ranveer saw the feint and moved to his left, bringing his sword down to block the downward strike that Abdali followed through with.

'You are not bad, boy. I'll grant you that much, but I've broken better men than you. Men like your father. He cried for mercy before I beheaded him.'

'No!'

Ranveer screamed and lunged at Abdali again. The Afghan again parried his blow with ease, kicking out with a heavily muscled foot at Ranveer's shin. As Ranveer staggered to keep his balance, Abdali kneed him in the face. Ranveer fell back, landing on a bed. The woman who had been hiding there screamed and ran away, and as Ranveer tried to get up, his mouth was full of his blood. Even before he stood up, Abdali was upon his again, bringing his sword down in a mighty slash aimed at Ranveer's head. Ranveer rolled out of the way just in time as Abdali's sword tore through the mattress, sending feathers and cotton filling flying through the air.

Ranveer spat out blood as he took his stance again. Abdali was smiling now, confident that he had the upper hand.

'So, you mongrel, it seems being the pet dog of a Mughal noble and getting an easy entry into the army does not make you a warrior after all. At least your father fought like a man till I gutted him.'

Ranveer was about to lash out again in rage when a voice spoke out to him.

Don't lash out in anger. That will always be your undoing.

Abdali had been taunting Ranveer, using his father's memories to make him lash out blindly, but as his father's words came back to him, Ranveer realized his mistake. Instead of attacking, he stood calmly and smiled at a puzzled Abdali.

'Thank you, Abdali, for reminding me so much about my father. Let me teach you a lesson he tried to teach me so hard.'

Abdali feinted towards Ranveer's right arm, but Ranveer did not take the bait. He stepped back and stood his ground. Abdali tried taunting him again, saying, 'At least your father fought before I cut him up.'

Ranveer felt his anger rising, but controlled himself, just circling Abdali, waiting for the Afghan to attack. Abdali probed with his sword, hoping to goad Ranveer into attacking, but Ranveer just stepped back again. After another failed feint, Abdali finally lost his temper and thrust his sword towards Ranveer's stomach. Ranveer blocked the blow and stepped back again. Now it was his turn.

'Abdali, I was always faster and fitter than you, and that was when you had both hands. I will just tire you out till you're panting like the overweight pig you are and then gut you.'

Abdali lashed out with his sword, but Ranveer blocked the blow and kicked Abdali on his injured right thigh. As the Afghan staggered back in pain, Ranveer reversed his sword and brought the heavy metal grip crashing into Abdali's face. Several of his teeth shattered as the big Afghan fell against a bed. Ranveer kicked the sword away from Abdali's hand, and stood over him. Abdali knew he had lost.

'Kill me and get it over with.'

'I'm not a coward like you who kills unarmed people. You always claimed to be a soldier so pick up your sword and fight.'

Adbali struggled to get back on his feet with his one good hand, and picked up his sword. He was out of breath, and blood flowed freely from his mouth. Still on his knees, he brought his sword up in a clumsy blow, but by the time his sword had even reached halfway to its intended target, Ranveer leaned back and with his sword held straight at shoulder level with both hands, put all his weight into a thrust towards Abdali. The sword penetrated Abdali's chain-mail armour just below his neck and came out the other side. The Afghan General dropped his sword and sagged down on his knees, impaled on Ranveer's sword. Ranveer kicked him away, taking his sword out.

There was the sound of footsteps behind him, and Ranveer turned around, ready to face any new threats. Instead, he saw Theo, Tatya Tope and several Maratha soldiers rush into the room. Theo looked at Abdali's body on the floor and Abu Bakr lying on a bed, and said to Ranveer. 'I think it's finally over, my friend.'

***

Thirteen

Arise Amir-e-azam.

Ranveer held the Royal *firman* while still down on one knee and then rose to face the Emperor of Hindustaan.

The other senior nobles gathered clucked appreciatively, but more than a few looked upon Ranveer with envy. Most of them were much older than Ranveer, and many had sided with Abu Bakr, only to change sides just as easily when Jawan Bakht took the throne six months ago after the fateful battle that had occurred in this very chamber. Ranveer could read their minds.

Got the position only because his father left it vacant. Hope he can fill those boots.

No doubt he will have favour with the Emperor after his role in the fighting. He may be a favourite, but he is a novice in the ways of the Court.

As Ranveer felt all their gazes on him, he realized the great irony in the situation. For most of his life, he had despised the artificiality and politics of the Court, even though his father had always wanted him to follow in his footsteps. To *settle down*, as he had put it. Ranveer had never really known what he had wanted, but knew that this was not the life for him. A life spent guessing what the Emperor wanted and trying to meet it before the others. A life spent in calculating which noble was in the Emperor's good books and trying to curry favour before one's rivals. A life spent achieving little more than navigating the politics of the Court to climb one rung after another in the Empire's hierarchy. A life that Ranveer had never wanted to be a part of.

Well, except now it seemed that his father had won out, after all. Once the new regime had settled down, the first order of business, as was usual in regime changes, was to tear down those who had been loyal to the old regime, and to dispense largesse in the forms of promotions and grants to try and create a loyal base of its own. Ranveer's promotion, as he well knew, was in part a repayment of the debt Jawan Bakht genuinely felt he owed Ranveer, and in part, shrewd politics. Qureshi was a role model for the new regime- fiercely loyal to Bahadur Shah Zafar's vision for the Empire in his life, and a true hero in death. Filling his position with his son was a sure way to get the vast sections of the nobility and the *mansabdars* who were loyal to him to support Jawan Bakht.

Ranveer looked up at Jawan Bakht and realized that the young man before him had changed much. Perhaps it was just the fact that sitting on the Peacock Throne made him look larger than life, or perhaps he had just matured fast in the past few months, but Jawan Bakht looked nothing like the young boy barely into his adolescence that Ranveer had first seen him as. As Jawan Bakht smiled at him, what Ranveer noticed most were his eyes. They had a hard edge to them, the eyes of someone who knew that he could not trust more than a handful of people. The eyes of someone who knew that, as had happened with his father, all his riches and splendour could be lost in an instant. The eyes of someone who was coming to grips with the terrible burdens that great power often brought with it.

'Ranveer, your promotion will bring with it much prestige and riches, but nothing compared to what you have endured and done for us. Today, you do your father's memory proud. However, I sense that there is something on your mind. Is there something else you want?'

Ranveer was not sure whether he should speak his mind, but he figured that if he did not speak up today, he would never again have a chance to change what direction his life would take. He had prepared the words that would follow at least a dozen times, and he kept his head bowed, but his voice was firm.

'*Jahapanah*, I want nothing for myself, but I do have a request that I hope you can entertain.'

'Anything you ask is yours today.'

Ranveer hesitated a bit, looking around at the nobles around him, trying to choose his words carefully.

'*Jahapanah*, all my life I have grown up looking at the great power and respect this Court commands, and the privileges that come with serving it.'

Several of the nobles leaned forward, surprised to see the young warrior speak with such polish before the Emperor. Ranveer continued.

'However, there are many in this Court perhaps more qualified than me to serve you and the Empire in such a capacity. There is however, one area where I may be of service- where I could do my bit to build back the legacy of your father, peace be upon him.'

Jawan Bakht, who had been initially irritated at having the honour he was bestowing rejected, saw the reaction Ranveer was having on the gathered nobles, and nodded to Ranveer to continue.

'I want to dedicate my service to the Empire in re-creating the *Ahadis*, and once again creating an elite corps loyal above all to the principles your father had laid down, a corps drawn from all religions, symbolizing the unbreakable unity of our nation. A corps that will be the bulwark against any future attempt to destabilize the Empire again, and one that I will personally lead in crushing anyone who tries to divide us again.'

Someone began applauding, and Ranveer looked back to see Ghalib in a corner, clapping. Several of the nobles joined in, and Jawan Bakht beamed.

'You truly do your father proud, and we are fortunate to have you in our service. I will still appoint you *Amir-e-azam*, with all the privileges that go with the rank. But follow your heart's calling, and create that force which was once the heart of the Empire, and ride at the head of the *Ahadis*.'

Ranveer bowed low and then stepped out the chamber. When he was out the door, he finally exhaled loudly in relief.

'You do realize that you have actually made the nobles resent you even more than if you had accepted the position and become one of them?' Ranveer turned to see Ghalib standing by the side of the door, his typically cynical smile on his face.

'Ghalib *sahib*, I don't understand. I am no threat to them and have no wish to be one. If anything, I want nothing to have to do with them or their politics.'

Ghalib chuckled. 'My boy, what you do not realize is that ambitious men like them most fear those who do not seem to covet power the way they do. Anyways, what will you do now?'

'I need to go fetch Maya, but before I leave this evening, I have an appointment with a friend.'

'Let me guess, an English friend who has been mysteriously missing these last few months?

Ranveer smiled.

'Yes, it seems Theo is back in town.'

***

'You know what I missed the most while I was away?'

Not getting any response from Ranveer, Theo tucked into his food and answered his own question, his mouth full of food.

'Hot *jalebis* at Ghantawala's shop.'

While Theo had already finished two servings, Ranveer had barely touched his food. He was torn between his joy at seeing his old friend again and also his nagging suspicions about what Theo's real agenda was. Theo must have noticed, for he paused to ask Ranveer if there was anything bothering him.

'Theo, on more than one occasion, we have placed our lives in each other's hands. So, will you at least give me one thing if I ask for it?'

'Anything, Ranveer. What do you want?'

Ranveer looked Theo straight in the eye.

'The truth.'

Theo looked into the distance, as if wondering what to say, and then answered.

'My friend, I have never betrayed you. If anything, I have staked a lot on your behalf, but I must confess that I have not been entirely truthful with you.'

Ranveer had been afraid that it would come to this, but now he was not sure how to react.

'So was everything you said at the *Diwan-i-khaas* the truth?'

The sparkle returned in Theo's eyes, and he replied with a broad smile, as if enjoying a private joke.

'I didn't say that either.'

'Theo, no more games. Were you sent by your government on a mission, and were you on that mission all along when you were with us?'

Theo paused, as if weighing in his mind how he should

best answer his friend's question. He looked around, and satisfied that nobody was looking in his direction, took out his hip flask and took a quick drink. He cleared his throat and then looked at Ranveer.

'When you do brave things like tell the truth, it's always best to get a drink in you. So, Ranveer, the short and truthful answer to you is yes and no.'

Ranveer, thinking that Theo was still avoiding the truth, lost his temper, slapping his palm on the table.

'Theo! Please be serious!'

Theo smiled, and then took another drink.

'My dear Ranveer, I am dead serious. Yes, I was sent on a mission, and no, I was not on that mission for most of the time I was with you. Now, order some more *jalebis* for me, and you shall have my full saga, if it does indeed interest you so very much.'

As the sweets arrived, Theo launched into his tale.

'So, I was in China, as I had told you, and my father, always desirous of seeing his son shine, asked me to volunteer for a new mission in Hindustaan. I've always had a gift for languages, so that helped, and soon enough I was inserted into this country. My early days were dull–just report on what was happening, how strong the grip of the Mughal Empire really was, what the other kingdoms were up to and so on. And then things got interesting.'

'What happened?'

'About three months before the Emperor was killed, my superiors told me that they had intelligence that something was afoot, and I needed to get closer to the Court and let them know if anything was happening that could shake the stability of the Empire.'

Ranveer was stunned.

'How could they know something was going to happen?'

Theo shrugged.

'Look, I am a small cog in a giant wheel. They have agents everywhere–and I would not be surprised if someone in the Royal Court was on their payroll. Anyways, so I got the job as a teacher at a *mansabdar's* house, and was well on my way to getting into the inner circles.'

'So why on earth did we find you in the desert in the condition that you were in?'

Theo hesitated and then answered with a wink.

'What I told you about my weakness for women was the truth, I am afraid.'

They both laughed, dissipating some of the tension between them. 'When you rescued me, and I sent a message to my superiors, they were actually thrilled, thinking I had earned the trust of someone like you–a rising officer, and son to a powerful noble. But then, I had to break ranks.'

'What do you mean?'

'When the Emperor was killed, my superiors told me that they wanted to support Abu Bakr. The thinking, I guess was that a weakened and fractured Hindustaan served them better. I did not do as they said, and chose to ride with you. The rest you know. They did sell Abu Bakr the rifles, but I knew nothing of it at the time.'

'What about the affair in the *diwaan-i-khaas*? The Royal parchment, the *Gurkhas*?'

'While you were in captivity, I managed to get in touch with my superiors and tell them of our plan. I convinced them that Abu Bakr was on his last legs, and that they were backing the wrong horse. My father being who he is probably helped convince them–but they bought into my plan and helped.'

'So they totally changed sides?'

'Our politicians are no different from yours–opportunistic bastards, all of them.'

Ranveer smiled and asked Theo why he had disobeyed his superiors.

'Was it because you indeed did not believe in their desire to grab more lands and subjugate their people, as you had told me once?'

Theo bit into a *jalebi* and replied.

'No, my friend, it had nothing to do with that. It had to do with the fact that I could not let you down. As simple as that.'

Ranveer looked at Theo and smiled, holding out his hand to shake his.

'I'm lucky to have a friend like you. So, what next for you?'

Theo shook his head, smiling to himself.

'They wanted me to accept a position as an envoy to the Mughal Emperor's court. Imagine, me a bloody bureaucrat! In that respect, you and I are alike, my friend.'

Ranveer looked up at Theo, 'What do you mean?'

'They want us to be replicas of our fathers and be what we do not want to be.'

Ranveer smiled and asked Theo what he wanted to be.

'Unlike you, the life of a warrior does not hold much attraction, though recent events indicate that I may once again find myself in harm's way. No, I was serious when I said that my heart was always in writing. So I have asked for some time off, which has been graciously granted.'

'What will you do with that time?'

'I will ponder my future, write my book, and fornicate with comely daughters of sundry *mansabdars* who have the poor judgement to hire me as an English teacher.'

Ranveer laughed out loud, and clapped Theo on the shoulder.

'That I am sure you will–just don't expect me to rescue you if you attempt to spirit yourself away dressed as a woman again. What will you write about?'

'Us. All of us–Iftiqar, the Rani, and the others, and the times we all saw together. It should make for quite a tale. I'll throw in a few tigers, fierce cannibal tribes and a few princesses who tried to seduce me, and the ignorant English masses will lap it up.'

Theo and Ranveer promised to stay in touch and then parted ways. As Ranveer walked past the Jama Masjid, he realized that even if on the surface, things seemed to have returned to normal, things could never really be the way they had been. Not after the upheavals of the past year. The changes were not obvious, but to someone who had grown up in Dilli, they were real enough. The bards in front of the Masjid were back, doing roaring business, spinning their yarns of the adventures of Abu Hamza, but there was a difference. Most of the children gathered in front of them were Mussalmans. There were few Hindu children around. That was simply because there were very few Hindu families left in the vicinity. Ghantawala had been an exception, but after the riots, most Hindu families had moved to areas where there were fewer Mussalmans, suddenly conscious that the relative peace and harmony they had come to take for granted could be suddenly and violently uprooted. That was but a microcosm of the changes across *Hindustaan*–the divide between Hindus and Mussalmans, while never fully bridged, had become narrower under Bahadur Shah Zafar, and while Jawan Bakht made all the right noises about following the erstwhile Emperor's policies on religious tolerance, the naked violence unleashed by the ghazis after the coup and the retaliation that had followed had opened old scars on both sides.

Dilli was by no means the only, or even the most acutely affected part of Hindustaan. Rumour had it that the Marathas had embarked on a huge militarization drive, training lakhs of new troops and importing new weapons from European powers. The Sikhs were quietly raising an army again. There was no open hostility but the signs were clear- the other kingdoms had learnt the hard way that the stability offered by the Mughal Empire could not be taken for granted, and they would learn to take care of themselves. The Mahant at Somnath had issued a rallying cry of 'Hindustaan for Hindus'. There were no takers yet, but Ranveer sensed that it was but a question of time before that cry came to haunt the Empire. He found the British incorrigible, but was even more convinced after his talk with Theo that they would continue to lurk in the shadows, waiting for an opportunity to stake their claim on Hindustaan once again.

There were so many things to worry about–not because he was concerned about them from a matter of state policy or politics, but because they brought home to him the troubled times in which he would have to begin his new life.

With Maya.

***

Ranveer was awakened in the dead of night by the sound of gunfire. He had been dreaming of an enemy with one arm hunting him, of women jumping off walls, and of Iftiqar dying in his arms. Dreams of the sort, that seemed to haunt him lately. The moment he heard the sounds, he reached under his bed and wrapped his hand around the loaded pistol he kept there at all times. A reassuring hand reached out in the dark and held his.

'Shh,, dear. It's nothing, just some kids lighting off firecrackers a bit early for Deepavali.'

Ranveer let go of the pistol and held Maya's hand. He turned to look at her, seeing her outline beside him. He cuddled up to her, grateful for everything she had meant to him, not least the fact that she was the one anchor of sanity and warmth in the last year or so when he had lost so much in his life and seen so much of what he believed in torn down. Maya leaned over and kissed him.

'Sleep now, my love or if you awaken the little one, then I'll have to pay with all the kicks I'll have to put up with through the night.'

Ranveer smiled and placed his hand on Maya's swollen belly. He knew he was perhaps just imagining it, but he thought he could feel their unborn child's heartbeat. In just over three months, he was going to be a father, and his life would come full circle. His son would be born in the very house where he had spent his childhood. Would he be a good father? Would he be able to protect his little family from the many storms that he knew loomed over the horizon? Most of all, would he be able to live up to all the trust, that Maya had placed in him?

He felt a little tremor beneath his fingers as the baby moved, and then settled down to sleep. Holding his wife and his unborn child, Ranveer realized that he had been looking for his destiny in all the wrong places. He had rejoined the Ahadis and in a short few months of intensive training, produced a fearsome force that was the envy of every other unit and the pride of the Empire. He kept hearing of how the Emperor held him in great favour, and how he was destined for great things. But none of that mattered compared to the two lives that were now linked to his.

As Maya drifted back to sleep, Ranveer lay on his back, waiting for the early hours of dawn when he would get up and exercise. If anything, he had taken to staying in fighting trim even more seriously over the last few months, knowing from hard experience that no matter how settled things looked today, he may be called upon to defend the things and people he held dearest once again. This time, he had decided, he would be much more ready than he had been.

He reached over to the table by the bed and felt for Theo's book, a thick volume that had reached him just a week ago. The volume had been written in both English and Hindustani, and had already earned some admirers in Dilli, and it was reported, back in England. From what Ranveer had learnt from Theo's letters, he had so far made just a few copies to pass among friends before he got it published. The title was a pithy one–Hindustaan– and as Ranveer lay in the dark, he thought that Theo had ended the book with a perfect last line.

It is difficult to end this tale, for in Hindustaan stories like life itself do indeed go through cycles of rebirth. Every story never really comes to an end; it merely leaves with it the seeds for its next telling to begin.

***

Glossary

Aayah	Nanny
Abba	Father
Acharya	Hindu holy man
Ahadis	Elite cavalry unit in the Mughal army
Amir-e-Azam	Noble commanding a force of at least three thousand men
Badmash	Rogue
Bandookchi	Rifleman
Bhumis	Local militia armed and paid by the Empire to keep the peace especially in areas outside the purview of central forces
Caravanserai	Guest house
Chacha	Uncle

Daal	Lentil soup
Dastak	Official document of identification-in intent, similar to passports today
Firangi	Foreigner–usually used for white men
Firman	Official decree
Ghazi	Literally 'soldier of the faith', usually used for Islamic fanatics
Gora shaitaan	White devil
Hakim	Doctor
Hanuman Chalisa	Collection of chants in praise of Lord Hanuman
Hazaari	Commander of a thousand men
Hookah	Pipe used to smoke tobacco
Howdah	Mount on an elephant for the rider (mahout)
Jahapanah	Emperor
Jauhar	Rajput tradition of women commiting ritual suicide by self-immolation instead of being captured by invaders
Jizya	Tax levied on non-Muslims, abolished in 1720
Kafir	Non-believer
Kahwa khana	Coffee house
Khalsas	Sikh warriors
Khooni darwaaza	Bloody gate. Popular name given to a gate in the Qila Mubarak where many executions took place

Kos	Unit of distance in use in Mughal times. 1 *Kos* is equal to 3.2 kilometers
Lakh	One hundred thousand
Mahant	Seer
Mansabdar	Lowest rank of noble in the Mughal aristocracy–commanding a force of upto five hundred men. Usually looked upon as lower ranked *Omrahs.*
Maulvi	Islamic preacher
Mukhia	Village headman
Omrah	Seniormost rank of noble. Each noble maintained an army in the service of the Emperor. The rank of *Omrah* began with the title of *Hazaari*, and included ranks up to the Amir-e-Azam.
Palki	Palanquin
Panchayat	Village council
Punkhah	Fan
Rajmata	Queen Mother
Rakshas	Monster
Seraikhana	Rest house
Sowar	Cavalryman
Topi	Hat